RAISING LUCY

SURRENDER, BOOK ONE

BECCA JAMESON

ACKNOWLEDGMENTS

I want to thank all my beta readers who encouraged me along the way and kept this book moving every time I had my doubts. You know who you are and how much you mean to me. I couldn't have written this book, much less this series, without all of you! Susan, Paris, Lea, Rose, Melanie—you guys rock!

Christa—there are no words. Love you bunches. I won't cry. I promise.

CHAPTER 1

Master Roman

"It's done."

I spin my desk chair around to find Julius, the manager of my club and the only man I would trust with the task I've assigned him. He drops a thick file on my desk. "You're sure?" I lift a brow, my heart pounding. If I pull this off...

Julius narrows his gaze. "Roman, you insult me."

I blow out a breath and open the file. Her picture is on top. I run my hands over the page, caressing it. Julius Martens is one of my oldest friends. He's also one of only two people who do not call me Master Roman or Sir. The other is our mutual friend Claudia Renault. Everyone else in my life refers to me by my preferred title.

"You think she'll be here tonight?" I ask, not lifting my gaze from her photo.

"I can't guarantee that, but if she doesn't show, we'll move to plan B or even plan C. This will work."

I nod.

Julius leaves me alone in my enormous office on the second story of my Seattle fetish club, Surrender.

I close my eyes, willing my heart to slow down. This reaction is so unlike me. I don't want any of my employees to see me nervous. I have a reputation in Seattle as one of the most severe Doms. I've earned that reputation intentionally. It's not just a reputation. It's my life. I'm demanding. I'm strict. I get what I want.

And I want Lucy Neill.

She is mine.

She is my girl.

My life.

My world.

She just doesn't know it yet.

CHAPTER 2

Lucy

I know it's a horrible idea for me to be out at a club tonight, but as I enter Surrender, I shake off my problems and force them to the back of my mind. They will still be there in the morning. Tonight, I need to escape. Tonight, I need to forget. Tonight may be the last time I'm able to do so for God knows how long.

Five hours ago, I was fired. *Fired.*

I have never been fired from a job in my life. I've been working as a receptionist for a small accounting firm, Martin and Sons, for two years. I'm a fantastic employee. No one has once complained about my work. I still can't believe they've terminated me on the spot without notice. The owner rambled on about outsourcing my position or some shit. I tuned him out after realizing I was being let go.

I don't even know what has possessed me to think a night at Surrender is a good idea. I should be at home scouring

LinkedIn for a job, but instead, I'm hiding from my problems like a coward.

Nope. I shake off the unease. I'm enjoying a night for myself. I deserve it.

The member in front of me signs in and walks through the second set of doors to enter the main club.

Cindy, the bubbly woman who runs the front desk, smiles at me and hands me the sign-in sheet. "Hey, Lucy."

I force a smile in return as I sign my name, a ball of anxiety growing in my stomach as I remind myself this is the last time I'll be entering Surrender.

Cindy spins around to pull a stack of papers off the printer and then sets them neatly on the corner of the desk. Something about their formality catches my eye. "What's this?"

Cindy sighs. "Applications. Any chance you're looking for a job? Master Roman is hiring an assistant."

I stop dead, blinking at Cindy. "Are you serious?"

For a moment, I think I'm imagining this conversation. I'm distraught. The only reason I've left my small apartment is to take my mind off my problems. I didn't make much as a receptionist, and my paycheck barely covered my expenses as it was. I don't have any savings. I'm basically screwed.

Cindy giggles, her voice drawing me back. "Of course. Fill out the application if you're interested." She leans her elbows on the counter so that her face is closer to mine. "I'll warn you, I've heard he's demanding. His assistants don't usually last long. This is the fourth time this year he's asked me to take applications."

My mouth goes dry as my gaze lowers to the form. "I got fired this afternoon," I murmur, as if she wants to hear my problems.

Cindy winces. "Damn. That sucks. Then maybe you're in luck." She shrugs as she shoves off the counter. No one else is currently in the reception area that separates the inside of the club from the street.

Could my luck really take this kind of turn? I find it hard to believe the universe has seen fit to shine down on me today.

Master Roman is the owner of Surrender. I've only seen him a handful of times. I've never spoken to him. He's elusive. Most of the time, his brow is furrowed, and he looks rather frustrated any time he walks through the club.

What I'm sure of is that I'm not the only one who stops breathing when he walks by. He's formidable. First of all, he's tall. Six two I would guess. And huge. The man works out. He's about forty with thick brown hair I'd kill to run my hands through. His eyes are an intense deep brown. If he looked directly at me, I would probably melt. His skin is tanned. And his hands… Every time I see them, I want them on my body. Who wouldn't?

The man always wears a suit. At least every time I've seen him. Perfectly starched shirt, tie, slacks, dress shoes. He oozes authority. He oozes dominance. He oozes confidence.

That's Master Roman. That's the man who is looking for a new assistant. I'm crazy for even considering it. But I am.

My hands shake as I take the top application and turn to sit in a chair in the reception area. One thing is for sure. There is no way I'm going to miss the opportunity. The inside of the club can wait. My entire night is looking up. Even if I don't get an interview, at least I will have tonight to pretend the future holds some possibilities.

CHAPTER 3

Master Roman

She's here. She's in my club. And she's filling out the application. As I watch her on one of the many security cameras in my office, I silently fist pump. It's not like me. I never show emotion. Of course, no one is watching.

I have seen her a total of four times before tonight, though I've known from the first moment I set eyes on her that she was mine.

I've spent the past month planning, plotting, figuring out how to make her mine. It's been a lengthy, coordinated effort, but tonight I'm hoping all the pieces fall into place.

I need to remain calm. I'm still sitting at my desk, trying to control my nerves, tapping my lips with two fingers as I stare at the monitor. To the casual observer I know I look the same as usual, but inside, I'm losing my mind. This has to work. There are no other options.

The first time I saw Lucy, she was wearing jeans and a pink sweater. Both articles of clothing were worn and neither fit her properly, which led me to believe she had purchased them at a thrift store. I later verified my belief.

Tonight. Damn. Just damn. That dress. My. God. My cock is stiff already, and I haven't even stepped into her presence. I'm hard from looking at her in the monitor. When she takes the clipboard and lowers herself onto the chair across from the receptionist, I come out of my seat to watch her closer.

She tucks her skirt under her bottom, but her thighs are bare, and the skirt isn't very long. It's long enough to be modest. It's street appropriate. But on Lucy, it's... *Fuck me.* I can't know her skin tone from the monitor, but I don't need to. I've been close to her enough times to know her skin is several shades lighter than mine and silky smooth. Flawless.

My heart is pounding as I watch her squirm in the chair as she fills out the application. The way she squeezes her legs together and crosses her dainty feet at the ankles. The way her long, curly, dark ponytail falls over her shoulder, the tips of her hair dangling down to her thigh.

She is precious.

Though I have visualized so many scenarios with her over the last month, tonight she is going to take my breath away. I can't wait to get closer to her. I will force myself to remain aloof and pretend I don't notice her, but it will be hard. *I* will be hard.

She's so young tonight. Not in years. In style.

Perfection.

My girl is small. No, she's not just small. She's petite. She stands at about five feet and is proportionately tiny throughout. Most people would have to do a double take to confirm she's even an adult. I've seen her identification though. She's twenty-two. Tonight...with that loose ponytail in her hair and that dress... Jesus, she looks young. I swallow, wondering if she is also wearing minimal makeup like every other time I've seen her.

Her glorious thick curls hang down her back when she tosses her ponytail over her shoulder. So far, I've only seen her with all of that hair gathered in a haphazard ponytail at the nape of her neck, or on one occasion, she'd gathered just the top layers and clipped them in that same spot.

Lucy has no experience with BDSM. It's obvious. I wonder what spurred her to get a temporary pass to visit my club. She has, nevertheless, come every Friday night for the past four weeks, which means she only has two guest passes left. I've been racing against the clock to figure out how to make her mine.

I close my eyes and take a deep breath, tapping my thigh with my fingers. It's out of character for me to be this distressed over a girl. It's never happened in all my forty years.

I have spent a great number of those years searching and hoping for the perfect submissive. Someone I can own. Someone who will be willing to enter into a fulltime relationship that suits my tastes. And my tastes are specific.

I believe in my heart that Lucy fulfills all my standards, even though it will take some time to convince her and train her. She has no idea how her life is about to change, but I know she will not regret my decisions.

Yes, I definitely have broken every rule I expect my employees to uphold. I never even hesitated. The first night Lucy came to my club, I watched her for two hours. Some of that time I was on the floor literally following her around as nonchalantly as possible. Some of that time I spent in my office watching her every move on my monitors.

She is timid and unsure. She is also intrigued and frequently aroused and flustered. I have watched her fidget from one foot to the other, squeeze her legs together, hug her small breasts tight against her chest, and even bite her nails—a habit I will break her of as soon as possible.

I have paid close attention to exactly how much time she watches each scene and how she reacts physically.

My dick is hard now and has been hard for four weeks as my suspicions and hopes were confirmed. She magnetically finds herself watching the strongest Doms. Demanding ones with serious expressions and humble subs. She has been mesmerized by submissives on their knees with their faces tipped down. She once watched an age play scene where a woman dressed as a young girl gave a blow job.

Lucy's face was completely flushed by the end, and her legs were crossed, making it easier for her to clench them together. When she fled the room and made her way to the bathroom, I almost went after her.

I knew it was too soon, but it bothered me that she might masturbate in the bathroom in my club. I don't want her to touch herself without my permission. I want to own her orgasms. All of them.

Luckily, I exercised restraint. In addition, she returned from the women's room minutes later, somewhat composed but in no way relieved. I know girls well enough to tell if they have recently come. Lucy did not have the moxie to orgasm in my club.

That provided me with the smallest relief. I exhaled and let my eyes close long enough to release my grip on the edge of my desk before resuming my obsessive monitor scanning.

Another night, Lucy spent almost an hour watching a Dom specifically play with his babygirl. She had on a frilly nightie and was sucking a pacifier. She didn't speak, and at one point she began to cry and then had a bratty tantrum.

My girl cringed and turned away.

I smiled and took notes.

My obsession is not innocent. I have crossed the line when it comes to Lucy.

After she left that first night, I pulled her paperwork and

memorized everything there was to know about her. I know she's single. She has worked for an accounting firm for two years. She doesn't have a driver's license. Instead she has a state ID. I know where she grew up, where she went to high school, and every place she has worked since then.

I also know I went way overboard when I hired two men to follow her everywhere she went. I did it for two reasons. One, her safety. I would never forgive myself if anything happened to her after I finally found her. And two, I needed to know who she spent time with, if she had a boyfriend, what kind of hours she kept.

I took it even further when I had someone break into her apartment while she was at work. I needed information. I got it. Nothing was stolen. No harm done.

The response from my PI's was mind boggling and made me extremely happy. It would seem she has no friends, only leaves her small, rundown apartment to go to work and the store, and never goes out at night. I can't imagine why a girl like her is so cut off from the world, but my investigator dug deep and has assured me she has never once been in trouble with the law and doesn't appear to be hiding or running from anyone.

I suddenly sit up straighter as Lucy returns the application to Cindy. She is smiling. Excited. She rubs her hands together. There is a God.

CHAPTER 4

Lucy

As I enter the main playroom at Surrender, my steps are lighter. It's absurd that I should feel any relief simply because I filled out an application, but I do anyway.

I glance around, taking in the number of people inside and adjusting to the dimmer lighting. The walls are painted black, as are the floors and ceiling. I love that part. The anonymity.

I smooth my hands down my dress as I wander farther into the space, and when I find myself crossing my arms, I force myself to stop and keep my hands at my sides.

I've learned a lot from watching the last four weeks, absorbing the rules most Doms have for their subs. In an odd way, I've forced some of those rules on myself just to pretend I'm someone's sub. That I belong to someone.

I fist my hands because it's the only way to keep them at my sides, especially tonight. Every previous week, I've arrived in jeans and a modest sweater or shirt. This is my last night, though, so I've forced myself to get more fully in the mindset of role play.

In order to keep from giggling at my imagination, I chew on my bottom lip. Role play. Right. Alone. It can't really be considered role play if I don't even have a partner. It's just me.

So, I'm wearing a dress. It's not fetishware. It's not even remotely provocative or revealing. It's actually kind of prissy. It's pink, which is my favorite color. A soft pastel pink. It's made from the same material as a polo shirt. In fact, the upper body is precisely that—collared and only slightly fitted, hugging my breasts.

There is no defined waistline. Instead it drops down to my hips, and the skirt is pleated, landing halfway down my thighs. If I were to twirl, everyone would see my panties. I have no intention of doing anything like that, but the thought that I could is somehow titillating.

I'm wearing pastel pink flats too. They are the most extravagant shoes I own, and I only bought them last year on a whim because they called out to me at my favorite local consignment shop. They were almost new, my size, and my favorite color. In order to justify them, I've worn them often to work with other pink blouses and shirts.

The dress is another story. I got it at a thrift store. I have no idea why I bought it. I've never worn it before tonight. Where would I wear it? It cost only a few dollars, so I have never worried about the expense, but though I loved it when I tried it on, I later realized it had no real use in my life.

The reality is that I look younger than my age in it. I wouldn't have worn it to work at Martin and Sons because anyone who came in would have thought I was one of the owner's kids instead of taking me seriously as the receptionist.

Tonight I spotted it in my closet and didn't hesitate to put it on. Now that I'm inside Surrender, I feel relaxed and more comfortable than I ever did in jeans. I feel young. Too young. Much younger than twenty-two. But that's the point. And I'm not alone. There are other women in this club who are dressed far younger than I am tonight.

It suits me in an odd way that I can't put my finger on.

I glance around, knowing I need to make the most out of my evening. It's my last night at this club. Even if I miraculously manage to get a job working for Master Roman, I still wouldn't return to his club as a patron. It would be weird. And if I don't get the job, well, then I'll be in such dire financial straits that my Friday night entertainment will be the last thing I think about.

A purring noise has me turning toward the right, half expecting to see an incongruent cat in the club before I remember that there are several members who engage in pet play. Sure enough, I see a woman on her hands and knees being led through the main room on a leash. I've seen her before. She has cat ears fastened to a headband and even a tail, which I assume is attached to a butt plug.

I follow her with my eyes, pondering the fascination of pet play. On the one hand, submissives who enjoy role-playing as a puppy or kitten don't seem to be required to make many decisions. They have turned over nearly every aspect of their lives to their masters, permitting themselves to be led around, fed, even caged.

While I watch, the man holding the kitten's leash attaches it to a bolt in the floor. He points at the floor, she curls up on her side, and he wanders away. She looks content. Relaxed. Happy.

Part of me can understand. After all, for the few hours she spends as a kitten this evening, she doesn't have to worry about whatever problems might exist in her real world. They aren't hers. She left them at the door.

However, I don't think I would enjoy being cut off from

communication like this kitten seems to be. My mind would race with the need for social interaction. I smile at the irony considering how introverted I am and how few people I have spoken to in this club.

As if on cue, a deep voice to my left interrupts my thoughts. "Enjoying your evening, Ms. Neill?"

I turn to find Master Julius standing near me. The tips of his fingers are tucked in the pockets of his black dress pants. His brows are drawn together, but his lips are lifted in a slight smirk. "Yes, Sir," I murmur. I've seen him every week, which isn't surprising since he is the manager of Surrender. Master Roman is the owner. I don't see him as often.

"I'll be wandering the floor this evening. Please let me know if you have any questions."

"I will. Thank you, Sir." It feels awkward referring to the men I encounter in the club as Sir, but I'm getting used to it. I haven't spoken to very many people anyway.

Master Julius slowly walks away.

I realize I'm still standing near the entrance to the main room. I haven't moved beyond this spot yet. Perhaps that's what led Master Julius to check on me. Forcing my legs to propel me forward, I inch around the room. It's growing crowded.

I pause to watch a submissive with gorgeous dark skin being caned by a Domme with nearly white skin and naturally blond hair. I recognize them. They often scene together. Perhaps they are a couple. When the cane lands on the darker woman's naked bottom, I wince. She isn't bleeding, but angry welts have risen all over the backs of her thighs and butt.

If I've learned anything in the past five weeks, it's that pain is not for me. I may not be able to pinpoint my precise kinks yet, but I'm not a masochist.

Unable to stop myself, I cross my arms and hug myself, turning my gaze away. I find myself lured to the corner of the room where a woman stands oddly facing the wall. I don't recall having seen her before. She's tall and a bit on the heavy side.

As I wander closer, I'm fascinated to realize she's wearing a frilly white dress and carrying a teddy bear. She has her thumb in her mouth. A man who is slightly shorter than her and slender steps up to her side. He sets a hand between her shoulder blades and presses her nose into the corner.

I can hear him as he admonishes her. "When I put you in time out, I expect you to keep your nose to the wall. Do you understand?"

"Yes, Sir," she responds. "I'm sorry, Daddy." She straightens her shoulders, presses her breasts against the walls, and keeps her nose right where the man directed her.

My breath hitches. I drop my arms to my sides and continue watching. The man paces behind her, lecturing her. "Do you understand why you're in time out?" he asks.

I swallow, my gaze on the woman. She drops her thumb from her mouth and clasps her hands behind her back.

Instinctively, I reach behind my own back and grab my wrist with my opposite hand. I rock forward and backward on the balls of my feet, feeling as if I'm the woman being chastised instead.

I glance around, feeling odd at my reaction and my behavior. It's dark in the room. I'm in the shadows. No one has noticed me. Nor would anyone care. Far kinkier things are happening all over the club than one woman watching a scene with her hands clasped behind her back.

"I'm sorry for talking back to you, Daddy."

He stops pacing and smoothes a hand down her back. "I know you are, little one, but you're still going to stand in this corner for fifteen minutes to think about your behavior. I have some things to take care of. If you fidget, your time will start over."

15

"Yes, Sir," the woman whimpers.

The man leaves her there, disappearing.

I can't move. I'm frozen in my spot watching this woman who is obviously pretending to be a young girl. She's sniffling. Her shoulders are rising and falling. But she doesn't move an inch otherwise.

My knees shake. I know I'm shivering, but I can't move. I'm mesmerized by the dynamic. I wait the entire fifteen minutes and then a tear escapes my eye as the man returns, hugs the girl/woman, and tells her what a good girl she is. He brushes her hair back from her face, wipes her tears, and snuggles her into his side.

When the scene is over and the two of them walk away, I find myself emotionally drained. It takes me several minutes to move from my spot, and I head for the women's locker room.

I need to lock myself in a stall for a few moments of privacy.

I need to wash the tears from my face and take some deep breaths.

I need to ponder what just happened to me and what it means.

It doesn't really matter, however, because I won't be returning to Surrender or any other club in the near future. Whatever discovery I might be able to glean about myself from watching that scene, it will have to be set on the back burner.

CHAPTER 5

Master Roman

As I watch Lucy flee the main room and enter the women's locker room, I draw in a deep breath, realizing I have not taken in enough oxygen for a very long time.

I've known for weeks that Lucy was born to be a little, or perhaps a middle. I've been in the lifestyle for over half my life. I've seen nearly everything there is to see. I've known many people, both men and women, who enjoy role-playing at many different ages. I'm familiar with the signs.

Lucy's inclination doesn't shock me. In fact, it's what drew me to her in the first place. I'm confident I sensed her kink even before she did. Nevertheless, I'm blown away by what I just witnessed. It was as if Lucy herself had been the submissive in that scene.

I take several more deep breaths, my gaze glued to the locker room door, wondering what she's doing in there. I've seen her aroused before, but I'm not certain if her reaction to what she witnessed is arousal this time or simply sub drop.

Does she fully comprehend what happened to her? I'd give anything in the world to go to her. Comfort her. Hold her. Stroke her hair. Someone needs to. She's in need of just as much aftercare as the woman who stood in timeout, if not more.

So many questions run through my head. Is she crying? Is she alone? Is she even able to stand on her own?

Is she touching herself? Did she get off on that scene?

My hands are fisted at my side, and I take a step forward.

"Don't do it."

I hear those words from behind me just before Julius steps around me and blocks my view. His gaze is stern.

I swallow hard. I've never once been this affected by someone. Not in my club or in any other club. I hope no one is watching me as closely as Julius is. I have a reputation to uphold.

Julius crosses his arms and stares me down. "You can't go in there. You know that."

"Were you watching?" I ask.

"Yes. Most of it. Enough to know you're salivating right now."

I roll my eyes, trying to make light of my reaction. Failing, I'm sure. At least in front of my closest friend. Julius knows me better than anyone alive. I can't hide from him. It's not possible.

"I sent Claudia in to check on her inconspicuously."

I groan. It's not that I don't think Claudia can handle Lucy. I know she can. Claudia is a Domme. One of the best. I've known her since college. Julius and I met her in a club we were members of at the time. She is perfectly capable of being discrete. I have no doubt Julius informed Claudia that he personally noticed Lucy dropping into subspace. There isn't a chance in hell that Julius would have mentioned me when he sent Claudia into the locker room.

My groan is not out of concern for Claudia's ability, but rather because I would prefer to be the one holding Lucy in my arms right now. Not Claudia.

Julius has the slightest grin on his face. Not so much his lips but the corners of his eyes. "I've never seen you like this."

I roll my eyes again, but there is no denying he is right. And why would I bother? "She's special."

"I see that, and may I remind you that you went to a lot of trouble and paid top dollar to that PI to learn everything about her. If you confront her now, you will ruin your plans. She needs to believe she randomly applied for the job as your assistant, and you need to pretend you've hardly noticed her before, if ever."

My breathing evens out. I nod. He's right. Of course. And I question my momentary weakness. It's so out of character.

"Monday, Roman. You can wait until then. You've waited years for the perfect submissive to come into your life. Two more days is not going to kill you."

Intellectually, he's right. But my heart is pounding, and I'm anxious to speed this process up. I hate that I need to interview her like the hard Dom I intend for her to see in me. Then I need to hire her to be my assistant and slowly introduce her to my world.

It's all planned out. I'd be a fool to break my own plans at this stage.

An outsider would examine this plot and find me to be manipulative and crossing the line. Perhaps they would be right. But I don't see it that way. I know in my heart what I'm going to do for Lucy is bring her out of the shadows and into the light, introducing her to a life she was meant to live.

Just because she doesn't know it yet doesn't mean I'm wrong. Every natural instinct in my body tells me I'm right.

The truth is even Julius doesn't know how far my reach has gone. He arranged the PI and made sure Cindy had applications at the front desk. He does not know I spoke to the PI several times myself and paid for extra services. He does not know I spoke with her employer and ensured she would be desperate when she arrived here tonight and found out I needed an assistant.

If I hire her and she turns out to be completely different from the woman I've been watching slowly process the lifestyle she's been exploring, I will let her go. I won't have a choice. I'll do everything in my power to find her another job so she leaves me in better shape financially and emotionally than she was when she arrived.

But I know in my soul she is the perfect woman for me.

My girl.

My little.

My life.

It can't go wrong. I can feel it deep in my bones.

CHAPTER 6

Lucy

I have never been more nervous in my life than I am at this moment, standing in this enormous dark-wood foyer of Master Roman's mansion. As I wring my hands together, I'm unable to keep my nerves at bay. I've arrived early, and the older man who opened the front door upon my arrival has instructed me to wait inside this imposing entrance area.

I shuddered as I watched the man walk away from me. He moved with purpose but not speed. He informed me his name is Weston. I'm not sure if that's his first name or his last. His expression was serious, and he hardly glanced at me before leaving me to fidget alone.

I still can't believe I've been granted this appointment. Interview, really. The truth is I both need and want this job. Badly.

Somehow Fate has stepped into my pitiful life like a ray of light. Things like this don't happen to me. Ever. I'm not the sort of girl who has good luck, or any luck at all.

I'm standing in the dark wood foyer of Master Roman's estate, and I can't believe I'll actually get this job. Surely, he will have had a chance to look over my resume and found me lacking by now.

Nevertheless, a woman named Nancy called me Saturday morning to set up an interview first thing this morning. Apparently, Master Roman is desperate. I wonder if he's even been informed of my qualifications or if his secretary simply set up this appointment without consulting him.

I shake that idea out of my head. I may not know Master Roman at all, but from what I've seen, it's unlikely anything in his life happens without his stamp of approval.

I have no idea in the world what the job entails or if I'm qualified, but I took the time Friday night to carefully fill out every detail of my job history on the application, praying Martin and Sons would give me a good review even though they had mysteriously fired me.

I'm a hard worker. Always on time. I stay late when required. Never complain. No one in the office ever reprimanded me a single time since I started working for them two years prior.

My discharge had come as a total surprise.

My luck a few hours later lifted my spirits. Hope alone was enough to help me sleep the past few nights.

Standing here in the foyer, waiting, is making me question my decision. This isn't just a house or even a mansion. It's an estate. I realize I'm in over my head. I know it, but I'm still intrigued. If Master Roman is willing to interview me, I will do my very best to impress him.

"Miss Neill." The voice startles me, and I jerk my gaze up to find the same older man returning. "If you'll follow me, please." He turns around and retraces his steps down the hallway.

I take a deep breath and follow him. The ceiling is very

high, and our steps echo on the hardwood floor. My entire concentration needs to be focused on not tripping over my own two feet.

I remain two paces behind the presumed butler as we round a corner and then continue down another hallway. Finally, he stops at an open door and motions with his hands for me to enter. Just as quickly, he continues down the hall, leaving me to realize every step I heard on the walk toward this room has been my own. This man moves silently. His presence feels like it's out of an old movie. I have trouble believing people still own homes like this and employ butlers like him.

The entire estate has the feel of old money. I would guess it was built or at least renovated fifty years ago.

Taking another deep breath, I enter the room. It's clearly an office, and it's enormous. The same dark wood paneling that covers the hallway extends into this giant room. The desk, situated several yards in front of me, is made of the same wood. It's large enough for at least four people to occupy it at the same time.

There are two comfortable chairs on the opposite side of his desk and across the room is a fireplace with a sofa and two armchairs angled around it. All three pieces of furniture are a deep brown soft leather. Also worth noting is the wall of bookshelves loaded with more volumes than I would own in a lifetime. Or even have the chance to read.

Master Roman is standing behind the desk, his leather chair at his back. He's so imposing and large that he actually makes the desk seem smaller. His gaze is on the paper he's holding between two fingers, hovering an inch above the wood surface. I'm staring at the top of his head, his thick hair messy from running his fingers through it. The fingertips of his free hand are tucked just inside his suit pants pocket. He's wearing exactly what I've always seen him in—dark slacks, starched white shirt, dark tie. The matching jacket is draped over his chair.

I hesitantly inch farther into the room, feeling awkward, unsure if he knows I'm here. I have never felt more out of my element as I glance down at my drab outfit and tuck a loose lock of hair behind my ear. I suddenly wish I had the skills to have put the long unruly curls up in a fancy bun or something. Instead, it's gathered in its usual ponytail at the base of my neck.

Before I can come up with the courage to clear my throat or speak, he beats me to it. "Have a seat." His voice is deep, sharp, demanding.

I flinch as his tone penetrates. I know almost nothing about him except that he's a Dom and he owns his own club. I've never heard a single person refer to him by any other name than Master Roman. I don't even know if that's his first or last name.

Before I take another step, I start trembling. Half of me is nervous as hell because there is no way I won't get tongue-tied and blow this interview. Half of me is concerned that if I look directly at him, I won't be able to speak at all.

Master Roman is the object of every girl's fantasies, mine included. He's larger than life, commanding, and intense. When he steps into a room, he fills it with both his size and his magnetism. Heads turn. People stop breathing. Panties dampen. Including mine.

I knew I would freeze up at this moment. I even rehearsed it in my head many times over the weekend as I paced my tiny apartment muttering to myself. And yet, here I am, exactly where I expected to be. Frozen.

Perhaps I've made a mistake applying for this position. I'm not at all sure I'm cut out to work for this man. Nor do I believe I'm qualified. Hell, I'm not entirely certain what

Master Roman is looking for in an assistant, but judging from the impeccableness of this office, I'm not the girl for this job.

Master Roman lifts his gaze. His brows are drawn together. "Do you have a hearing problem?"

I jump in my spot then find the will to move toward the chair opposite his desk. "Sorry," I mutter.

As I lower my shaking body onto the chair, I realize the paper he's holding is my application. While he continues to peruse it, I take the opportunity to soak in his frame. He's even taller than I remembered. Over six feet. A giant compared to my ridiculous five-foot frame. His shoulders are broad. I guess him to be about forty, but his ever-present serious expression gives the impression he's much older. He's intimidating to say the least.

Obviously, he's a Dom. After all, he owns the club —Surrender.

Without lifting his gaze, he speaks again. "It says here you've been a receptionist with Martin and Sons for two years."

"Yes." I chew on my bottom lip, concerned that this is the first moment he's had a chance to read my application. I feel incredibly inadequate. I'm surprised he hasn't laughed out loud yet and told me to get out of his office.

He lifts his sharp gaze and stares at me. "You'll address me as Sir."

I stop breathing and nod. "Yes, Sir," I murmur.

"And, though I won't permit you to raise your voice in my home, I'll at least need you to speak at a level I can discern."

I force my voice higher, sitting up straighter at the same time. "Yes, Sir."

His gaze lingers a few more moments on my face and then lowers back to the paper. "Do you have family in the area?"

That is the oddest question to choose to start this

interview, but I shake my head. "No, Sir. My parents have both passed. It's just me."

He looks my direction again. "No siblings? Aunts? Uncles? Grandparents?"

I shake my head again, still shocked by his line of questioning. What does it matter how much family I have?

He lifts a brow. "Speak, please. I don't respond well to timid head shakes and nods."

I swallow the fear that is climbing up my spine, fighting hard to keep from crying. I have no idea why I'm suddenly emotional. It's not rational. If Master Roman finds me lacking, fine. Why should I care that he has so many quirks? No wonder he has gone through three assistants in the last year.

"Lucy." He speaks my name sharply, his voice raising.

I realized he's still waiting for a response. "No, Sir. I don't have any family nearby. My only relative is a grandmother I never see in Chicago." Is this a problem?

"You live alone?"

"Yes, Sir." I sit up straighter, forcing myself not to squirm on my seat. I've never been so unnerved in my life. He's so intimidating. He makes me feel like a small child instead of a grown adult. Every piercing glance from him shrinks me, and I start to tremble.

He's staring at me as if I'm in trouble for some transgression I'm not aware of, and it makes me squirm. I'm too warm. I'm a little weirded out by my reaction. Half of me would like him to continue to reprimand me. His narrowed gaze alone is making my nipples hard.

I like this feeling. A lot. Does he know what he's doing to me? He seems like the kind of Dominant who probably knows exactly what he's doing to me. That thought makes me flush. He's interviewing me for a job as his assistant. Not a submissive.

When Master Roman's gaze returns to my application once again, I glance down at my body, partly to confirm I'm the twenty-two-year-old I know myself to be instead of the small, trembling girl.

I'm wearing my most professional outfit, but it seems quite lacking all of a sudden. Navy pleated skirt and matching jacket. White blouse. Navy flats. I have never owned or worn heels out of fear that I would land on my face if I attempted such a thing.

"You can't possibly have made enough money to afford your apartment and utilities working for Martin and Sons."

I lick my lips. "It was tight. I got by."

When he slowly closes his eyes as if he's fighting extreme frustration, I quickly add, "Sir."

That seems to soothe him because although he doesn't comment, his face relaxes marginally.

I'm out of my element. This man is a Dominant of the highest order. He obviously expects his employees to submit to him. As that thought fully seeps into my system, I shudder. Does he want *me* to submit to him? As his assistant? And what would that entail?

I draw in a long breath, careful to keep it silent, as I squeeze my thighs together and cross my ankles. It takes every bit of self-control to keep from shivering. The idea of submitting to Master Roman at his club has definitely entered my mind. It enters the minds of every submissive in Surrender. He's that powerful. Both men and women covet a scene with him.

I have never actually seen him dominate a single member or guest, however. I'm not sure anyone else has either. If he has, it's been on nights when I wasn't there, or else he takes his submissives to a private room.

I do not have full membership to Surrender. I have a temporary guest membership for six visits. Friday night was my fifth. I'm also aware that I didn't make enough money to have actually joined after my sixth visit.

I first went to Surrender a month ago on a whim that was way out of character for me.

I don't know a single member, nor had I ever been to a fetish club. What I had done was bury myself in books from the moment I'd learned to read. As soon as I was past puberty, I switched from childhood mysteries to romance novels. By the time I graduated from high school, I had read more erotic books than most grown women.

I'm an only child. My father was old when I was born, and he passed away when I was only ten. My mother found out she had advanced breast cancer the following year and died when I was eleven. I moved from my small hometown in rural Missouri to live with a maternal grandmother I had never met in Chicago at that tender age.

Making friends was hard for me. The kids made fun of my Midwest accent from day one. I didn't mind, though, because I was an introvert. So, I buried myself in books. Reading saved my life.

Reading erotic novels fueled my curiosity, which led me to explore the fetish world. I don't have a computer, but I learned over a year ago that the public library has a shocking lack of security on their computers. It took me no time at all to open a FetLife account and absorb every detail I could about the community. That's where I stumbled upon Surrender, the local club, and somehow managed to find the willpower to get a guest membership.

I still can't believe I walked through the door that first night four weeks ago. Alone. Eager to explore. Wanting to sate my curiosity.

Am I submissive? I'm still not sure. But I know my body lights up when I watch women submit in the club. I don't even care if they submit to other women or men, though men usually make my heart beat faster, probably because of their sheer size.

I jump in my seat as Master Roman rounds the desk and then leans his butt against the front, his feet inches from mine, perfect unscuffed black dress shoes catching my eye. "Should you decide to work for me, I would pay you far more than the ridiculous salary requirement you listed."

I swallow, my eyes widening. He speaks as though he's about to hire me. I'm shocked. We've discussed nothing except the fact that I have no local family.

"However," he narrows his gaze, "I need to be sure you understand a few things." He crosses his arms, staring down at me intimidatingly. I can still see his hands though. Enormous. I don't know why I'm so intrigued by them. Probably because it's impossible not to wonder what it would feel like to have them on my body.

I jump when he continues speaking, yanking my thoughts away from his hands. "I require very long hours. I would expect you to be here at seven o'clock sharp every morning. I can't guarantee what time you will leave at night. Sometimes I work twelve or more hours six days a week. In addition to your salary, you'll make time and a half for overtime."

I stare at him, doing the math in my head. That's a lot of hours. But hell, what else do I have to do? It's not like I have friends. I have work. I have books. I don't even own a television. I can't afford one, and I don't care. I have always preferred reading to watching mindless TV.

"Would that be a problem for you, Lucy?"

"No, Sir." My voice squeaks. I need this job, and it's starting to seem as though Master Roman is leaning toward offering it to me. Besides, I suddenly feel a strong urge to be the person who doesn't quit in three months. Apparently three weaker women have not been able to hack the demands.

If long hours were what broke them, I will not be affected by the time constraints of other people.

Though I don't yet know how much he intends to pay me, if it's more than I was making and includes benefits and overtime, I know I will find the will to make this work. I have to.

He scrutinizes me for a long time, his gaze lingering on my face for a while and then trailing down my body. "I provide medical insurance and a 401K. Your starting salary would easily be double what you've been making, but I don't like to listen to excuses about my employees needing to leave early, come in late, or take time off."

A 401K? I hardly even know what that is. I certainly never intended to have one in my life. I at least understand it's a retirement plan. This job is looking better by the moment. So what if Master Roman is gruff and demanding and keeps long hours?

"What, exactly, would I be doing for you, Sir?" I ask, proud of myself for keeping my voice even and sounding intelligent.

"Whatever I want." He pauses.

I part my lips, thinking to ask for a few more details.

Luckily, he elaborates. "Working for me can be extremely boring at times. For that reason, you'll need to get a good night's sleep every day. I expect you to be near me at all times, mostly for the sole purpose of taking care of anything I might need ranging from coffee to lunch to finding a book in my library to sorting papers, filing. The list is long. The labor isn't difficult. I'm demanding, and I'm certain my three previous assistants were bored. I often caught them nodding off. I won't tolerate sleepiness. If you have been enjoying late nights out with friends, those days are over. You'll come here rested and sharp and ready to serve me."

Serve him? So, let me get this straight. This man is offering me way more money, health insurance, and a savings plan. In exchange, he wants me to stay near him for long hours with very little required of me. Who in their right mind would turn this down?

On top of everything else, he's the sexiest man I've ever set eyes on, so the view will be constantly spectacular. My biggest challenge will be not squirming in his presence as my mind wanders to thoughts of kneeling before him and letting him dominate me.

I shiver at the thought, my stupid panties dampening again. I have zero experience being submissive. I'm still not even sure I *am* submissive. If my reaction to Master Roman is any indication, however, it's probably safe to assume I have my answers.

I've done my research. I've watched people submit at Surrender on five occasions. Maybe that's enough to know what I might like. On the other hand, perhaps it's a very bad idea to take a job working for a man I clearly would rather submit to.

If he gave me a choice right now to take this job or explore D/s with him, I would be hard-pressed to turn down the offer of submission. I've heard of girls who train under men like Master Roman. I wonder if he only dominates seasoned submissives or if he ever trains anyone.

I also wonder if he has any intention of dominating me, or if he's done so with any of his previous assistants. Unlikely, I decide, which is disappointing.

Master Roman shoves off the desk and wanders back to the other side. "Since you haven't run from the room, I assume I still have your attention."

"Yes, Sir." I shake my inappropriate thoughts away.

"And you're still interested in the position?"

"Yes, Sir." My heart pounds. Could I be so lucky?

"Good." He finally lowers himself into his giant leather

desk chair and pulls it up to the desk. "Can you start immediately?"

"Yes, Sir." My luck is skyrocketing now. I can do this. I will not disappoint him. If he wants someone to stand around at his beck and call every day and endure his gruffness, I'm the girl for the job.

"You'll need a physical. I require regular checkups of all my employees. I'll make an appointment for tomorrow morning with my physician." He picks up a business card from his desk and reaches across to set it on the far side. I'm close enough to take it out of his hand without standing, nor does he seem to think it's necessary just yet because he continues speaking.

"Assuming you're in good physical condition, I'll expect you to start the following morning. Wednesday. Does that work for you?"

"Yes, Sir." I try not to show too much emotion. The truth is I'm excited and elated.

"Excellent. I have several staff members. You'll need to learn their names." He picks up the phone on his desk and speaks directly into it without dialing. "Nancy, Lucy will be joining us starting Wednesday. Would you please provide her with a uniform and see her out? She's leaving my office in a few minutes." He sets the phone down without waiting for a response.

Uniform? I don't even need to provide my own clothes? This just keeps getting better because the truth is, I'm seriously concerned about fitting in with his household using my current wardrobe. Martin and Sons was relatively lax. I always wore a dress or slacks, but I don't own anything fancy. Honestly, my clothing is as frumpy as possible, most of it acquired from second-hand shops.

When Master Roman speaks again, I jump in my chair. His gruff tone is going to be hard to get used to. "As you know, Lucy, I'm a Dominant. I don't leave that at the club. It's who I am. I demand respect from all my employees at all times. You, as the newest employee with the lowest status in my household, will speak to every single person you encounter with respect, addressing them as ma'am and sir. Even the gardener. Your status here is as I deem it unless and until I decide otherwise. Have I made myself clear?"

"Yes, Sir." I'm trembling, and I can hear it in my voice.

"Everyone who works for me has a job to do. I expect you to keep that in mind at all times. You will not speak to anyone unnecessarily unless they have instigated the conversation. If you have any questions, you will bring them to me."

I nod, slowly, my mouth too dry to speak.

He lifts a brow. "That will be the last time you use a non-verbal response to answer a question, Lucy."

I swallow. "Yes, Sir." My voice wobbles.

He narrows his gaze, and I worry for a moment that he might change his mind and fire me before I've even left his office. "As long as you do as you're told and stick to the tasks you're assigned, you'll get along just fine. I will warn you that I will discipline you in an appropriate manner to fit the offense if you choose to willfully disregard my instructions."

My voice is barely a whisper as I once again squeeze my thighs together tighter. "Yes, Sir." The visual of him disciplining me in any way overwhelms me. I picture him spanking me or putting me in a time out. I know that can't be what he meant, but I can't stop the mental picture.

His gaze lowers to my lap, mortifying me. He can't possibly know that his words have aroused me. I would die if he assumed such a thing.

Did his other assistants receive this same lecture before they started working for him? Surely they did. I'm not somehow special. And yet, as he continues to stare at the way my hands are gripping each other in my lap with my bare knees pinched tight and my heels bobbing up and down, I fear he might just call me out on my plight.

His word choice runs through my head over and over. Respect. Discipline. What does he mean when he says discipline? Would he dock my pay or have me clean toilets?

My body jerks as I picture his huge, strong hand on my bottom, spanking me. Ridiculous of course and totally inappropriate thoughts. I really need to curtail my roving imagination or I'll get myself in trouble.

His gaze slowly lifts. "Work on raising your voice, Lucy. If you mutter constantly so that I need to ask you to repeat yourself, I will quickly grow weary."

"Yes, Sir."

"You may go now. I'll expect you Wednesday morning. Seven sharp. Do. Not. Be. Late." His attention instantly lowers to his desk, and before I manage to stand, he appears to be already engrossed in a file on his desk. I've been summarily dismissed.

It occurs to me that perhaps he treats all his new hires in such a dismissive manner in order to weed them out and test their strength. If he thinks I will break from his sharpness, he is wrong. I'm not like other assistants he's had. I'm desperate. I need this job, and the promise it holds far outweighs the challenges.

I stand as tall as possible and pad quietly from his office. There is no way I can keep my shoes from clicking on the hardwood, however, so I make a mental note to invest in rubber-souled shoes immediately.

CHAPTER 7

Master Roman

Holy fuck. What just happened?

I continue to stare at the papers in my hand as the sweetest little girl I've ever encountered nervously pads from my office. I can see nothing. I have no idea what paper I'm holding. But she doesn't know that.

Did I push her too far? Did I scare her too badly?

I don't think so. I think I hit the ball out of the park. I did my best to read her every reaction and respond accordingly. She may not know it yet, but she is so perfectly submissive in every way. The exact kind of girl I have spent my life looking for.

She is young. I don't care. She is also a blank slate that no one has tarnished to the best of my knowledge. If she has any skeletons I did not find, they can't be very big. I will extinguish them until they do not exist.

The way she fidgets and blushes and wrings her hands

made my cock swell to the point of aching. Her breathing and shocked expressions and muttering and biting her lip all made my pulse increase by the minute. And when she squeezed her legs together, I nearly came in my pants.

It took incredible restraint not to demand she strip off her clothes and kneel in front of me. I almost believe she would have done it too.

But that's not how I want our relationship to start. I want to earn her submission. I'm not patient enough to wait months or years, so I will push her every day, but I have enough willpower to encourage her not so subtly to recognize the sort of girl she was born to be.

Specifically, my girl.

Her life so far has seemed messy and confusing. I haven't dug deep enough to know what her childhood was like, so I can't say for sure if she leans toward the role of a submissive little due to a childhood trauma or if she comes by it naturally. I will take care of her either way.

I have dabbled in age play over the years with many women, none of whom were interested in anything permanent. I have also known for most of my adult life that I won't be satisfied until I find a little who needs comfort, protection, boundaries, direction, and discipline. Not for two hours a night once a week but full time.

I run my hand over my face and take a deep breath, mentally reviewing every moment of the past hour. Lucy far exceeded my expectations. She wasn't simply timid. She was also strong-willed. Determined. She not only needs this job, she wants it. She knows I've fired three women in less than a year. She intends to prove she can fill their shoes, probably more for herself than anyone else.

I have no idea if Lucy can do the job I need filled. I don't even care. It's not why I hired her. I hired her to get her under my roof and my thumb. I hired her so I could keep close tabs on her while I watch her blossom into the perfect version of herself.

Hell, I hired her because the thought of her being anywhere else for even an hour at a time had started to make me nauseous. I will keep her long hours and work her hard for the first few weeks, and then I will move her into my home. Surely, when she sees the benefits, she will not balk. Her commute is not going to be pleasant, and she doesn't have a car. Her apartment is abysmal on top of that. When I propose free room and board so that she no longer has to commute, she will have been with me enough days to jump at the opportunity.

I need the time to get to know her better anyway. It will take me several days to read her and decide which direction to guide her. I have no idea what age range she might end up falling into as a little or even a middle, but I do know she wants to please me already. She is determined to make me proud of her. She won't intentionally do anything to disobey me. And she won't enjoy it when I punish her.

I spent far too much time inquiring of her work from her previous employer, pretending I was simply someone with whom she had applied. They had nothing but praise for her performance, which pleased me. I learned she is punctual and loyal. She takes responsibility when she makes a mistake. She tries hard to ensure everyone around her is pleased.

I smile as I remember she is also messy. Her work is excellent. Her organization skills are lacking. The inside of her apartment is a disaster. She keeps her clothes strewn across the floor, dishes in the sink, and books placed everywhere. I cannot wait to discipline her for her lack of organizational skills.

I know she reads a lot, which I approve of. I know what

sort of literature she prefers, which has been informative. Many of the books in her apartment are library books, and the vast majority of those are either erotic romance novels or information about the fetish world.

I have to adjust my cock as I picture her learning about my world through books. I can't be sure how much she knows, but from her reactions to me, I have to assume she is still very green.

I have used restraint by not putting cameras in her apartment, which means I have no idea if she masturbates. However, I do know she doesn't own a vibrator. Nor does she keep condoms or birth control in her apartment.

There are so many milestones I cannot wait to watch her achieve.

But I will force myself to remain patient with her, as patient as a Dom like me is capable of.

Tomorrow she will see my personal physician, Dr. Pruitt, at a clinic she has no idea only sees lifestyle patients from eight to ten in the morning one day a week. Thank God that day happens to be a Tuesday. If I'd had to wait several days to get her in, I might have lost my mind.

I'm not just sending Lucy there to intimidate her, unnerve her, or freak her out. I'm sending her there to make sure she is healthy, and I will insist she return for frequent visits for the same reason.

I've already warned Dr. Pruitt and his nurse, AnnMarie, that Lucy is not only new to the lifestyle but also isn't aware of her submissive tendencies yet. The doctor will go easy on her this first visit. Subsequent trips will prove more trying.

I wish I could be with her in the office or at least a fly on the wall as she is examined. I close my eyes again and picture her shaking with nerves as Dr. Pruitt examines her. I have no idea if she's ever even been to a gynecologist, but considering her financial status and the fact that she doesn't seem to have a boyfriend, there is every possibility she has not.

She's so innocent.

A blank slate.

Mine.

CHAPTER 8

Lucy

I spend Monday afternoon cleaning my apartment. Elated. Unable to stop smiling. My primary intention is to keep my mind occupied so I don't freak out over my good fortune. My secondary intention is to find my inner tidiness.

The truth is Tidy is not my middle name, and this concerns me. Master Roman's home is pristine. His office doesn't have a scrap of extraneous paper in sight. There isn't a dust bunny to be had.

I'm not a disaster when it comes to work. I maintained a decent workspace at Martin and Sons. However, I know it's not in my nature. The reason I kept papers filed and messages organized was because I needed to do so to keep my job.

My bedroom in my apartment is forever cluttered. Even though I don't own many clothes, two thirds of them are usually on the floor except when it's laundry day. I don't have a dishwasher, and my sink is filled with dishes until I run out and am forced to wash them. I don't own a vacuum. I somehow manage to wipe down my bathroom counter every few months when the hair starts to annoy me.

And yet I've taken a job with the king of domination. What am I thinking?

You can do this. You can do this. You can do this. I've repeated that mantra over and over all day. How hard can it possibly be? All I need to do is show up at seven every morning, run around obeying Master Roman's orders, keep my voice at a reasonable level, and stay off everyone else's radar.

I giggle as I think of the word *obey*. Master Roman certainly made it clear that I was to obey him like a child. Perhaps I should have been more intimidated than I was and turned down the offer.

But I don't have that luxury. I need the money. I don't have savings or relatives to bail me out. If I hadn't stumbled upon this opportunity and taken this job, there's a good chance I would be evicted and homeless in weeks.

I also have an unexpected new problem. I didn't sleep a single moment last night. Every time I started to doze off, visions of kneeling at Master Roman's feet yanked me awake. Why couldn't I just have a normal dream like a regular person and wake up smiling and refreshed?

Nope. Not me. Instead, I bolted awake over and over because my body was heated with arousal. I repeatedly kicked the covers away and found myself sweating as I rubbed my thighs together. About a dozen times I considered masturbating to the images assaulting me, but I forced myself not to act on the impulse.

I feared I would be much worse off if I succumbed to the temptation and then had to face my new boss on Wednesday with fresh visions of kneeling naked between his legs with my head on his thighs. When my mind wandered to sucking him off in the process, I had moaned in the dark.

So, I'm cleaning. Deep cleaning. I even went to the store to purchase cleaning supplies. I also splurged and got myself a small vacuum. I figured with my new salary I would be able to afford it by the time the credit card bill came.

Most of the time, I try not to think about my credit card debt. It's not outrageous, but it is enough to make me nervous, considering I have lived paycheck to paycheck for two years. Before that, my life was even less consistent. I was waiting tables.

I know I could make ends meet easier if I had a roommate, but the truth is I don't like spending that much time with other people. I never have. As a child, I was mousy and quiet so that no one would find out my father was verbally abusive, and then when I went to live with my equally mean grandmother, I never bothered to make friends.

I was an outcast from the day I arrived in Chicago. My grandmother made sure I knew every day how inconvenient it was for her to finish raising me. She made it perfectly clear that as soon as I turned eighteen and graduated, I was on my own.

I learned quickly that the best way to keep Grandmother Strickland off my back was to be as quiet and unobtrusive as possible, make good grades, and stay out of trouble. I tended to slip in and out of her house without making a sound. She fed me and provided me with a roof. That was it. I often thought I should be grateful. If she'd turned me away, God knows what might have happened to me in the system.

My world was filled with books. I went to the library at least three times a week. I often read two books a day. I never watched television because my grandmother only had one TV, it was always on her channel, and she was always watching it. I never spent one more minute than absolutely necessary in the same room as her.

I turned eighteen four years ago and graduated two weeks later. The next day, my grandmother made it clear that her job was done. She gave me enough money to last a few weeks on my own and basically showed me the door. It wasn't unexpected. I packed my few belongings, bought a one-way bus ticket to Seattle—I'd always wanted to go there—and never looked back. In all this time, I have never even tried to contact her. I have no idea if she's still living or not. In fact, until this morning when Master Roman inquired about her, I hadn't thought about her in months.

I count my blessings that I have never been homeless. I've been close on a few occasions, but I've scraped by. The fact that I kept the same "secure" job for two years made it possible for me to get a credit card in the first place, and though I have tried to never abuse it, there have been months when it came in handy to get me by the last few days until I got paid.

I've never had a car. I take public transportation. I live a simple existence. Maybe for the first time in my life I can finally get ahead. Maybe I can pay off my bills and buy a few nicer outfits. Maybe my luck has turned.

Speaking of clothes, I glance at the package sitting on my small, wobbly kitchen table, realizing I have not looked inside to see what uniform Nancy has sent home with me.

Part of me has been reluctant to take a peek. Part of me has been holding off to maintain the mystery.

Suddenly, I can't wait any longer. I drop the rag I've been using to clean my kitchen counter and wipe my hands on my oldest pair of jeans—the pair with holes at the knees that weren't there intentionally when I bought them.

It's absurd that I'm holding my breath and my hands are shaking as I open the oddly wrapped package. Instead of using a grocery sack or a paper bag of some sort, Nancy had carefully folded the contents into a piece of brown paper, tying it with string. It looks like a parcel someone would have brought home from a department store in the eighteen hundreds.

I carefully untie the string and let the paper fall away. My breath catches to find a bra and pair of panties. How weird is that? When Master Roman said I would be provided with a uniform, I pictured a skirt and blouse, not undergarments.

I slowly pick up the plain white bra and look at the tag. I stare at it for a moment, wondering how the hell Nancy or Master Roman or anyone else would know my size. The panties are also plain white. Neither piece has any lace or silk to them. Both are cotton. Even weirder, the panties are full briefs. They are in my size, but I've never seen a pair of underwear with that much material.

Although I am not made of money and buy most of my clothes from thrift stores, I have always purchased my undergarments new from a supermart. I have never owned anything quite this modest. I'm going to feel like a ninety-year-old woman in them.

Trying not to think about the implications of including panties and a bra for me, I set them aside and reach for the next item. Surprisingly, it's a decent-looking navy dress. It has short sleeves and a modest neckline. The skirt is pleated, and when I fan it out, I realize it flairs out all the way around but will hang loose close to my thighs. It looks a bit short, but maybe it's my imagination.

Another shocker is the shoes that were hidden under the dress. Who provides their employees shoes? *The same man who also provides underwear.*

I pick them up, chuckling inside as I notice they have rubber soles which will keep me from making any noise on the hardwood floors throughout Master Roman's home. They are flat and brown leather with narrow shoestrings. I assume they are intended to go with other outfits in the future.

Naturally, they are also in my size. I close my eyes and take a deep breath, unsure if I ever want to know why the hell anyone could have purchased all these items to specifically fit me. And, more importantly, how did they do so before I even interviewed for the job?

I'm going to try not to think about all the implications of that question for as long as possible and instead I head to my bedroom to hang up the dress. The last thing I want to do is arrive wrinkled for my first day on the job.

After hooking the dress to the back of my bathroom door, I stare at myself in the mirror. Should I get my hair cut and styled? Have my nails done? Invest in some better makeup?

Master Roman did not mention any of those things. I'm not even sure if he paid close enough attention to me to notice. If someone were to ask him right now what color my hair was, he would probably shrug and say, "whose hair?"

I giggle. I'm also exaggerating. He might have been serious and intense, but he did stare at me long enough to take in whatever seemed to interest him. It might be prudent to wait a few weeks before I invest any more future, hard-earned money in hair and makeup. There is still the chance I will get fired on the first day and then I'll be stuck with no job and more credit card debt.

I pull my hairband out to free my messy, indistinct, dark curls, wincing as one gets caught. I have never been able to manage my hair. It's unruly. If someone were to grab a curl and stretch it out, it would probably reach my butt. I used to cut it myself on occasion, but it always ended up crooked, so I don't do that anymore.

Instead it's long. My shampoo bill is high. My conditioner bill is higher. I have never had the luxury of investing in other hair products that would probably tame the mop, nor have I ever been taught how to manage it. So, now I sigh as I fluff it out, creating a disaster.

Nope. There is no way I can show up for work with it

down. The hairband not only keeps it out of my face, but it also keeps it from poofing out in every direction.

I shift my gaze to my face and sigh louder. My skin is pale because I rarely go out in the sun, and there's rarely sun in Seattle anyway. I own cheap mascara that I use sparingly on my already dark eye lashes. My eyebrows are probably too large, but again, I know nothing about plucking them. On the bright side, my cheeks are often rosy from stress or embarrassment, so that cuts down on my blush bills.

I giggle. *Blush.* As if.

I own clear lip gloss, but only because it keeps my lips from being chapped.

Am I attractive?

My smile fades as I consider that question. I truly don't know. I have never even cared. For the last ten years since I hit puberty, I have mostly hidden from society, which was easy enough behind my hair.

I'm short, and I know I'm underweight. I'm lucky I have any boobs at all, but proportionately I would say I did well. They're never going to sag by any stretch of the imagination, but I can fill an A-cup.

I have never dated anyone. The closest I've come to a relationship is watching other people at Surrender the past five weeks. How pitiful.

And that brings up another depressing thought. First of all, my temporary membership was only for one more visit anyway. But, more importantly, there is no way I would continue to frequent a club owned by the man I now work for as his assistant.

Too bad. I was enjoying myself at Surrender. Not that it mattered from any angle since I was now either out of money or working for the boss. But, I had been learning, and I think in my mind I was making progress.

I hadn't managed to reach a point in five visits where I had the guts to try anything, but I had spent hours watching. No one had asked me to do a scene, and there was no way I would have accepted such an offer.

I know several things about myself now. I get aroused when I watch women submit. I get even more aroused when the Dom is firm and demanding. My panties get wet when a sub is disciplined. And, I would give anything to have a Dom treat me like I'm precious and worth disciplining.

I've read all of this. I've studied it. I have no idea how any of this research and information is going to change my life other than to frustrate me in the middle of the night when I'm supposed to be sleeping so that Master Roman doesn't ever catch me tired.

I need to put the entire experience at Surrender out of my mind. It's done. It's in the past. At least for now.

CHAPTER 9

Lucy

I am right on time for my eight o'clock appointment Tuesday morning with Dr. Pruitt. For some reason, I get the feeling that news of my tardiness would get back to Master Roman before I left the building.

It wasn't easy to get to the clinic since it's several miles from my apartment and required two bus changes. But I left my home at six thirty and am relieved to have made it on time.

A receptionist takes my name, hands me a clipboard with a stack of papers to fill out, and tells me to have a seat. I'm nervous for no good reason. It's a physical. Nothing more. I've had other physicals in my life. Not many. But some. The doctor is going to look in my ears, take my blood pressure, hit my kneecaps with that triangle thing, and done.

I know I'm perfectly healthy. This is a formality. I force myself to fill out the forms and return them as quickly as possible to the receptionist. Anything to get this over with.

I try not to fidget as I look around the room. The other patients waiting catch my attention. There is a woman next to a gruff man who seems like a Dom. She has her hands folded in her lap and her gaze toward the floor. Obviously, my mind is totally warped if I've started thinking people around me are in the lifestyle.

Another woman about my age is sitting across from me with her feet planted firmly on the floor and her gaze also downcast. Her hands are in fists on her thighs. She is chewing on her lower lip.

I jerk my gaze to two men and then to a woman with a younger man and then to a man by himself. Yep, I'm losing my mind because it seems like everyone in the room came from a fetish club. Irrational, of course. Clearly, I didn't sleep long enough last night. My brain is so clouded with thoughts of BDSM that they're infiltrating my waking consciousness.

Moments later, someone calls my name. "Lucy Neill?"

I'm relieved to exit the twilight zone and jump to my feet.

A woman waits for me at the entrance to the offices, and I follow her down a hallway that has about six exam rooms, three on each side. She opens a door and motions me to enter. She smiles at me oddly and then tells me a nurse with be with me shortly.

I am unrealistically nervous. *This is a doctor's office. Get a grip.*

I'm still standing in the middle of the room when the door opens a minute later, and I jump, a slight squeal escaping my lips.

The woman who enters has a serious expression, and she lifts a questioning brow. "Are you okay?"

"Yes," I assure her, smoothing my hands down my jeans.

I judge her to be about sixty. Her gray hair is in a severe bun. She glances at a chart and then meets my gaze. "You're a new patient. Master Roman sent you."

"Yes." I wonder why she knows who sent me and why she calls him by that formal club name.

She hands me a light blue folded paper gown and says. "Please remove everything and put this on. It opens in the front. You can drape this piece over your lap. Dr. Pruitt will be in shortly." As she reaches for the door handle, she turns back to meet my gaze. "Miss Neill, you are obviously totally new to the lifestyle. Let me make a suggestion before you get yourself into trouble."

I'm stunned. Speechless. Staring at her with my mouth hanging open.

She continues. "Dr. Pruitt only sees lifestyle patients on Tuesday mornings. Every patient in this clinic right now is either directly or indirectly involved in some form of BDSM."

I clear my throat and interrupt her. "I'm starting as Master Roman's assistant. I'm not really in the lifestyle."

She smiles, but her expression is condescending and screams that I am a foolish girl. "Lucy, everyone Master Roman knows is in the lifestyle. Employees and acquaintances alike. Even if they don't realize it yet."

I'm even more shocked now. She has no idea what she's talking about.

"Word of advice, Lucy, since you're new to Master Roman's employ. You should err on the side of caution at all times and address everyone you come in contact with as sir or ma'am. Including me. It's what he would expect."

With those words hanging in the air, she leaves.

I stare at the door for several long seconds, repeating everything she has just said in my head. *Everyone Master Roman knows is in the lifestyle, even if they don't realize it yet.*

Is she correct?

I can't even process that information. I don't want to. If I stopped to consider the implication, I wouldn't even know what answer I want. Part of me is screaming that she's wrong.

I've been hired as an assistant. Part of me is trembling at the idea of submitting to Master Roman. Is that what he truly expects?

I'm stunned. I also hadn't expected to get naked this morning. For a routine physical?

Taking a deep breath, I try to calm my racing heart, set the paper gown on the exam table, and turn around to remove my clothes. My hands are shaking. I need to move faster. The worst imaginable thing will be if Dr. Pruitt comes in before I'm situated.

I rush to remove my shoes and socks and then my jeans, T-shirt, bra, and panties. I'm shivering by the time I arrange the ridiculous paper gown around my shoulders and tug it across my chest. My butt is exposed, and I grip my legs together as I cover thighs with the larger folded paper napkin.

I wait for several minutes. The room is too cold. I start shaking. I can't catch my breath either as my mind wanders wildly to absurd thoughts. I'm twenty-two years old. I've never even been to a gynecologist. Why would I? I've never needed birth control because I've never had a boyfriend and thus never had sex.

No person in the world has seen me naked since I was a toddler, and I have no memory of that. I force myself to breathe. In. Out. In. Out.

Finally, a soft knock resounds through the room and then the door opens. A man, who I presume is the doctor, enters followed by the stuffy older nurse.

The man is cleanly bald with a goatee. I think he's about fifty. He smiles at me briefly and glances at my chart. "Lucy Neill. Master Roman sent you."

"Yes." Again, this is odd information. And why does the doctor refer to my boss as Master? The nurse did too.

The nurse shoots me a look, her eyes wide with suggestion.

I clear my throat. "Yes, Sir. I'm starting a new job with him tomorrow."

He inclines his head to one side as he meets my gaze again. "Relax. It's just a routine physical."

I swallow and say nothing.

He looks back at his file. "It says here you're twenty-two. Single. No allergies. Do I have that correct?"

"Yes, Sir."

"You've met my nurse, AnnMarie," he states as he picks up my wrist and checks my pulse.

I glance at the surly woman. "Yes, Sir."

Dr. Pruitt says nothing while he peers into my eyes, my ears, my throat. He hooks his stethoscope on his ears and sets the incredibly cold flat metal on my chest between my breasts. He listens, moves the cold disk, and listens again. He switches to my back. "Sit up straight, please, Lucy."

I jerk my spine taller.

"Deep breath in."

I inhale.

He listens.

We repeat this several times.

Finally, he rounds to my front. "When was your last physical?"

"I'm not sure. A few years ago maybe. I don't get sick often."

He frowns. "You should always have regular checkups."

I nod. It's not like I can do anything about the past now.

He pats my thigh. "If you're working for Master Roman, it won't be an issue. He's a stickler about health."

I'm not surprised.

"What form of birth control do you use?"

"None. I haven't…needed it," I murmur.

"So you use condoms for protection?"

I'm going to die of mortification. "I haven't had sex," I murmur.

He doesn't flinch. "Good. I'd sure like to hear that more often these days. At your age, I recommend using something. Just to be safe. You never know when you might meet the right person." He smiles.

I nod. I've never considered birth control before. Why would I? And as ridiculous as it sounded to think that I might meet someone, I find I like the idea of pretending I'm a regular woman who might have sex. So I respond, "Okay."

"I recommend the Depo-Provera shots. A lot of women your age are using it nowadays. Your periods will probably stop entirely, which also has the added benefit of reducing cramps and PMS."

"Okay. That sounds good. Sir."

"Have you ever had a pap smear?"

"No." My face heats up. Is that necessary? Today?

"Are your periods regular?"

"Yes, Sir."

"'Kay, I'm going to check your breasts and do a vaginal exam today. A woman your age needs to start regular well-woman checkups."

I can't breathe.

He sets a hand on my back, the other on my shoulder. "Please lie back, Lucy. I'll be quick. Trust me. This is painless. It'll be over in moments. Then you'll be on your way."

I'm trying not to hyperventilate as I recline. I stare at the ceiling while Dr. Pruitt pulls the napkin robe to one side, exposing my breast, and uses the pads of his fingers to press around my nipples. "Do you regularly perform self-breast exams?" he asks.

"No, Sir," I mumble.

"You should start." As he marginally covers the first breast and exposes the second one, he continues rambling about how I should check myself for lumps. I can hardly pay attention. I don't breathe until he covers my second breast.

Nurse AnnMarie has a hand on my shoulder. I don't look at her face because I don't want to know if she's smirking condescendingly at me or providing a soothing motherly expression.

I close my eyes and focus on the backs of my eyelids as Dr. Pruitt lifts my feet onto stirrups and gently opens my legs. He is quick. I'll give him that.

I flinch when the cold speculum hits my most private body part and grit my teeth while it slides inside me. I feel nothing else, and then it disappears as quickly as it was inserted.

In moments, the doctor has a hold of my arm and he's helping me to resume sitting. "Everything looks great," he declares as he makes several notes in my file. He smiles at me when he meets my gaze. "AnnMarie will be back to give you the first shot. You'll be good for three months with that. Do you have any questions?"

I shake my head. I don't even have any nouns or verbs. There is no way I could respond if I wanted to. Whatever. In a hundred years when I have a free night off work, maybe I'll meet a knight in shining armor, he'll sweep me off my feet, and I'll be glad I've been taking birth control.

"Okay. It was nice to meet you, Lucy. We'll let you get dressed now. AnnMarie will get your sorted out."

In less than a minute the nurse returns with a syringe in hand. She gives me the shot and then leaves me to get dressed.

I cannot get out of this office fast enough. Two strangers have just stared at my vagina. I wasn't prepared for that. I'm still trembling. I probably will be for the rest of the day.

CHAPTER 10

Master Roman

I am in my office early Wednesday morning. Too early. The truth is I have not slept much since Monday. I hope the arrival of Lucy will help me relax, though that is probably wishful thinking. The next weeks will be trying. Difficult.

Waiting for her to understand.

Waiting for her to know.

Waiting for her to be mine.

I adjust my tie as I stare out the window, my gaze seeing nothing of the impeccably groomed backyard I know to be there. Instead I'm in my head.

Am I doing the right thing in hijacking Lucy's life and making it my own? I can't be sure, but I have to trust my gut. I'm not usually wrong.

I'm a Dom in every way. Always have been.

My club, Surrender, is aptly named. The Dominants who frequent my club are seasoned and knowledgeable. My members are well-vetted. They must abide by strict rules, or they can find another club. I don't mess around when it comes to safety, and I don't give second chances to anyone.

I've owned Surrender for fifteen years, and in that time, I have watched over the club as it grew into the premier coveted location in Seattle that it is today. I'm well aware of my reputation as a Dom, however, most of the lore is just that, lore.

It is true that I am a demanding Dom with high expectations for my submissives. It is true that I'm difficult to get along with and go through personal assistants about as often as it rains in Seattle. It is also true that I don't play with anyone in my club.

I decided years ago when I first bought the place that it would be in my best interest to remain aloof and keep gossip about myself to a minimum. For this reason, although I keep a close eye on everyone else who comes through my front doors, my personal liaisons happen inside my club before it opens, after closing, or on nights when it is not open.

Surrender is open Wednesdays, Fridays, and Saturdays. I try to make a point to pop in at least for a while every night we are open. I don't always stay long. Julius has had things well under control at the club for years, and we have acquired the most efficient staff over the years that we are confident everything will run smoothly even if neither of us is there.

Surrender is not my main source of income. It's not even a primary source. I inherited my money, and I work hard for the wealth I've added to it. I come from a long legacy of money going back to my great grandfather. I also come from a long line of Dominants. It's in my blood. My father was a Dom and my grandfather before him. Unfortunately, both of them are gone now, but I have inherited the family estate and maintain it to the same standards as they did.

I'm a perfectionist. Perhaps that's what makes me a Dominant. I expect everyone who works for me in my home, in my professional life, and at my club to do the highest quality work possible. And in return, I pay them well, far better than they could be making anywhere else.

Not to imply that I haven't earned every cent I make. I have a master's degree in business, and I know how to manage not only my money but the finances of over a hundred clients as well.

They say I'm a financial god. I never dispute the facts.

I have worked hard. I have earned my place in society and inside my club. I have everything a man could possibly want.

Except one thing.

Her.

CHAPTER 11

Lucy

I have not slept enough. I know this, but there is nothing I can do about it. I was so nervous about this morning that I couldn't sleep for more than a few restless minutes at a time. I tossed and turned all night. Every time I drifted off, I had ridiculous dreams.

Master Roman starred in all of them. He was dominating me. I was usually on my knees in a position I'd learned from watching at his club. He didn't even have to touch me for me to wake up over and over in a sweat, my panties wet from arousal.

Each time I fell asleep, the dream picked up where it left off, slowly progressing. He was so intense, circling me, staring at me, judging me…

In my dream I was dressed in a thin, white, transparent gown and nothing else. It reached midthigh. My knees rested on a pillow, but I was shaking from holding the position so long. That's how real the dream felt.

Even now, as I sit on the public bus, staring out the window, my nipples are tight points and my panties are wet. I'm wearing the plain white panties and bra Nancy provided me, though I hesitated for a long time before putting them on, thinking about wearing my own underwear. Who would ever know?

In the end, I put on the approved underwear, visions of my dreams still haunting me enough to worry that Master Roman just might check for himself. Ludicrous, yes. Out of the realm of possibility? No.

The bus comes to a stop, and I get off, glancing at my watch. It's six thirty. I have half an hour to get to Master's home. I have meticulously checked and rechecked the early morning routes several times to ensure I would not be late. It's only going to take me about ten minutes to get there from here, so I don't need to walk fast. This is a good thing since I don't want to arrive sweating and out of breath.

Lucky for me, it's late summer so it's not snowing or freezing cold in Seattle. I'm also fortunate that it isn't raining this morning. At some point I'm going to need to make other arrangements to get to work. I can't count on walking a half a mile every day in rain, sleet, or snow. But for today, I've been granted good fortune from the weather gods.

I'm wearing everything Nancy provided, but I have added a lightweight, white sweater just in case it gets chilly either outside or in the house. The shoes are not something I would have chosen for myself, but they are thankfully comfortable for walking.

The only thing about the dress that stood out when I put it on this morning is that it's a bit shorter than I would normally be comfortable in. Most likely, that's just me. Other women my age probably wear far shorter dresses and skirts. I've just never been outgoing enough or wanted to draw that kind of attention to myself.

59

Even though I walk slowly, I still arrive at Master Roman's estate fifteen minutes early, which is probably a good thing. I ring the bell outside the gate on the main street and wait for a response.

Suddenly, the gate swings open without anyone speaking to me through the intercom. Of course, whoever mans the gate would have been informed of my arrival this morning. They probably also have pictures and a bio knowing Master Roman.

Nancy has instructed me to use a side entrance instead of the front door, so I walk toward the left of the house and around to the back. I hesitate, wondering if I should knock or just go in. I'm still standing there when the door suddenly opens and a round woman in her early fifties is smiling at me.

"Good morning. I'm Evelyn. You must be Lucy."

"Yes, ma'am," I respond, remembering I've been instructed to do so now by both Master Roman and eerily the nurse at the clinic.

Evelyn holds the door for me and backs up. "Come on in. You don't have to knock. This door is always unlocked when I'm in the kitchen."

I step inside to realize I have entered an enormous kitchen filled with amazing smells of several things cooking. My stomach starts to grumble, and I cringe, embarrassed.

Evelyn chuckles, her whole body moving. She is the first person I have met in this house who has smiled. "Don't you worry. I'll be calling you to breakfast in about an hour."

I'm shocked. I wouldn't expect to eat breakfast here. In fact, I had fretted over what to do about lunch all day yesterday, finally deciding I should wait and see what Master Roman's schedule was like. In the future, I would bring a sandwich. I figured that today I would be too nervous to eat anyway.

Evelyn turns toward a pot boiling on the stove. "You look

surprised. I guess no one told you. You'll eat all your meals here. Master Roman feeds all his employees." She turned to wink at me. "Or rather I do."

"All my meals?" I ask, surprised.

"Yes. Of course. Seven in the morning is too early for most people to have eaten yet. I'll have your breakfast ready by about eight. You'll break for lunch at noon and dinner at six. If you lose track of time, someone will come get you or Master Roman will send you. Master Roman works long hours. I'm sure he informed you that you would often be here late at night."

"Yes, ma'am."

Evelyn smiles again. "Well, don't let me keep you. Go on through the kitchen. You'll figure out where you are in the house when you step into the hallway."

I nod and head toward the far side of the room. At least I don't have to worry about bringing a lunch or leaving the estate to find fast food.

Sure enough, as soon as I enter the hallway and shut the door to the kitchen behind me, I am oriented. I'm in the same hallway that leads to Master Roman's office.

The kitchen is a world apart from the rest of what I've seen of the house. It's white and bright with white tile and counters and cabinets. As soon as I shut the door, I'm standing in another dimension. Darkness. Dark paneling, hardwood, paint. Everything is a deep brown. Stately, I assume.

Taking a deep breath, I pad toward Master Roman's office, smiling as I realize my shoes are silent on the wood flooring. There is no way the selection is a coincidence.

Luckily, the door is standing open because I have no idea what the protocol is for my arrival each morning. Master Roman is sitting at his desk, head down, deep in thought. I step inside, pull my shoulders back, and clear my throat. "Good morning, Sir."

He lifts his gaze. "Ah, Lucy. Good. Right on time. I like that."

"You won't have to worry about my punctuality, Sir. I promise," I reassure him. I have never been late to work in my life. I am worried about the transportation to this estate, but I will figure it out in a few days. I can't really afford to take a taxi or Uber until I get paid, but if my salary is truly going to be as high as Master Roman has insinuated, I can surely afford something more reliable than the city bus.

"Excellent. I need you to read over some employment papers and sign them this morning." He stands as he tells me this, holding a file folder in his large hand. "Follow me."

I rush across the room as he turns to open a door at the far corner. He enters the second room I had not noticed the other day, and I follow. It turns out to be a smaller office much like the one I've just walked through. Same dark paneling. Same dark wood desk in a smaller version. There is an armchair in a deep forest green velvet and a loveseat in a deep brown leather across from the desk as if the occupant might at times entertain guests.

"This will be your office. Originally, when the house was built, this was probably a coat room or something. There have been several renovations over the years, however, which have left this odd room off my office. It's perfect for an assistant's space."

He is correct, and I'm suddenly glad I won't be sitting in his office all day working. It would unnerve me to be in his presence all the time. "Yes, it is, Sir."

He nods toward the windows—two giant windows behind the desk that reach floor to ceiling. "The best part is the view of the grounds." He turns back to face me. "The worst part is there is no other entrance other than through my office."

"Oh." I glance around. He's right. The wall opposite the desk, behind the love seat and chair, is covered with built-in bookshelves. They are about half full, though I'm not close enough to see what sort of literature occupies them.

"There is a bathroom across the hall from my office, so anytime you need to use it, you'll have to pass by me. It can't be helped." He is frowning, though I'm not sure if he finds the arrangement annoying or if he just frowns as a general rule.

"I'll be sure to sneak past you quietly, Sir."

His frown deepens. "I prefer you do no sneaking at all, Lucy."

I swallow. Obviously, he didn't hear the humor in my statement. "Yes, Sir," I murmur. It doesn't seem worth it to attempt to explain my intended meaning.

"I see you didn't practice raising your voice to an audible level since Monday."

I wince. "Sorry, Sir. I'll work on that."

"See that you do. It's annoying." He sets the file he's holding on the pristine desk and leaves the room. He does not shut the door.

I take a deep breath and shuffle over to the desk, taking only a moment to glance out the windows. The scenery takes my breath away. The focal point is an enormous waterfall cascading over artfully arranged rocks into a built-in hot tub. The deck is surrounded by beautiful plants and flowers and tables and chairs. A very large party could be held out there.

I quickly turn away from the view, knowing I can see it any time I want. I need to make a good impression here today. Staring out the window won't accomplish that.

As I carefully take a seat in the comfortable leather desk chair and roll up to the desk, I wonder what really happened to the three previous women who had this job and couldn't hack it. If Master Roman treats every employee with the same harshness as he has me, I'm not really surprised, but I'm not like other people.

Where did he hire the other women from? Does he always hire his assistants from applications at the front desk of Surrender? That seems farfetched. Then again, since he obviously takes his Dominant role very seriously, it's possible he won't hire anyone who isn't familiar with the lifestyle. The man lives bossy twenty-four seven.

I thank God I visited the club the five times I did. At least I understand the demanding way of Doms from watching. I don't feel prepared to be on the receiving end of so much dominance at all, but perhaps I'm less shocked than I would otherwise be if I walked into this home without any warning.

I open the folder, noticing that every piece of paper inside is precisely stacked. Nothing Master Roman does is messy. I glance toward the open door and my breath hitches when I see that his desk and mine are directly in line with each other. If he were to glance my direction, he would be looking right at me.

"Is something wrong, Lucy?" he asks without moving a millimeter. His head is facing down, his eyes seemingly focused on his desk. And yet.

I jump in my seat, jerk my attention back to my desk, and speak loud enough for him to hear me. "No, Sir." *Jesus.* Not only is the man bossy and demanding, but he has amazing peripheral vision.

I don't permit a single muscle besides my hands and my eyes to move for the next hour while I carefully read all the paperwork and fill out the necessary parts. Most of it is standard employment information, but under the circumstances, and considering who my new boss is, I take no chances with anything.

I'm careful the entire time that my chair doesn't roll any direction. I don't shuffle my feet or lean my elbows on the desk. I figure the sooner Master Roman learns he can trust me, the sooner he will ease off a little. Could be wishful thinking on my part.

I feel more nervous than when I arrived after filling out the details about my life. I have no local next of kin. I don't have friends whom someone could contact in an emergency. I have nothing but my grandmother in Chicago, and putting her down as a contact seems fruitless.

Surely he will judge me for being so introverted and shy. What twenty-two-year-old doesn't have girlfriends?

I remind myself that half the reason Master Roman was willing to hire me probably stemmed from the fact that I am available to be at his every beck and call seven days a week. I can work long hours. I don't have a husband or kids or even a boyfriend or friends. This may have been precisely why he hired me.

After ensuring I have filled out all the information and signed in every necessary spot, I push away from the desk and stand. I have no choice but to return the papers to him. He hasn't specified otherwise.

I hold my breath as I enter his office and approach his desk. I'm loath to interrupt him, nervous about his reaction. I don't know enough about his personality yet to know if he doesn't like to be interrupted or if he has an angry side. "Is there anyplace specific you'd like me to put these, Sir?"

"You may leave them on my desk," he answers without looking up. "I'm sure Evelyn has your breakfast ready. You should go eat."

I feel dismissed, and I'm not sorry. I'm not sure I can actually eat anything, but maybe Evelyn at least has tea or something that will settle my stomach. Besides, a break from the intensity that is Master Roman will help me catch my breath.

CHAPTER 12

Lucy

Finding my way back to the kitchen is easy, and I'm instantly calmer. I blow out a breath as Evelyn lifts her face and smiles at me. "I hope everything is going well for you so far, dear."

"Yes, ma'am. Just fine."

She points at a small table that sits at the far side of the long island. "Your breakfast is ready. Sit. Eat before it gets cold. Master Roman will want you to get back in half an hour."

Half an hour is far more time than I need to eat, and I'm still not sure I can eat. "Thank you, ma'am." I wander to the white table she has indicated. There is a bowl of steaming oatmeal, a plate of berries, and a glass of milk.

I take a deep breath, trying not to panic. I hate milk. Always have. I don't even like it on cereal. Oatmeal I can probably eat but not today. Berries I can manage. "I don't usually eat breakfast, ma'am," I inform her as I take a seat.

She glances my direction, her hands covered in flour. I

realize she is kneading dough. "Breakfast is the most important meal of the day. Trust me, you don't want to wait until lunch to eat around here. And," she tips her head down slightly to look at me over the top of her glasses, "Master Roman is a stickler about food. I suggest you eat." Her tone is still pleasant, but I hear the warning behind it. It might not be her own personal warning. It probably comes from Master Roman. I should appreciate the head's up.

"Thank you, ma'am."

My hands are shaking as I pull out the chair and lower myself into it. Something is odd about this table. I can't put my finger on it. As soon as I plant my feet and pick up my spoon, I realize what's different. It's small. It's my size. The chair and table are both proportionately my size.

I have never once been able to reach the floor with my flat feet when sitting on any chair on earth. Until this one. Very strange. The table height is lower too. And frankly, even the spoon I'm holding is a bit smaller than regular spoons.

I glance at Evelyn. I figure she is about five two. Two inches taller than me. Maybe she likes her table this way. And I suppose some silverware is smaller. Probably a coincidence.

I taste the oatmeal. It's still warm. It has brown sugar sprinkled on the top. It's not from a package torn open and tossed with hot water. It's the real deal. It tastes good, and I decide I should be able to eat most of it. I fork a berry next. Fresh. Ripe. Delicious. I can't remember when I've had fresh fruit. I can't afford it.

I eat, finding it goes down easier than expected, but the milk has me nervous. I'm very full and slowing down when Master Roman appears in the room. He heads for the counter and picks up a steaming cup of coffee. I can smell it from several yards away.

I set my fork down and wipe my mouth on the cloth napkin while Master Roman leans his butt against the counter and meets my gaze. He's frowning. "Something wrong with your milk, Lucy?"

I swallow. "I've never liked milk, Sir."

"It's good for you. It has calcium and protein."

I bite my lower lip. "I'm sorry, Sir. I've never developed a taste for it."

He stares at me for several seconds and then nods toward the glass. "Drink it and meet me in my office." With those horrifying parting words, he shoves off the counter and strides from the room.

I follow him with my gaze, staring at his back until he's gone, and then I shift my gaze slowly back to the glass on the table. Did he seriously just order me to drink milk? I know he's a Dom, but I'm not *his* submissive, and that's going too far.

I remember what Nurse AnnMarie said to me at the doctor's office yesterday. *Everyone Master Roman knows is in the lifestyle. Employees and acquaintances alike. Even if they don't realize it yet.*

I squirm in my seat at I stare at the milk. I feel like a child. Oatmeal and milk. On an ironically small table that is just my size.

And I'm turned on.

It makes no sense. No one would be aroused from the way Master Roman bosses people around. Would they? Finally, knowing the clock is ticking and unwilling to blatantly defy the man I've been working for just one hour, I pick up the glass, hold my breath, and down it as quickly as possible.

It's not quite as bad as I imagined, but I'm still glad there are two berries left on my small plate, and I grab them both with my fingers and stuff them in my mouth to cover up the taste.

I feel a twinge of mischievousness for not using my fork and almost giggle as I wipe my fingers on my napkin and rise from the table. I pick up all my dishes and utensils and head toward Evelyn and the sink. "Where would you like me to put these, ma'am?"

She smiles at me. "In the sink is fine, dear. I'll take care of them. You can run along and see what Master Roman needs from you."

I hesitate, staring at her profile. Run along? She's older than me. Almost thirty years older than me. I suppose she would see me as more a young girl than an adult, especially considering my size and the fact that I have unruly curly hair pulled back in a ponytail.

Suddenly, Evelyn's gaze comes back to mine and she adds, "Oh, there is a fresh toothbrush in the guest bathroom if you'd like to brush your teeth after meals. It's under the sink in a wrapper."

"Thank you, ma'am." Without a word, I quietly set the dishes in the sink and exit the room, knowing the rest of the day and the near future is going to be a series of odd challenges. I can do this. I must.

I take a deep breath and leave the kitchen on silent feet.

CHAPTER 13

Master Roman

If I live through this trial, God will surely grant me a special place in heaven. My life has been upside down for weeks, from the moment I first saw Lucy in my club. It's been a hurricane since she came to my home Monday morning to interview. But today has been more like a tsunami.

When she tipped her pretty face up to me in the kitchen, eyes wide with shock that I had told her to drink her milk… God, I nearly came in my pants. I know for certain she drank that milk as soon as I left the room. I watched her shift in the seat and sit up straighter. I have shocked her, but I feel confident she will thrive under my direction. My firm demands will make her heart pound.

Lucy is a blank slate, but she is so totally ripe for training. Her responses and mannerisms are screaming for someone to dominate her.

Patience. I need an abundance of it. I will ruin everything if I move too fast and scare her. She is so pure and precious and untouched. Even though she had been in my club five times, she has never scened with anyone.

Of course, that had never been an option. Every member of my club knew within an hour of her first appearance that she was off limits. No one even looked directly at her. They weren't rude, but they knew better than to approach her, especially because this was the first time in the fifteen years I have owned this club that I have ever made such a proclamation.

I need to tone down my demeanor for the rest of the morning or she might not return tomorrow. I have the time. I've made the time. I've carved out the next month to ensure she learns what it means to submit to me and realizes her true nature.

Sure, I have work that needs to get done, but I won't be traveling or seeing many clients in my home office. The bare minimum is what I have planned, and my staff knows it.

I have met with Nancy—my house manager, Evelyn—my cook, and Weston—my butler. I have many other employees, but those three have been with this household for years. They know me better than I sometimes know myself. They can anticipate my every need often ahead of me.

Over time, the rest of my peripheral staff will understand this arrangement, but for now, the only thing that matters is that those three manage things in the express way I have dictated.

And they will too. They are paid well to do as I request. They enjoy working for me. And in addition, all three of them worked for my father before he died. If anyone thinks I'm an excessive dominant with outrageous quirks, they did not have the pleasure of knowing my father and grandfather.

Those men were far more formidable. They could make anyone cower, and I'd seen them in action as I grew up. Is dominance genetically inherited or learned? I would never know. It didn't matter.

As Lucy steps back into my office, wringing her hands in front of her, I can feel the tension rolling off her in waves. She's nervous. Probably confused. Understandable, and I want some of that edge to remain, but I need to soothe her a bit also.

I rise from my chair and point to one of the chairs directly across from my desk. "Sit." I considered ushering her to the sofa across the room, but then decide that might be too intimate and tempting, so I lower myself back onto my desk chair and wait for her to sit across from me.

She sits with her back straight and her hands folded in her lap in much the same way she sat Monday morning. Professional. Nervous.

I lean back in my chair, trying to appear casual, rubbing my chin between two fingers and my thumb. There are things about her I want to know. There are also things I need her to know. "Tell me about your childhood."

She frowns. "My childhood, Sir?" Her cheeks pinken. Odd.

"Yes, it's that time between birth and eighteen. I'm making conversation. Getting to know you," I point out.

"Oh." She licks her lips and sits up straighter, but she bounces one knee. "It wasn't very interesting, Sir."

I lift a brow, lean back, and steeple my fingers in front of my mouth. "I'll decide that." Now I'm even more curious than before. The PI didn't dig too hard because I didn't feel it was necessary. Perhaps I have errored.

She glances away from me. "I grew up in a small town in Missouri. My father died when I was ten and my mother when I was eleven. Then I moved in with my grandmother in Chicago until I turned eighteen when I came here. That's about it."

I don't like her answer. She spoke too fast, glossed over her parents' deaths as if they meant nothing, and left her grandmother to move across the country right out of high school? There is much more to this story. Perhaps she never got over her parents' deaths and it hurts too badly to discuss it.

"It must have been really hard to lose both parents so young."

She blinks at me.

"Lucy?"

She shrugs. "I don't really remember, Sir."

I don't believe her. In fact, my curiosity is far more piqued now. I sit forward and set my elbows on my desk. After staring at her several moments, I decide to let this topic go for now. I don't want to alienate her. I'll delve into this further another day.

I change the subject. "Why did you get a temporary pass to my club?"

She squirms, which I'm quickly learning makes my cock hard every time. I can't decide if I want her to keep doing it or take her over my knee. For now, I will scowl. I glance at her lap, frowning, until she gets the hint and stops moving her sweet little ass.

Finally, she speaks again. "I just wanted to check it out."

"Just so we're clear, you won't be returning."

Her eyes widen. "Okay, Sir."

"I don't permit my home employees to have membership in my club."

"Okay, Sir. I wasn't intending to actually join anyway, Sir."

I tip my head to one side. "Why? Did you not find my club to be to your liking?"

Her face flushes a darker shade of red and she shakes her head. "No, Sir. That's not it. I couldn't afford it."

"I see. Well, on my salary you can, but you won't. Nor will

you join any other local club. Understood?" I realize my voice has gotten gruff.

She is biting her bottom lip, and she releases it before I have a chance to either demand that she do so or possibly jump over the top of the desk to take it in between mine. "Yes, Sir."

"I won't have gossip tainting my employees. Their private lives are their own, but since I'm the owner of a club, it could cause unnecessary issues for my staff to belong to any club, especially my own." I hope I have sufficiently explained myself.

It is true that my home employees don't belong to clubs, not even my own. But in Lucy's case this decision has far more to do with my claim on her than anything else.

It's not that many of my employees don't enjoy the lifestyle or participate in it. Most of them do. But they do so in private. I prefer there be no public scrutiny of my personal staff.

"I understand, Sir. Your point is moot. I have no intentions of joining a club." Her knee is bouncing again.

I narrow my gaze at her. "You must have enjoyed visiting Surrender. You returned four times."

She swallows. God, I love to watch her squirm. The more I speak with her, the more certain I am of my initial assessment. Lucy Neill is not only submissive but will thrive under my thumb.

She is fighting an internal war. I watch it unfold on her face and in her body language. She has the inner strength to straighten her spine and take my dominance. I make her nervous. Hell, I make most people nervous. But she intends to stay. And I'm so damn proud of her already. It's difficult to keep my face rigid and not smile.

She flattens her hands on her thighs and rubs them slowly, her face dipping toward the floor. "I wanted to see what it was all about."

"Submission?" I watch her so closely.

"Yes, Sir," she whispers.

"Why are you embarrassed?" I ask, gauging her every movement. I desperately want to set my hand on her thigh to make her stop jiggling her leg, but I also don't want to draw attention to her body language right now. I like how authentic it is while she isn't being self-conscious about it.

She lifts her face again. "I'm not sure, Sir."

"Well, there's no reason to be embarrassed about your submissive tendencies. Many people have them. Right now, it's working in your favor. I wouldn't have hired you if you weren't subservient. I need my assistants to easily obey orders without questioning them.

"As you well know, I have been through several assistants lately. People think they can hack it. They tell themselves they can tolerate me because the pay is good. I'm sure you've given yourself a similar pep talk more than once."

She smiles slightly for the first time all day, and it radiates all around the room and makes my cock harder than it's been since Friday night.

I realize at that moment I want to see her smile often for the rest of her life. It might take a while to get to the point where she does so frequently, but I intend to persevere. Getting soft on her now would not bode well for me in the long run, however. She needs guidance and rules and structure before she is permitted laughter and free time and...pleasure.

I continue. "The point is, I want you to know that I feel confident in your ability to do this job. I'm a good judge of character." When she flinches, I release a chuckle before I can stop myself. "Touché. I suppose that wouldn't appear to be true considering how many assistants I've had lately."

Her face reddens, and her mouth falls open. "Sir, I meant no disrespect."

I lift a hand. "None taken. You're right to wonder about my judgment. However, just so we're clear. In every one of those instances, I knew from day one the women would not work out. All I could do was hope they proved me wrong."

She nods slowly. "Why did you hire them?"

I offer her a smile. "Because you didn't apply."

CHAPTER 14

Lucy

By the time I get home from my first day at work I am a mess of emotions. Master Roman has spent the entire day confusing me. He has so many facets. He can go from gruff to laid back to laughing without warning.

Okay, laughing is too strong a word. He smiled once for a millisecond and might have given a half-chuckle at his own expense for the same length of time.

It's late. I'm so drained from the stress of the day, I want to drop into bed. Instead I find myself heading for the bathroom while stripping out of my clothes and dropping them along the way.

The reason I turn on the water and start to fill the tub is because Master Roman all but demanded it in his parting words. *"Go home, Lucy. Take a long, hot bath. Get eight hours of sleep. I'll see you in the morning."*

As I slide into the hot water, I try to remember the last time I've taken a bath and come up with nothing. In fact, if it weren't for my crazy cleaning spree on Monday, this tub would have been too gross to lie in. I've used it as a shower and nothing else for the two years I've lived here.

I suddenly wish I owned bubbles and sigh. I would never own such an extravagance even if I were the sort of person who took baths. Bubbles cost the same as an entire loaf of bread and some American cheese. I could eat that for lunch for a week. Bubbles are an extravagance I cannot afford.

Perhaps by my first paycheck I will be able to. I close my eyes as I admonish myself. There will be no bubbles until I'm out of credit card debt and the rent is consistently paid on time without me having to scrape the last few dollars together.

The water feels good. It is soothing. I start to drift off, my mind wandering in a direction I should not permit. But I can't help it. Before today, I have imagined submitting to Master Roman on a number of occasions. All of those daydreams have evolved out of my imagination.

Now? Now, I have actual material to work with, and my thoughts run wild. The thing is, I know Master Roman is a Dom, so visualizing me on my knees before him is so easy. After all, he certainly has someone in his life who kneels in front of him.

I jerk my eyes open, my mouth drying at the thought of another woman submitting to him. I grip the sides of the tub, stiffening. Why does that bother me so much?

I wonder how many submissives Master Roman has had in his life. How many of them has he trained? But more importantly, does he have one now?

As I release the edges of the tub, I force myself to calm down. Jeez. First of all, it's none of my business whether or not Master Roman has a submissive or even twelve of them. I'm his assistant. Nothing more.

Second of all, when would he have the time? The man is a

force to be reckoned with. With the exception of the time he spent talking to me after breakfast, the man worked non-stop all day. He was either on the phone or buried in a file or clicking away at the computer.

I was near him for twelve hours today, and nothing about his body language suggested he was wrapping things up when he excused me. In fact, he had muted his phone to glance my direction and bark out his final orders to bathe and sleep, dismissing me.

In truth, every day has twelve other hours in it. Perhaps Master Roman sleeps five of those and spends seven in some dungeon playroom with nine women, or men. How would I know? And, it's none of my business, I remind myself.

The water begins to cool, but I find I'm enjoying my soak and not done analyzing my day, so I turn on the hot water to let it warm up again. I sigh as my limbs relax. I know my brain is not going to shut down and permit me to sleep no matter how tired I am.

The absurd thing is that I truly didn't do much today. After breakfast, and after our weird chat, I spent some time familiarizing myself with his filing system which I discover is located in my office, taking up a good portion of the wall I had not paid any attention to.

Master Roman keeps his space free of clutter. Even his file cabinets blend into the décor, making it appear that he has nothing to do and no work happens in his office or mine.

I worried the entire time, mindful that I would need to become far more organized or risk his wrath. Lord knows how he might react if I left a paper on my desk at the end of the day or a file cabinet not quite closed.

He hasn't said as much to me, but it doesn't take a rocket scientist to pick up on his need for order in all aspects of his life.

My mind wanders back to the idea of submitting to him.

How much "order" does he insist upon in that area of his life? How meticulous are his submissives? Does he require them to shave their legs on Mondays and Wednesdays for example?

I giggle. I wouldn't put it past him. I picture myself again, kneeling at his feet, arms behind my back. Would he gather my hair and braid it like I've seen a few Doms do at his club? Would he want me to cut it? After all, it's unruly. Or...would he wrap his hand in it and yank my head back.

I squirm in the bathtub, squeezing my thighs together. I'm turned on. More than I have been in the previous few days since I first went to Master Roman's house. I slide one hand between my legs and stroke my fingers through my folds. Even though I'm submerged in water, I know I'm wet.

When I flick my fingers over my clit, I jump and bite down on my bottom lip. Holy shit. I've been aroused many times in my life. After all, I read a lot of erotic romance novels. They make my life interesting and give me a reason to get up each day. As an introvert, I'm grateful to the millions of authors out there who provide me with entertainment.

I have not, however, ever had an orgasm. I have tried a few times lying in bed late at night after reading a particularly risqué chapter, but I have never succeeded. I'm not even sure orgasm is a real thing, or perhaps not for me.

Tonight, though... I flick my clit again and flinch. Nerve endings that have never been this close to the surface or this sensitive come to life. My belly flips over and tightens inside. My legs shake. I slide my finger lower and push it up inside me. Slowly. I've never done this before. The only thing that's ever been inside me is tampons...and Dr. Pruitt's speculum. It's tighter than I expected.

I have never actually seen a male penis in the flesh, but I'm pretty sure they are significantly larger than the opening I'm examining.

My body slips lower in the tub, and I lose my grip on the edge, nearly going underwater. Sputtering, I jerk to sitting, grab both sides of the tub, and pant into the silence of the room.

I stare down at my small breasts. My nipples are hard points. The globes feel heavy. There is a throbbing between my legs. My entire body is shivering. The water has cooled again.

I rise from the water and step out of the tub carefully, afraid my legs won't hold me or that I might slip on the linoleum. After toweling off, I make my way to my bedroom, open a drawer, and pull out an old T-shirt and panties. My standard nightwear.

As I shrug into my clean underwear, I remember that I need to open the package Nancy has sent home with me tonight. Tomorrow's clothes. It seems beyond odd that she would provide me with an outfit every night for the next day, but then again, everything in Master Roman's world is a bit off kilter.

Nancy has instructed me to bring my "soiled" clothes from the previous day back each morning to be sent to the laundry. She used the word *soiled*. As if I were playing outside all day and got my knees dirty.

I'm still shaking from the arousal I'm fighting to ignore and exhausted at the same time as I pad back to the living room and grab the package. It's tied with string like the today's had been. In it, I find a pleated beige skirt and pastel pink blouse. At least I won't be wearing the same thing every day. My favorite pink flats would go with the outfit, but I worry that I'm not supposed to wear anything I wasn't instructed to wear, so I shove that idea to the back of my mind.

I chuckle as I head to the bathroom. This job could quite possibly prove to be extremely boring over time, but at least I will have some surprises to look forward to: the following day's clothes and every meal.

After my breakfast experience, I worried about what I might be expected to eat for lunch and dinner. I was relieved when my lunch consisted of vegetable soup and a ham and cheese sandwich. The best part was the glass of water.

If Master Roman expected me to drink milk for every meal, we would end up in a confrontation for sure. I might be able to hold my breath and suck down one glass in the morning, but if I had to do so more often, I'm not sure I wouldn't end up vomiting on the kitchen floor.

I ate that meal alone at the same oddly small table in the corner of the kitchen. I had no idea where everyone else was eating or what they had been served. I didn't dare ask.

Dinner was much the same. At six o'clock, Master Roman ushered me to the kitchen where I once again ate alone. Meatloaf, mashed potatoes, carrots. Blessed water. I'm not fond of cooked carrots, but I dragged them through the mashed potatoes and ate every bite anyway. This was the first day in a long time when I've had three solid meals and didn't end up with a grumbling stomach in the afternoon.

Evelyn was sometimes in the kitchen working at the counter while I ate. Sometimes she would leave for a few minutes and return. She made limited small talk, encouraging me to finish up and get back to the office. At least she smiled warmly.

The same could not be said of Nancy. I have yet to see her smile. Her face is usually permanently blank. I'm not sure if it's her personality or genetics.

The third person who is also a fixture in the house is Weston. He is older than both the women, or at least appears so. He moves slower, and I have no idea what his job is except to man the front door in the event someone arrives. To my knowledge the only person who came or left today is me.

I hang tomorrow's clothes up in the bathroom, set my alarm, and slide into my bed. I'm both tired and wired at the same time. Thoughts of the day are not going to make it easy to sleep.

In fact, when I close my eyes, I instantly picture myself on my knees again. What is it with that visual? It's disturbing that I can't shake it. I'm also still aroused, and this renewed imagining gets my pulse beating faster and draws my attention to my sex.

Perhaps tonight is the night I could stroke my clit until I finally experience an orgasm. More than likely I will again be left frustrated and sore, losing sleep to visions of kneeling before the formidable Master Roman. I still won't be able to reach that elusive place.

Sighing, I roll onto my side, curl up in a ball, and take several deep breaths. Luckily, that's the last thing I remember. Blessed sleep takes over.

CHAPTER 15

Master Roman

I'm alone in my home gym, silently working out harder than usual. Pushing my body to its limits. Fighting off images of Lucy. Unsuccessfully.

The day was long. I pushed her hard.

She exceeded my expectations.

I shouldn't have kept her as late as I did. I took a risk. If I push her too hard, she might quit, and that's the last thing I want. On the flip side, I also don't like her going back to her own apartment at the end of the day either. I hated knowing she would walk to a bus stop and then travel for over half an hour before walking again to get to her apartment. It's not in the safest neighborhood.

I jump on the treadmill and start jogging, trying to burn off my frustration. Lucy has been living in that apartment for two years without incident. I have to trust that nothing will happen to her between now and the day I convince her to move in with me.

That day can't come soon enough. In fact, preparations are already under way. Nancy has made all the arrangements. Before the end of the week, a bedroom will be ready for Lucy. I have my doubts that Lucy will be ready to use it yet, but I want to be prepared.

She is skittish, nervous around me, but also intrigued. There is no doubt she knows she is submissive or else she wouldn't have come to my club for five nights to watch. Memories of watching her fidget as she stood mesmerized by every sort of apparatus in Surrender make my cock stiff even as I jog.

I adjust my dick and pick up the pace, desperate to chase the images away. I'm growing more possessive of her in my mind. I can't picture myself bringing her to Surrender or any other club. I want her all to myself.

She's a loner, but I can't know for sure if that's by accident or design. I've pegged her as introverted. She's quiet and reserved and spends a great deal of time chewing on her lower lip while hiding in the shadows.

A noise behind me has me jerking my gaze around to find Claudia strolling into my gym. She's smirking. "Sorry. Didn't mean to startle you. Weston let me in."

I turn off the treadmill and hop down, grabbing a towel to swipe across my face. "What's up?"

She wanders around my gym, dragging her fingers over several pieces of equipment. Even though it's late in the evening, her blond bob is still perfect, as is her makeup. In twenty years I've rarely seen her not completely put together. She is still wearing a tailored skirt and matching suit jacket in gray. Her blouse is a pale yellow and looks fresh as if she's just gotten dressed. I know she hasn't.

I wait for her to speak her mind.

She finally stops, leaning her ass against a piece of equipment. "Julius told me you hired Lucy. How's it going?"

I smirk. "Today was her first day. It went fine. If you've come here to lecture me—"

She holds up a hand. "Of course not. What good would it do me anyway? I just want to make sure you know what you're doing and that you're following all the rules you expect every member of your club to follow." She lifts a brow.

I cock my head to one side. I'm sure Julius has informed Claudia about my nefarious methods, but the truth is Julius doesn't realize how far I went to accomplish my goals. Yes, he arranged a PI and is well aware I made sure Lucy applied for a job with me, but that's all he knows. Which means, that's all Claudia knows. "If you're asking me if I intend to get consent every step of the way, don't insult me. You know me better than that."

"Do I?"

"Claudia..." I warn. She may be a Domme, but she's not *my* Domme.

"You've taken over her life, Roman."

I nod. "Yep. And it's a good thing too. Her previous job sucked. They were taking advantage of her. She wasn't making enough money to afford the absolutely shitty apartment she rents. She's skinny. It's obvious she hasn't eaten a proper meal in years."

"And that gave you the right to interfere? What if she loved that job?"

I groan and drop down onto a bench. "Get off my back. I'll take care of her, and you know it. If I'm wrong about her— and God help me I can already assure you I'm not—I'll let her go. I'll give her an amazing severance package and help her find another job. Happy?"

She doesn't smile. "Don't be an ass. I know you well. You've never done anything like this before. I'm worried about you."

I throw out my arms. "Maybe the reason I've never taken a

fulltime sub is because I've never found the right girl."

She narrows her gaze. "How old is she?"

I shoot daggers at her with my eyes. "Don't go there, Claudia. Ageism doesn't become you. She's legal."

She rolls her eyes. "You know I'm the last person who would judge someone by their age. I've been with people twenty years older than me and twenty years younger. But none that I intended to keep around."

"You never intend to keep *anyone* around," I point out.

She laughs. "Good point. Just...please, be careful and take things slow. I know you're an amazing Dom, but don't let your personal attraction cloud your judgment. You'll hurt her if you push her too hard."

I know Claudia means well, and she's right, but she doesn't know Lucy the way I already do. And I will heed her advice. "You have my word."

Claudia heads for the doorway. "Invite me over to meet her officially soon. If she's going to be part of your life, I want to get to know her."

"I will. As soon as she's more settled."

"I'll hold you to it." She turns to smile at me and then leaves the room. I can barely hear her footfalls as she walks away.

After a few minutes, I exit my home gym and take the stairs from the basement to the second floor two at a time. I lock myself in the master bedroom and beeline for the shower, stripping along the way.

I toe off my shoes and drop my clothes in the hamper before entering the shower. There is no door. When I renovated the master bath a few years ago, I had a walk-in shower and a large jetted tub installed. I've never used the tub, but as I stare at it now, I picture Lucy lying in it someday.

That's absurd, of course. Lucy won't be entering my bedroom. The set of rooms I'm preparing for her is in another wing of the second floor. She will reach it from a back set of stairs. She won't have permission to wander freely in my home.

If I'm right about her—and I'm growing more certain by the hour—she will thrive on the structure. She will be happier than she's ever been when she finally submits to me fully and permits me to train her to be the best version of herself.

Claudia has valid points. I understand and appreciate her concern. But this feels right. In my bones. It has from the moment I saw Lucy, and so far, nothing has changed my mind. Everything has solidified my opinion.

I'm beginning to suspect she is a middle, not a really young child but someone closer to puberty. I still can't know for sure what age suits her, but that's not important. I'll explore several with her. There is no rush. If needed, she can spend weeks at a time living in different age brackets until I determine what age is most appropriate for her.

As I stand under the flow of hot water, letting it sluice down my head, I close my eyes. I've spent the majority of my adult life looking for the perfect submissive. I've known I wanted a little for almost as long as Lucy has been alive. She's young. Is she too young? I don't think so.

A twenty-two-year-old woman can know her mind and what she wants out of life. Far better than I probably did at that age.

My dick is so hard there is no avoiding the need to jerk off. I sigh as I finally permit myself to wrap my palm around the length and drag it slowly up and down my shaft. I tip my head back, eyes closed, and pretend Lucy is on her knees in front of me, that it is her fingers on my cock, and that she is about to lick the tip.

I flatten my other palm on the tile wall to steady myself as I grip my dick harder and jerk faster. It doesn't take long for me to come, long jets of my semen squirting into the spray of water. I've done this every night for a month now. Thirty-three nights to be precise.

I also haven't been with another woman in that time. At first, I tried to shake her image. I attempted to scene with a few of the women I normally play with. I couldn't get into it. It wasn't fair to them. My mind wandered. I haven't dominated another woman since that first weekend.

I'm pretty particular and discreet with my dominance. Even though I own the club, I don't scene when it's open. I have regular submissives I trust who meet me before the club opens, usually on Saturday nights, to scene. I find I'm more relaxed during opening hours if I've already gotten my own need to Dominate out of my system. Plus, I prefer to monitor my club and be fully involved in my job when I'm there.

When I'm not at Surrender during business hours, Julius handles everything. In the past year, I've turned more and more responsibility over to him. Often I have only come to the building one or two nights a week and only for a few hours. But since first spotting Lucy five Fridays ago, I have been in the club every open hour. I wasn't willing to take the risk that she might show up when I wasn't there. I wanted to watch her every move for the entirety of her six visits.

Instinct told me she might stop coming at any time. She might find herself overwhelmed or even spread out her six visits.

Those days are over. I'm lucky enough to have arranged for her to be under my roof now almost fifty percent of the time. It's not enough, but it will have to do for now.

I shiver. The water has grown cold. I quickly rinse my body and turn off the dial. I need sleep. I need to be on my game again tomorrow. I need to ensure Lucy is properly groomed to be mine. Every decision I make with regard to her training makes a difference.

I will not fuck this up.

CHAPTER 16

Lucy

I'm early. It's my second day of work, and I'm ridiculously punctual. I'm early because I woke up after only a few hours, unable to go back to sleep. After flopping around from side to side in my bed for over an hour, I finally gave up and got in the shower.

The bus makes me nervous. Since I was dressed and ready to go earlier than necessary, I left my apartment and made my way to the bus stop. I'm going to stress about the bus every day, so I tell myself this way is better. If I get on the earlier bus each morning, I won't have to worry about it being late or not coming at all.

This plan has a problem though. It's dark outside. And probably not safe. In fact, a man drives by me slowly at one point, his window down, calling out to me. He laughs when I ignore him and pick up my pace.

There is no reason for me to wait for the bus I took yesterday, and as soon as I board an earlier one, I know I will prefer it. There are far fewer passengers. I don't have to share my bench with a stranger.

I'm not nervous when I arrive at my stop. Even though it's still dark, I'm in a better neighborhood. I walk as slowly as I can toward Master Roman's home.

Nevertheless, I arrive at the ridiculous hour of six fifteen. I wait until six thirty to ring the bell, and am immediately buzzed in.

When I reach the rear entrance, Evelyn opens the door before I can reach for it. "Goodness gracious, girl. The sun is just peeking over the horizon. You don't need to arrive this early every day." She ushers me inside, and I close the door behind me.

"I couldn't sleep, ma'am, and the bus makes me nervous. I don't want to arrive late." I have no idea why I've shared so much information with Evelyn, but she doesn't seem annoyed.

She shoots me a smile as she returns to the kitchen island where she is already hard at work herself. I wonder if she lives here. Probably.

"Master Roman won't like the idea of you wandering around outside in the dark. He'll have a fit."

I freeze in my spot. My face heats up as a flush rises. The last thing I want is for Master Roman to get involved in my transportation issues. I don't want him to think for a moment that it's a problem. I need this job. If he feels I don't have adequate transportation, he might fire me.

I consider asking Evelyn to please not mention my problem to Master Roman but decide against it. It's probably better to hope she lets it go or forgets. Tomorrow I'll waste more time before I come into the house. After all, Master Roman's mansion is not in a dangerous location. I could bring a book and sit outside the gate reading in the mornings before seven. I'm confident the streetlight will be sufficient to see the pages.

Of course this plan will only work during the summer. As soon as winter falls, I'm going to have an entirely new problem on my hands. But I'll deal with that in the future. Hell, if I really manage to keep this job and make as much money as my contract implies, I will be able to take an Uber here instead of the bus. That will save me hours of stress and worry.

Taking a deep breath, I quietly shuffle down the hallway and enter Master Roman's office. Like yesterday, the door is open.

Master Roman is standing behind his desk, looking for all the world as if he's already been hard at work for hours. His brow is furrowed when he meets my gaze. "Did you take the bus to get here, Lucy?"

I swallow. How has he already learned of my situation? There is no way Evelyn could have informed him of my problem during my short walk from her kitchen to his office. "Yes, Sir. I don't have a car."

He crosses his arms and stares at me, lips pursed before he finally parts them again. "Don't do it again. It's not safe. It's dark. You must have left practically in the middle of the night, and then you spent fifteen minutes pacing outside my gate before ringing in."

I flinch. I lift my hand and nearly slap my own forehead as I realize there must be a camera outside. Of course there is. I stop myself from reacting just in time and lower my hand to my side.

Master Roman rounds the desk and then leans his butt against the front, arms still crossed. "Weston monitors my camera."

"I see, Sir. I'm sorry to have bothered him. I didn't want to come inside too early." My voice is too low. I know I'm frustrating him. But he doesn't realize his order to stop taking the bus would mean total disaster for me. I don't have the means to afford other transportation, especially not until after I'm paid.

I knew this would be a problem as soon as it got cold or snowed, but I hadn't anticipated facing the issue so soon. I can't pay an Uber tomorrow. I don't have even five dollars in cash until I get paid.

My hands are shaking, and I'm fighting against the flush and rising emotions. Part of me is about to cry. The last thing I want to do is tell my new boss that I can't afford an Uber. He might think I'm wasteful if I don't have enough money saved up for such things.

Master Roman narrows his gaze. "From now on Weston will pick you up in the morning and bring you home at night."

My mouth falls open. I'm speechless.

Master Roman rounds his desk and lowers onto the seat.

I force myself to speak. "That's not necessary, Sir. I don't want to put him out."

"You're not. He's my employee. He does what I instruct him to do." Master Roman doesn't look at me as he speaks. He has already grabbed his mouse. His attention is on his computer screen. "This discussion is over, Lucy. Go to your office. I left you plenty to do."

I stare at him for a moment, uncertain about how I feel. Part of me is grateful. Most of me is unnerved. I need this job. If Master Roman decides the burden of getting me to his home isn't worth it, he will fire me.

Finally, I shuffle across the room toward my office. The door is standing open. I leave it that way. Master Roman has never insinuated that I should close it. In fact, I'm confident he prefers to be able to keep an eye on me, and he likes to be able to call out to me easily.

I find a pile of folders and loose papers stacked in the

center of my desk. A handwritten note is on top instructing me to spend some time familiarizing myself with his filing system. He's also left me a folder of things that need to be added to files that are already in the drawers.

I'm grateful to pick up the stack and move to the wall of cabinets. It puts me out of Master Roman's direct line of sight. I take the time to carefully open every drawer and ensure that I know how his system is set up and where everything is. In the future, hopefully when he requests something, I will be able to easily grab it without opening ten drawers first.

"Lucy." When he calls out my name, I jump in my spot. "It's time for breakfast."

I glance at my watch and realize more than an hour has passed. I close the last drawer, return the stack of papers in my hand to my desk, and then step into the main office. "Thank you, Sir."

He lifts his gaze. "Tell Evelyn I'll be in shortly to grab a cup of coffee. And, Lucy…"

"Yes, Sir?"

"I don't want to find you arguing with anyone about what you're served. Evelyn will provide you with healthy, nutritious meals every day. I expect you to eat what's in front of you without complaint."

"Yes, Sir." I gulp as I turn to leave. I know without a doubt I'm about to find a glass of milk at my spot. Sure enough, when I enter the kitchen, I see the milk first thing, and then I pray that I only have to choke it down in the mornings.

"Good morning, Lucy," Evelyn chirps as I take my seat.

"Thank you for making my breakfast, ma'am," I respond. "Master Roman says he'll be in shortly for coffee."

"Of course, dear."

I eye the milk and decide to get it over with first. It will probably taste better while it's cold, and then the rest of the meal will wash it away. Pancakes this morning. And sausage. I haven't had either in a long time. My mouth waters.

I hold my breath while I down the stupid, disgusting milk and then pick up my fork and take a large bite of fluffy pancake before I inhale again. It works. I don't taste the milk. I've lived.

When Master Roman enters the kitchen several minutes later, he eyes my food and my empty glass and almost smiles before leaving without a word.

I sit up straighter and squeeze my legs together as I turn my head to watch him stride from the room. I've pleased him. It sends butterflies to my belly and makes my nipples stiffen.

I'm shocked by my reaction, though I shouldn't be. His intense dominance is heady every time. Even without words, he has dominated me.

It's hard to finish my food because my stomach is still fluttering as I am unable to shake the visual of his approval from my mind. Somehow, I manage, and then I set my dishes in the sink, thank Evelyn again, and head for the hallway restroom to brush my teeth.

When I return to Master Roman's office, he isn't there. The room is quiet. This is probably a good thing after the way my body has reacted to him just a few minutes ago.

I hurry across to my side door and resume filing. When I've finished, I open the next folder and see that he has left me several letters, correspondences, that need to be mailed out. I busy myself with that.

CHAPTER 17

Lucy

An hour later, I hear Master Roman's footsteps before he calls my name. "Lucy."

Just as I'm about to rise from my desk, he fills the doorway with his enormous presence and wanders inside. "Stay there," he instructs. He glances around the room, probably to ensure I haven't made a mess of things.

Finally, he saunters to the large picture window behind me and leans against it casually, arms crossed. "Tell me about your childhood."

His question startles me. My childhood? Again? Why is he so inquisitive about my childhood? "Sir?" I don't see how my upbringing has anything to do with how I do my job. I'm concerned. Again. And on edge. I sit up straighter and fold my hands in my lap. My palms are sweating, but I don't dare wipe them on my skirt.

He sighs. "You are a unique girl, Lucy. I want to understand you better."

I lick my lips. I'm trembling slightly now. He notably doesn't call me a woman, but a girl. It makes me feel something deep inside that I can't put my finger on. It's not a bad thing. Just a curiosity.

"You aren't in trouble, Lucy. Relax. Tell me about your childhood," he repeats.

"Um, okay. Well, I was born in rural Missouri. You already know that. And I lived on a small farm with my parents until my dad died."

"How did he die?" Master Roman interrupts.

"He had a heart attack."

"Wow. I assume he was young."

I shrug. I don't really know how old he was. He seemed old to me at the time, but then again, I was ten. "I guess so."

"And your mom. Was she devastated? I bet it was hard for her."

I find myself shaking my head unintentionally, and then wish I could take the action back. This is not something I want to discuss with anyone, let alone my nosy, dominant, new boss.

"Did your parents not get along?" he asks.

My shoulders lower and so does my gaze. "My father wasn't a nice man. He probably died because his stress level was so high his heart couldn't take it." That's the truth.

Master Roman hesitates. "Was he abusive?"

"Emotionally, I suppose. He was always shouting. My mother could not please him. I don't think I ever heard him speak in a normal voice."

Master Roman's voice is lower and kind when he speaks again. "I'm sorry, Lucy. That must have been rough. How did your mother handle him?"

"She didn't. She never fought back. She just listened and then tried to fix whatever he was ranting about."

"What about you? Did he yell at you too?"

I lift my gaze, feeling stronger. This isn't so bad. Who cares if Master Roman knows my stupid secrets? "I'm not sure he even knew I was alive, to be honest. He rarely looked at me. I learned at a young age to keep quiet and not draw attention to myself. I don't think he wanted kids, so he ignored me. It was like he pretended I didn't exist."

Master Roman's face widens in shock. He opens his mouth, but it takes him a moment to speak. "Did you have friends? Did you go to other homes and see how other children lived?"

I shake my head. "Rarely. I was introverted and shy. I still am. I didn't care if I had friends. I went to school on the bus and came home and went to my room. I did my homework and read most of the time."

Master Roman stops frowning. His expression is one of genuine curiosity. "Did your parents have enough money? Did you at least have dolls and toys to play with?"

"No. I had very little. I had a crib when I was a baby, and then my mother took it apart when I got too old for it. She put the small mattress on the floor and told me one day when she could afford it, she would buy me a regular bed. That day never came." I suck in a breath and glance away, unsure why I've revealed so much.

"You lived in that house on that small mattress until you were eleven?" His voice is stunned, but also a little angry.

"Yes." I force a wan smile. "I was smaller than most girls. It's not as if I was hanging off the edge of the baby mattress. When I went to live with my grandmother in Chicago, I finally had a regular twin bed. It wasn't pretty or anything, but it was an improvement."

"Did you know this grandmother?"

I shake my head. "No. Never met her. I don't think she and my mother got along. I didn't even know she existed until my mother died and a social worker came and got me. I'm not surprised. The woman was cold and distant."

Master Roman's eyes draw together, and he runs a hand through his dark hair. "Jesus."

"I've said too much. I'm sorry, Sir." I lower my gaze, my legs shaking.

He shoves off the window and comes to me, extending his hand in front of me.

I stare at it.

He shakes it. "Come."

I lift my smaller hand and set it in his, fully aware of our size difference. The warmth of his touch is immediate. I calm slightly as I rise to my feet. I'm shivering. It's not cold. I'm nervous.

Master Roman leads me to his office and then he releases me when we reach his desk. He sits on his chair, opens the bottom drawer of his desk, and then pulls out a pillow.

I'm so confused as he sets it on the floor at his feet and points to it. "Kneel."

I can't breathe as I lower to my knees at his feet. My heart is pounding. My hands are shaking so badly that the only way I can stop them I to clasp them together. Instinctively I do so at the small of my back. I keep my face tipped toward the floor.

"Good girl. Don't move." He rises and pads across the room.

I think he's going to leave me there with my uncertainty and doubts, and then I hear the door snick shut and the lock engage. I'm so relieved that I blow out a breath. I would have been mortified if Nancy or Evelyn or Weston walked in to find me on my knees.

Master Roman returns to his seat, facing me, but I don't meet his gaze. I keep mine lowered. I can't stop the shaking.

His voice is low and full of command and understanding at the same time. "Pull your shoulders back, Lucy. Straighten your spine."

I follow his instructions.

"Spread your knees wider."

It's hard to obey that instruction on the wobbly pillow, and it's awkward, but I manage. Instantly, I feel exposed. I realize my panties are damp. My boss has managed to arouse me in short order. I hope he doesn't know it. Just because he has me on my knees does not mean he's thinking anything sexual about me. He's a Dom. They dominate. Not always for sexual purposes. I know this.

He leans forward, putting his elbows on his knees. His face is inches from mine. "Take a deep breath and let it out slowly."

I do as he says. I can't not. My heart rate slows.

"Good. Again. Keep breathing."

For several minutes I do just that. I'm still shaking, but I'm calmer.

"Can you feel yourself relaxing?"

"Yes, Sir."

"Good. Submitting can help lower your stress. It's soothing." His voice is so gentle. "Just follow my instructions, and you'll feel the tension ebbing."

I say nothing, concentrating on breathing and the tone of his voice.

"You haven't told many people about your childhood, have you, Lucy?"

"No, Sir."

"In fact, you didn't really have a childhood, did you?"

"I guess not, Sir." I've never thought about it that way, but he's right.

"Don't let it embarrass you. It's not your fault."

He's right again, but I still wouldn't want to run around whining about my past to random people. It's part of the reason why I don't have friends. I don't have to talk about my painful past if I never get close to anyone. And though I've considered making something up over the years to gloss over my life, I'm not good at lying. So I've chosen to remain introverted and unreachable.

Until now.

Until Master Roman.

"I want you to stay in this position for a while longer, until I tell you to move. You'll feel much better afterward." He turns toward his desk and grabs his mouse, his gaze landing on the screen.

I can't see it because it's angled away from me. Besides, I'm keeping my gaze on the floor. "Yes, Sir." This I can do. This is the first time I've submitted to anyone. I've watched at the club. I've read about it. But I've never participated.

I like it. I'm relaxing with every passing moment. I should feel weird submitting to my boss when I'm supposed to be working. But it's kind of his fault. He's the one who asked me all those personal questions. He's also the one who brought me in here to kneel at his feet.

He doesn't seem upset. In fact, if I had to guess, I would say he's content. Less stiff than I've usually witnessed. Perhaps he gets just as much out of dominating me as I do out of submitting to him. Of course he does.

Finally, he turns to me and cups my face. The warmth of his hand makes me tip my cheek into his touch. I sigh. "Such a good girl. I'm proud of you. Is this your first experience with submission?"

"Yes, Sir." My voice is steadier. I lift my gaze to find him smiling. He's a conundrum. The stern man who always seems to be almost angry is nowhere to be found. He's staring at me with kindness and affection and...pride. He's made me feel better, and he knows it.

"It's time for lunch. I want you to go wash up and catch

your breath and then head for the kitchen. After lunch, you can get back to work." He's gripping my chin now. "But Lucy, this was a breakthrough for you. You're submissive. Your entire outlook on life will be better if you regularly submit yourself to someone else."

I don't move. My eyes are wide. Who does he think I would possibly submit to besides him?

Stupid question. He answers my thoughts immediately. "I'm going to work with you. Help you find yourself. Consider it part of your job. I'll start small and keep it simple at first. Your job is to do as you're told. I promise you'll feel better with every passing day. Every aspect of your life will improve if you get the release you need."

"Yes, Sir." My voice is breathy. My entire body is on fire beneath his touch. Does he have any idea how many butterflies are accumulating in my stomach? How heavy my breasts feel under the blouse and bra he essentially provided.

I wonder if Nancy chooses my clothing each day or if he has a hand in it. Does he know exactly what I'm wearing under my skirt? Did he touch the panties?

My thoughts are rambling and absurd, but I shiver at the thought that he might have fondled my underwear before I put them on. My eyes slide closed at the visual.

"I'm not going to ask you what you're thinking right now. Because I know it would embarrass you. But keep in mind that in the near future I will insist you share the thoughts that go with the flush on your face and the way you're chewing on your bottom lip." To emphasize his point, he plucks my lip from between my teeth with his thumb, rubbing it soothingly.

I gasp.

He smiles. "Go eat your lunch before I change my mind and insist you share your thoughts." He releases me.

I scramble to my feet, feeling almost drunk as I hurry from

the room. There is no way I could possibly have told him what I was thinking. And yet, there was also no way I would ever be able to lie to him or deny him anything.

I need to be aware of this problem. It's going to bite me in the butt very soon.

CHAPTER 18

Master Roman

"There are no words to describe how perfect she is." It's Sunday evening. I'm sitting in my library in one of the enormous leather arm chairs that flanks the fireplace, swirling the scotch around the edge of my glass and staring at Julius.

Julius smiles. "I'm not surprised. You always were a good judge of character. Of course she's exactly what you expected."

"And then some." I take a sip. "Thanks for handling the club for me this weekend. There is no way I could have come in."

"I'm surprised you let her have Saturday off, to be honest."

"It was hard, but I pushed her this week. She's only been with me three days. I made it until late on her second day to get her on her knees. She was a natural. She was nervous, but she never balked."

"Be careful, man. She's so green. You'll hurt her if you move too fast. Or lose her."

"I know. You sound just like Claudia. I don't need an intervention."

Julius laughs. "Thank God."

"Besides, that's why I gave her Saturday off. I also left her alone for the rest of the day on Thursday. I didn't command her to kneel in front of me again until Friday afternoon. You can't know how many hours I have spent pretending to concentrate on my computer screen."

Julius chuckles. "You're whipped, man."

"She's the one."

"I hope so." He takes another sip from his own glass. "Are you still convinced she's a little?"

"Probably a middle. I don't think she'll be suited for single-digit ages, but I'll give her options. I pulled every detail about her childhood out of her. Made her tell me about the first ten years on Thursday and then her teenage years on Friday."

"And?"

"It was hard to keep from reacting. Her dad was an asshole. Her mother was weak. And then her grandmother was a cold bitch. She had no one. For eighteen years she had no one in her court. She kept her head down and worked hard in school and then moved to Seattle the minute she became an adult. Four years ago."

"That's rough. It explains a lot."

"Yeah, and in her case, I think the reason she gravitates toward age play is because she essentially missed out on her childhood. It's like it never happened. I don't think she was sexually assaulted or even physically abused. She was neglected. I bet she never had a doll or pretty clothes. And worse, I don't think anyone hugged her or told her she was good and pretty and perfect."

"Not even her mom?" Julius asks. His brow is furrowed in sorrow. Not concern this time.

"Maybe. When she was younger. Certainly not her grandmother. What Lucy craves is love. Approval."

"A Daddy," Julius points out.

I sigh. "Maybe, but I wouldn't dare use that term in front of her. Ever. If she figures that out eventually or comes up with it on her own, fine. If not, I won't harp on the semantics."

"Good idea."

"Did you see her grades? She made straight A's. She's bright. Even with no advanced education, she's an amazing assistant on top of everything else. If she had been able to go to college, she could be anything she wanted to be."

Julius tips his head to one side. "If?"

I shrug.

"You realize you could make that happen for her, right? I mean if this works out."

I scrunch up my face. "Not sure I could do that."

Julius narrows his gaze. "You can't or you won't? Because those are very different things. I can see your mind working. Make sure you don't smother her. She may be submissive and even a little, but that doesn't mean you should stifle the rest of her life."

I shudder and then lean back and stare at the ceiling. "Right now, I'm focused on convincing her to move in with me permanently. I can't stand that she sleeps in that damn run-down apartment every night. It's not safe, and I don't like it."

"And you think she'll agree to move into your mansion and never leave the premises? Because that's fucked up, and you know it."

Julius is right. "One thing at a time. First, I need her here in my home. I need to work with her. See what makes her hum. Then I'll face the future."

"How much are you going to tell her?"

"Not sure yet. It's hard. I'm not sure how self-aware she is.

She missed out on her entire childhood. It's going to take some time to help her see what is clear as day to me. I promise I'll at least explain my intentions before I move her in. I'm going to have to play with a variety of ages until we get it right. I'll start high and move to younger ages a few days at a time."

"And by high you don't mean sixteen, do you?" Julius guesses correctly.

"No. Twelve. Before puberty. I don't think she misses high school. I think she was hardened by then and more like an adult. It's the years when she should have been free of responsibilities that she truly misses."

Julius takes another drink. "Is the release she needs strictly age play, or do you think it's sexual?"

"I *know* it's sexual. The signs are there. She flushes when she submits to me. Hell, she flushes at other times too."

Julius laughs. "Roman, there are no other times with you. You're always a Dom."

I shrug. "Right. Well, still, I see the signs. I've watched her squeeze her breasts with crossed arms and pinch her legs together. When I make her spread her knees on the pillow, she gasps. I'd give anything to see how wet she gets. It's killing me."

"I admire your patience. Such as it is. I think I'll take a household poll."

"About what?" I narrow eyes, knowing he's kidding.

"The over under on how many more days you let her live in that apartment before she's under your roof."

I smirk. "Not many. I can assure you of that. I have Weston picking her up in the morning and dropping her off at night, but I hate that apartment. I hate that she's not safe."

"Admit it, you're a control freak, and you hate that she might be touching herself without permission."

I groan. "Don't remind me. We're hardly at a place in our

relationship where I can command her not to masturbate. It's too soon."

"I'm betting you hold out until about Friday." Julius laughs as he finishes his drink and stands. "I need to get home. I've hardly seen Beck and Levi this week."

Beck and Levi are Julius's roommates, for lack of a better term. Julius owns a home he inherited that's just as large as mine. When he met Beck and Levi many years ago at the club, the three of them fell in sync together, dominating women as a team. As a group, they are formidable. Women line up to be trained by them. They do not disappoint.

I rise with him. "Tell them hello for me and apologize on my behalf. I appreciate you stepping in for me more lately. I know I've been preoccupied."

Julius smirks. "That's putting it mildly, but I'm glad you've found someone that makes you happy. I hope it all works out for you."

I nod and shoot him a grin. "What about you? When are you going to stop hiding behind your bachelor status and claim someone of your own?"

He rolls his eyes. "Never, and you know that better than anyone. Once burned..."

"Not every woman is a conniving bitch, you know. There are others out there."

He turns to face me again as we stroll from my office. "I'll never know. Three months is all I'm willing to give a woman. Not a day more. They know that when they sign on with us. Beck and Levi agree. Keeps our lives uncomplicated."

Keeps their lives unfulfilling, but I don't say this. He doesn't need to hear this from me today. "Thanks for coming over. I appreciate the company."

"Good luck this week."

"I'm going to need it." I follow him to the front door and

then stare out into the night for several minutes after he leaves.

CHAPTER 19

Lucy

I'm emotionally exhausted. It's Friday afternoon, the last day of my first full week of work. I made it. I've never worked so hard in my life. Nor have I experienced submission like this before either.

True to his word, Master Roman has insisted I submit to him at least once every day. It feels like a bit of a stretch since truly I'm always submitting to him. He's that kind of Dom. It never ends. But he has ordered me to my knees on several occasions. Sometimes in my office. Sometimes in his.

Sometimes he sits next to me. Sometimes he leaves me alone with my thoughts for a while. He always insists on the same posture, back straight, shoulders back, hands clasped behind me, face toward the floor, knees parted. I've started to immediately slide into a zone when he commands my submission. It's like meditating.

He's nosy too, always prodding into my personal life, asking me questions about my youth and why I moved to

Seattle and how I've managed since then. I can hear the pride in his voice when he speaks about my ability to survive on my own. He's impressed.

The only times he has touched me have been to correct my posture and then to cup my face or grip my chin and force me to look at him when my time is up. I live for those moments. He has no idea.

I don't know how long this can go on. I'm exploding with desire for him. It scares me that he might not feel the same way. I have no way of knowing. This could all just be an exercise he's putting me through that has no sexual implications for him whatsoever.

I've learned how to please him more every day. I eat what Evelyn prepares without complaint. I work hard. I know he's impressed. I stay late without a word. I've learned new things, especially on the computer. I'm proud of myself. I can do this. At least, I think I can.

I've stopped worrying that he might fire me. My main concern now is that I'm falling for him, and I want more. I wake up most nights sweating and aroused from dreaming about his hands on my body. The idea is so farfetched, but I can't shake it. How long can I go on like this with this unrequited lust? It could be my doom.

"Lucy." His voice reaches me from his office, making me jump in my seat.

I realize I've been daydreaming and worry he might have noticed. I don't shake as often as I did a week ago, but my hands are trembling as I go to him. I notice the door to his office is closed, a sure sign he intends for me to submit. I wonder if the rest of his staff knows what happens in this office when the door is locked. I have pushed that thought out of my mind a dozen times a day. No one says a word. If they suspect anything, they keep it to themselves.

Master Roman drops my pillow to the floor and I

immediately kneel before him, assuming the position he has taught me. Instant relief. As always.

Instead of resuming his work, he continues to face me. And then he rises, and I think he might leave the room. He doesn't though. He sets his hand on my shoulder and circles me. Slowly. Until he is back in front of me, stroking my neck and then my cheek.

Finally, he returns to his chair. "Look at me."

I lift my gaze. This is out of character for us. He's never asked me to face him while I'm on my knees. I'm worried. I have to tip my head back a bit to meet his gaze. From his spot on his desk chair, his head is higher than mine.

"Relax. You're not in trouble. I have a proposition."

I don't move. I don't even breathe.

"You realize from our work the past two weeks that you are deeply submissive, right?"

It hasn't been quite two weeks, but he's right. "Yes, Sir."

I feel like he can see under my skin. I know he can. His gaze is intense. Heated. "I want you to explore the possibility that you are best suited as a little. Do you know what a little is?"

"I think so, Sir."

"You've seen littles at my club." He leans forward. "I saw you watch them play."

I hold his gaze, but it takes every ounce of my strength to do so without looking away.

"You're intrigued by the idea of assuming the role of a young girl and having someone take care of you."

He isn't asking me. He's telling me. He knows me better than I know myself. It should be unnerving. Instead I feel understood.

"That kind of role play is intense. It takes a lot of commitment. If I lead you down that path, I have to be very careful and always aware of where you are emotionally."

I swallow. I have no idea where he's going with this.

"I want you to explore a variety of ages until you figure out what age suits you best. Everyone is different. Every little has different needs. You're so new to the lifestyle that you can't possibly know.

"If you had a specific incident in your childhood that left a gap where you weren't nurtured for a few years, I could easily pinpoint what age you need to revert to in order to find comfort in that range, but in your case, it's your entire childhood. You missed it. No one cared for you properly. You didn't have the nurturing other kids experience. We'll start with age twelve, the time when you moved to Chicago."

I nod. It's all I can do. Agree.

"Without exploring the possibilities, it would be impossible for me to know what you need. Maybe you even need more than one thing. Are you willing to explore this craving?"

"Yes, Sir." Those two words are barely audible. I'm tense. I want this. I don't yet know what it is, but I want it.

"I want you to move into my home. I've prepared a room for you in the west wing. I want you to take the weekend to pack your important belongings and move here Sunday night." He stops talking and watches me.

I know my eyes are wide. I'm shocked. A million things have been running through my head, but I'm not prepared for him to suggest I move in.

"I know it's a huge step," he continues. "But I've worked out all the details. I have a contract written up for you to look over. It basically states that I will take care of breaking your lease and removing anything from your apartment you don't want. I will store your belongings while you live under my roof. I will provide everything you need while you're here. Everything I'm already covering as your employer as well as room and board.

"You will have the ability to break our agreement at any time. If for any reason, you want to leave my home or my employment, I will not stop you. And, I will provide you with the financial ability to get back on your feet in a better apartment than the one you're living in now."

I blink. He's talking slowly but it all sounds so fast.

"I know it's a lot to consider." He taps a file on his desk. "I have the contract right here. I want you to take it to your office and read it over carefully. You'll find that I've left nothing out. You can't lose. The worst thing that could possibly happen is that you change your mind and move out. You'll be better off financially. I've included a sizeable severance package."

I lick my lips. They are suddenly so dry. So is my mouth.

"Do you have any questions?"

About a hundred. "Why would you do this?"

"Because my dominant side is attracted to your type of submission." His words are vague.

"Would we, uh…"

"Say it," he demands.

I swallow. He knows what my question is. "Would we have sex?"

"I hope so, but I'll never pressure you."

I blow out a long breath. All this time I've been wondering if he is attracted to me in that way, unsure. He's given me no indication one way or the other.

He smiles. Knowingly.

I look away. I can't stare at his face any longer. I'm suddenly embarrassed.

He reaches out and cups my face in that way that warms me. "You have no idea how attracted to you I am. I've looked for someone like you for half my life. Yes, I'd want to include sex in our relationship, but only if it suits you and not until you're ready."

I'm ready now. I shudder.

He chuckles. "Go back to your desk. Read through the contract. Mark anything you want to ask me. We'll discuss it again when you're finished."

My legs are wobbly as I try to rise, and my fingers are unsteady as I take the folder from his hand.

Master Roman meets my gaze, not releasing the file just yet. "I'm a firm Dom, Lucy. I will demand a lot from you, but not more than I think you can handle. You'll have a safeword that you can use at any time. During the first weeks of this experiment, I will expect you to submit to me at all times. If you haven't noticed, you already submit to me twelve hours a day. It won't change much. You'll have free time to yourself in the evenings in your room."

"Will I still work for you?"

"Yes. For as long as you want. It isn't a requirement. We'll take it day by day."

That confuses me, but I nod anyway. I need to get out of his office. I need oxygen. I need to think. I need to read through this contract.

I need to get my hand steady enough to sign it.

Because there is no way I would turn down this offer.

Not a chance.

CHAPTER 20

Lucy

I have all my belongings packed in a few boxes ready by the door when Weston shows up to get me Sunday night. He acknowledges them and tells me someone will be sent to pick them up and deliver them to a storage unit the following day.

I leave my apartment for the last time, glancing back. I don't feel nostalgic. I'm not attached to the dingy place. But I'm nervous. And I have every right to be. I'm embarking on the craziest journey of my life. I have no idea if I'm making a good decision or not.

I've spent the past forty-eight hours second guessing myself over and over and then tossing and turning. I have not gotten enough sleep. I have made a long list of pros and cons. Even though I signed the contract and agreed to this arrangement before I left Master Roman's home on Friday, I know I can still back out. I can back out at any time. Even before we start.

The reason I'm not more concerned is because I own so

very little. Nothing in those boxes is overwhelmingly valuable or important to me. If for some reason I'm making the most horrible mistake and find myself on the street tomorrow homeless and without my meager possessions, I won't have lost much.

If Master Roman hadn't hired me two weeks ago, there's a good chance I would have ended up on the street having left everything behind anyway. I've checked my bank account ten times over the weekend. Master Roman deposited my first paycheck on Friday. It's still there. It's more than I've ever made in a month. I don't think he could take it back out. He doesn't have that kind of power. It's mine. I won't go without food.

I ride to the mansion in silence, sitting in the front passenger seat as I have every day since Weston started chauffeuring me to and from work.

It's dark when we arrive, and I follow Weston through the rear door like I always do. He faces me with a nod and then shuffles off to wherever the man goes. I've never figured that out.

Evelyn is not in the kitchen. The only lights on are above the stove. The kitchen is spotless. I've never seen it so bare.

I step farther into the room, wondering what I'm supposed to do next. As I step into the hallway, I hear Master Roman on the phone. I head toward his office. The door is ajar, but I don't want to disturb him. I've never entered his office when the door was closed.

In truth, I've never found it to be closed except on the occasion when I'm inside and he locks it.

Suddenly, someone clears their throat from down the hallway, and I lift my gaze to find Nancy approaching. Her face is stern. It always is. I don't think she has another expression.

"Good evening, Lucy. Master Roman is busy this evening.

He asked me to show you to your room and help you get situated. He'll try to come up later before you go to sleep."

I'm half relieved and half disappointed. Nancy makes me nervous. But at least I'm not expected to submit to her. I have no idea what Master Roman will be expecting of me right away.

I follow Nancy farther down the long hallway. Though I have been in this hallway every day, I have not ventured farther than the office and the bathroom. I've never been upstairs.

The stairway is dark like the rest of the house. The wood paneling and floor gives the entire house a daunting feeling. The stairs curve around as we ascend, so that when we arrive on the second-floor landing, I have no idea which way I'm facing.

I'm surprised when Nancy stops at the first door on the left at the top of the stairs and opens it. "This will be your room," she announces as she flips on the light and then steps back to permit me to enter first.

I enter and then freeze. Shocked. So many things about this room make me gasp. For one, it's decorated for a young girl. The focal point is a white, twin-sized, four-posted bed. The comforter is my favorite shade of pastel pink. It's thick and fluffy and has ruffles all around the sides. The matching sham is also ruffled in airy pink material. Leaning against the pillow is a stuffed bunny, white with pink ears. It should probably alarm me, but instead it makes me smile.

Master Roman told me we were going to explore age play. I marginally understood his intention, but I did not expect it to extend to my bedroom. There is a nightstand beside the bed with a Hello Kitty alarm clock sitting on it. That also makes me smile.

A white bookshelf sits along the wall to my left. It has several books on the shelves as well as a few knickknacks and a doll. To my right is a closet. It has a lock on it. The walls are painted in a soft pink.

There is a white wicker chair at the foot of the bed. It looks like an inviting place to sit and read.

The room's window has shutters that are already closed. I'm not oriented enough to be able to imagine what side of the house the window faces. A pink ruffly valance hangs from above the window. It matches the comforter.

There is a door next to the bookshelf, and Nancy rushes past me to open it. "There is an attached bathroom," she announces.

It seems I'm meant to follow her, so I do, stepping into the small room. It's mostly white. The walls are even painted white. The tile is white. The vanity and oval mirror and tub and toilet too. A soft pink towel hangs on a rack next to the tub. I notice there is no showerhead or curtain. I guess I'll be taking baths.

Nancy points to a small square door with a handle next to the sink. "This is a laundry chute. You'll be expected to keep your room tidy at all times and put your clothes down the chute when you take your bath every evening."

"Yes, ma'am." It feels awkward getting these instructions from Nancy instead of Master Roman. I wonder how much she knows and then decide she obviously knows a lot or she wouldn't be so calm.

"Master Roman will be instructing me to leave your clothes out in the morning and your nightgowns in the evening." She points to a folded pink garment on the vanity that I hadn't noticed.

"Yes, ma'am," I murmur when she pauses.

She nods. "Good. It's important to understand that Master Roman runs a tight schedule here, as you know. We all follow his rules. It's his home."

"Of course." I try to hold her gaze as she keeps speaking.

"You'll be escorted to your room in the evening by eight o'clock at the latest. You'll be expected to bathe first, and then you may spend the next few hours reading. Lights out is at ten o'clock. Your room is on a timer. The lights will literally go off on their own at ten. You're expected to be in bed by then and sleep eight hours."

I nod. I'm uneasy receiving all these instructions from Nancy, but I accept that it's obvious she will have a lot of control over my life, so it will be best if I treat her with respect and earn her affection. "Yes, ma'am."

"Do you have any questions?"

"No, ma'am." I have about a dozen, but they aren't for her, and I'm not sure I could even form words if Master Roman himself were standing in this small bathroom with me.

"Good. I'll leave you to bathe now. If Master Roman is able to, he will come up and tuck you in before ten. If not, be prepared for the lights to go out. You're not allowed to leave this room without permission."

"Yes, ma'am."

She nods again and then leaves, shutting the door to the bedroom behind her. The snick of the door makes me jump in my spot. I stand in the doorway between the bathroom and bedroom and let my gaze wander around again.

The room is so pretty. I chew on my bottom lip wondering if it's rational that I feel a bit excited. Master Roman has spared nothing. He told me we were going to experiment with age play, and he meant it. I'm obviously going to be about twelve starting right now.

My stomach is in a tight ball at the prospect of having no responsibilities other than to do as I'm told. It's as if Nancy is my nanny. I can live with that. She's a stern nanny, but she's not mean. I decide it would be a good idea to take my bath quickly in case Master Roman shows up. I don't want to miss him. Nor do I want to disappoint him.

I'm wearing a pair of jeans and a T-shirt, the only personal items I have with me at this point. I don't even have a purse. I don't own one. I've carried my ID and my only credit card for emergencies in a pocket on my person for all of my adult life. It has always seemed safer, and I've never been frivolous enough to carry lipstick or anything else.

I open a drawer in the bathroom to find a pink brush and comb. I tuck my ID and credit card under them. I survey the rest of the space and find a pink toothbrush in a holder on the vanity, cherry-vanilla lotion under the sink, shampoo and conditioner next to the tub. There is also a bottle of body wash and cotton-candy scented bubbles.

The smile that spreads is genuine. I've rarely had bubbles. Hell, I've rarely taken a bath. I shed my clothes, set my shoes under the small chute door, and open it. For a moment I hesitate, wondering if I will ever see these clothes again after I drop them into this dark abyss.

It's like a final acceptance of my situation that I finally release my clothes and turn around to get in the tub. As the water rises around me, I open the lids to all four bottles. They are a matching set, the scent the same cherry-vanilla as the lotion I found. There is also a razor along the edge of the tub, which tells me Master Roman must expect me to shave. I've already done so that morning, so I will leave the razor for another day.

My hair is long and thick and unruly. It's difficult to wash it and rinse it in the tub, holding my head under the spout, but I manage. After coating it with conditioner next, I lean back and take a deep breath.

I should be nervous, and to a certain extent I am. But I'm also excited. The prospect of submitting so thoroughly to the man I've been lusting after for weeks is exhilarating. I can't believe he's chosen me to move into his home and submit to him like this. I'm honored.

I close my eyes and take several deep breaths, luxuriating in the hot water with bubbles floating all around me. I permit myself this reprieve for only a few minutes, and then I rinse my hair and release the stopper in the tub to let the water drain.

After drying off with the fluffy pink towel, I reach for the nightgown. It's the prettiest article of clothing I've ever held in my hands. As I slide it over my head, I feel like a princess. Never in my childhood did I own anything that delicate, nor did I own anything that made me feel so pretty. It's cotton and soft, but also thin and frilly at the hem. It's sleeveless too. Only a few inches of material rest on my shoulders before it drops loosely over my small breasts, teasing my nipples.

I glance at the counter when I realize Nancy has not left me any undergarments. It would seem I'm expected to wear nothing but the nightgown. It isn't very long. It reaches my midthigh though. Long enough to cover my bottom.

It takes me a while to comb through my hair, and then I locate a hairdryer under the sink next to the lotion and do my best to take away the majority of the moisture, leaving it damp. If I dry it any further, my curls will be wild and out of control.

I should have gotten a haircut over the weekend. It's far too long. The spring of curls shortens it a bit, but at this length, the weight is enough to extend it.

It's too late now. I'll have to address the need to get it cut with Master Roman in the near future.

I put the lotion on my arms and legs mostly because I love the smell of it. I find a container of moisturizer and put it on my face. There is no makeup in the bathroom. Not even lip gloss. Apparently I'm not expected to wear any. And if Master Roman wants me to role-play as a young girl, it's not surprising.

I hang my towel on the rack, making sure it's straight, and

then I pad to the bedroom and peruse the bookshelf. As I squat down, I'm aware of my nipples beading against the front of my nightgown and my exposed bottom. It's an odd feeling. I've never slept without panties before.

I half expect the books to be age appropriate for a young girl, but I'm wrong. Most of them are educational volumes about the lifestyle I've embarked on. I select one called *Being the Best Me: A Little's Guide to a Happy Life*. If Master Roman has left me these books, I presume he intends for me to read them.

I'm giddy inside as I slide under the covers and literally sigh against the amazingly soft sheets. They are cool against my skin, and I have to lift my bottom to tug my nightgown down to my thighs. I settle in with the bunny to my left and open the book.

My mind is wandering like crazy though, making it impossible for me to concentrate on reading. Instead I hold the book open, but stare at the ceiling.

I'm in Master Roman's home. I'm in a bedroom fit for a young girl wearing a nightgown equally suited for someone half my age. I'm excited. This is absolutely something I want to explore. I vow to be the best submissive I can be so that Master Roman smiles at me and calls me his *good girl*. He has said those words to me twice now, and both times I shivered at his approval.

CHAPTER 21

Lucy

I'm still staring at the ceiling when a knock sounds at the door. I flinch, clear my throat, and say, "Come in."

I'm elated to find Master Roman entering. He looks incredible and far too large for the room. He is smiling as he comes to the side of the bed and then sits on the edge. He reaches for my cheek and holds my gaze. "I'm sorry I couldn't be the one to show you around, my little blossom. I had to take a phone call."

I blush when he calls me his blossom. I like that even better than *good girl*. "I understand. It's okay, Sir."

His smile broadens. "Do you like the room?"

"I love it, Sir."

He takes the book from me, glances at the cover, and then sets it on the nightstand. His other hand is still stroking my face, and my entire body is alive with arousal.

I have the covers up above my breasts, but he lowers his large hand and toys with the top of my nightgown at my shoulder. "You look so pretty in this bed wearing this nightgown."

"Thank you, Sir."

He leans closer and inhales, his eyes closing partway before he rights himself. "That scent suits you. I'm glad I chose it."

I'm surprised he selected it himself, and I wonder how many of the things in this room were personally chosen by him. I don't ask. But I do remember my earlier concern. "I didn't have time to get a haircut, Sir. Would it be possible for me to get one in the near future?"

He picks up a lock of my hair that has fallen over my shoulder and runs his fingers down the length. "Not a chance. I love every inch of it."

I'm shocked, but also intrigued by the fact that he seems mesmerized by the thick curl in his hand. I bite my bottom lip as he sets his hand on my hip next.

"I'm going to be very strict with you, Lucy. I want you to fully get into the role we're playing. Immerse yourself completely. You have nothing to worry about except obeying me at all times."

"Yes, Sir." My voice is breathy. Wetness has leaked between my legs, and without panties, it's running down my crack. I'm so turned on by this game we're playing.

He strokes my thigh. Even through the comforter, this is the most he's ever touched me. "You're squirming." His voice is playful. "Lie still."

I try not to move as heat rushes up my face. I hadn't realized I was moving at all, and I'm a bit mortified.

He smirks. "It's adorable. I love that I affect you that way."

I don't know how to respond.

He meets my gaze again and holds it. "I have a few personal questions so that I'll know what I'm working with."

I flush further, concerned about what he might ask me. "Okay, Sir."

"How many men have you slept with?"

I swallow. Yeah, this is embarrassing. Will he care? "None, Sir," I whisper.

He takes a deep breath, smiling. "I like that. Have you fooled around with any boys?"

I shake my head, tucking my lips between my teeth. His choice of words has put me deeper in the role. *Boys. Fooled around.*

This conversation was bound to occur eventually. I know that, but it's still awkward. I'm a twenty-two-year-old virgin with no experience.

"Are you aroused now, Lucy?"

"Yes, Sir." I can barely hear my admission. Will he touch me more intimately?

"Good. I like that too." He leans forward and kisses me on the forehead. "You need to go to sleep now, Lucy. Tomorrow will be here before you know it. Nancy will wake you up at six. She will bring you your clothes at that time too. I expect you to dress, comb your hair, and be downstairs in my office by seven. You'll be expected to submit to me at all times, but you'll still have duties in my office."

"Yes, Sir." I nod, wishing he wouldn't go, but knowing he is about to. I love the weight of him pressing into my side and the way his hand roams around, touching me everywhere except where I most crave contact.

"I have one rule I expect you to obey at all times, Lucy." His face has lowered, his voice serious as he eyes me, ensuring he has my attention. "You will not touch yourself unnecessarily. Beyond bathing and using the bathroom, you will keep your hands to yourself. Do not play with your little titties or your pussy at any time without my permission. Understood?"

I can't breathe. I can't even move. I'm too shocked to blink.

For one thing, I've so rarely explored my sexuality in the first place that his instructions aren't necessary. For another thing, I've never been so turned on in my life, not even the first time he had me kneel before him.

I clench my thighs together. My breasts feel swollen and achy. My nipples are tight and puckered, rubbing against the soft material of my nightgown.

He lifts a brow when I don't respond, and then he continues speaking. "Your orgasms belong to me now. I decide when and how you are permitted to come. I will dole them out when I think you've earned them. I need a verbal response from you that you understand this hard rule."

I swallow. My mouth is so dry. "Yes, Sir." I don't have the ability to tell him there is no way I would masturbate under his roof anyway. That his rule is completely unnecessary. I'd be too worried about getting caught. I can't speak beyond to agree.

"Good girl. If I find you disobeying this rule, you will not like the punishment. It will be severe. I'm not opposed to attaching your little wrists to the posts on your bed at night. Nor will I hesitate to install a camera in your bedroom to ensure you keep your fingers away from your greedy little pussy."

I swallow even harder. "I won't touch myself, Sir."

"Good girl." He closes the distance between us and kisses my forehead again. And then he shoves to standing and leaves me staring after him, speechless and shocked.

He pauses at the doorframe and faces me. "You're an amazing submissive, Lucy. I know you're going to enjoy exploring a variety of ages until you either get them out of your system or find the one that suits you best. I want you to know that from this moment forward, you don't need to worry about anything that shouldn't concern a child. Let me take that weight off your shoulders. Let yourself enjoy all the stages of growing up that you missed."

"Thank you, Sir," I murmur.

He gives me one last smile and then leaves, shutting the door behind him.

I stare at the last place he stood for a long time. When the lights suddenly go off, I flinch and then try to slow my rapid breaths.

I'm aware of several things. The bed is the most comfortable place I've ever slept. The sheets are soft enough to make me sigh. Master Roman is going to take care of me.

And I've never been so aroused in my life.

I wonder if my wetness will be noticeable on my nightgown and sheets. Will someone see that I was aroused? I'm not sure why I care. Everyone in the house obviously knows I'm role-playing with Master Roman. I'm his little girl now. No one has judged me.

For a fleeting moment I wonder how many other girls have stayed in this room. How many women has he moved into this house? I shudder. I don't want to know the answer.

I curl onto my side and close my eyes, but my nipples ache, and my sex is throbbing. I can't shake the words Master Roman spoke from my mind. *Do not play with your little titties or your pussy at any time without my permission.*

It's not just the meaning behind the instruction that has made me shiver with desire. It's the choice of words. *Titties. Pussy. Greedy.* It's almost as if he's reprimanded me in a dirty way. Admonished me ahead of time.

I clasp my hands together between my breasts under my chin and concentrate on lying very still so that my nipples will not abrade against the nightgown. It's futile because every time I breathe, I'm aware of their growing sensitivity.

Did Master Roman know what he would be doing to me when he verbalized his rule?

It takes me a long time to relax and fall asleep, and when I do, I dream of Master Roman stroking his hands down my naked body. He touches the tips of my breasts. He even attaches my wrists to the posts of the bed. I know I'm writhing under the comforter as I sleep, but I can't seem to wake up.

CHAPTER 22

Master Roman

The moment I shut Lucy's bedroom door, I draw in a deep breath and then blow it out slowly. I lean against her door for a long time, unable to walk away. I've never been as affected by a woman as I am by Lucy.

She takes my breath away with her innocence and shock. When I told her not to touch herself, I thought she was going to stop breathing.

It was precious.

She is mine.

This has to work between us because I'm falling harder for her every day. I close my eyes and remind myself that she is young and so very new to the lifestyle. Even though she seems pleased with her room and the arrangements I've made for her so far, there is always a possibility that she will eventually burn out and balk at living this life.

I want her fulltime. Even though I have her in my home

and totally under my care, I've given her an out. I had to. It's imperative that she not feel trapped.

I need to watch myself too. I must be careful not to get too attached. Ever. It's the reason why I've arranged for her to have her own room, far from mine. She needs to sleep in her own bed. I need her to sleep in her own bed. I need the few hours I'm alone in the night to regroup and remind myself this might not last.

I shove off the door to her room and wander through the house, taking the back stairs she's been told to use and then walking aimlessly around the first floor. My staff is amazing. I know I'm fortunate to have them. Because they worked for my father and even knew my grandfather, they are completely aware of my preferences.

I've never moved a woman into the house before, but they know where my tastes lie. They weren't surprised when I hired her, nor were they surprised when I called them together to inform them she would be moving in. They respect my privacy. And I'm certain they will respect Lucy's too.

Having Nancy get Lucy settled in was partly intentional. I want Lucy to see Nancy as someone of authority around here. It's not untrue, of course, but having a woman in and out of Lucy's room creates a certain feel. Nancy is like a headmistress at a boarding school. She has a stern vibe that suits her role in my scenario perfectly.

I will be the one making all the decisions where it comes to Lucy, including her clothing, bedding, and toiletries, but having Nancy deliver her things every morning and night will add to Lucy's experience.

The worst part about this entire scene is that I can't plan too far ahead. I can't know how Lucy will react to my domination. I will have to take everything one step at a time.

This entire experiment could blow up in my face before breakfast tomorrow.

I take a deep breath as I pause in my library to stare out into the night through the floor-to-ceiling back windows. I shouldn't doubt myself. I watched Lucy for several Friday nights. I've had her under my thumb for eight full days. I know she's submissive. I also know she's more than prepared to experiment with age play.

If I'm honest with myself, she has also more than exceeded my expectations so far. I can't believe how perfectly smooth our time went as I tucked her in. She had obviously stepped into the role and embraced it.

I know she has needs that stem from a missing childhood. I get that. But how long with they last?

This is my primary concern. I must guard my heart. If I fall too hard for her, I could find myself blindsided by her departure from my life. It's possible she needs me as a transition. Someone to help her heal and gain self-confidence. She could leave.

I shudder, leaning my forehead against the cool glass of the window.

Who am I kidding? I'm already in this too deeply to extricate myself. All I can do now is force myself to stick to the plan of sending her to her room for eleven hours a night. Without that separation, I know I could easily grow even more attached than I already am.

CHAPTER 23

Lucy

Childhood music fills the room at the same time the lights come on. I bolt to a sitting position and glance around, my heart beating fast. It takes me a few seconds to realize where I am and what I've committed to. I turn toward the Hello Kitty alarm that is blaring "It's a Small World" and push the button on the top. It stops.

A knock sounds at the door.

"Come in," I call out in a scratchy morning voice.

The door opens and Nancy steps in. She's holding a pile of clothes, which she sets on the wicker chair. "I hope you slept well, Lucy."

"Yes, ma'am." I did. Once I finally convinced my mind to stop running and was able to ignore the ache between my legs.

She smiles at me, her expression softer than last night. "Excellent. You'll have plenty of time to get dressed each morning. I'll bring your clothes in every day. Put your nightgown down the chute. Use the bathroom. Wash up. Comb your hair. Master Roman will expect you in his office by seven. You can use your extra time to read or relax, but don't fall back asleep." She narrows her gaze, and I shudder, imagining what kind of trouble I might be in if I snooze and don't show up at seven. "Yes, ma'am."

As soon as she leaves the room, I slip from the bed and pad to the bathroom. It was weird sleeping without panties. I feel exposed. I use the toilet and then lift my nightgown over my head and deposit it in the clothes chute. It must extend a significant distance because I can't hear anything, not even the swoosh of my clothes.

Naked, I quickly return to the bedroom and glance at the door. It doesn't have a lock on it. So far, the only two times someone entered, they knocked first and I invited them in. Will that always be the case, or is there a chance Evelyn, Nancy, or Weston might enter without knocking? What about Master Roman?

Uncertain, I decide to dress quickly. I grab the pile of clothes and return to the bathroom, shutting that door behind me. There are shoes on the bottom of the pile, and I set them on the floor. My pulse picks up. The shoes are black Mary Jane's, the kind a child would wear to a private school.

I take a deep breath and rummage through the rest of the pile. On top is a white blouse. The material is thin and starched. Under the perfectly folded blouse is a pair of panties. My hands are shaking as I lift them. They are full cut, pink, and covered with brown teddy bears. The kind a child would wear.

I *am* a child. I need to remember this. I'm playing a role. I'm stepping back into my childhood. The one I missed out on.

My hands are shaking as I step into the panties and pull them up. I've never owned sexy lingerie in my life. However, the white cotton underwear I've worn for the last ten years have always been bikini cut. It feels awkward putting on something that rises so high on my belly.

Under the panties is a skirt. I lift it next and hold it up. The pattern is a plaid combination of gray, pink, and purple. It's pleated and short. Without even putting it on I'm aroused. It's not going to extend much below my bottom, which will make me constantly aware of the little girl panties I'm wearing underneath.

Why does this arouse me?

I glance back at the vanity and freeze. My eyes slide closed. They have not deceived me. There is no bra. The only thing left is a pair of white socks.

My fingers tremble as I set the skirt down and put the blouse on. I button it up without looking in the mirror. Next, I step into the skirt and zip it at the side. I grab the socks and sit on the edge of the bathtub to put them on. They are my size but clearly intended for a child. I fold them down and then put on the Mary Jane's.

When I stand and look around, I confirm there is no bra. I step back into the bedroom and look around the chair and the floor. Definitely no bra.

I return to the bathroom and lift my gaze to the mirror. My breasts are small, modest, and pert, but my nipples are a darker shade of pink, and I can sort of see them through the thin material of the blouse if it presses against me.

In addition, the material is starched and slightly itchy, which means every time I move, my attention is drawn to the sensitive tips. I pinch the blouse at my chest and try to pull it away a few inches, but it fits me too snuggly to get the relief I need. I'm going to struggle to ignore my plight all day.

Could it have been a mistake? An oversight? Maybe Master Roman forgot, or Nancy. Or she dropped my bra somewhere. That thought makes me even more nervous as I picture a bra lying in the hallway. In fact, just to ensure that isn't the case, I quietly open the bedroom door and peek out. Nothing is on the floor in any direction.

I shut the door again and shuffle back to the bathroom to brush out my hair, and then I find a clip in the drawer and secure it at the back of my head.

My hair full and the curls are everywhere, but it can't be helped. I brush my teeth next and then return to the bedroom. I stand in the middle of the room for several minutes, thinking. Worrying.

I continually brush my hands down the front of the skirt. It's covering my bottom, but only by a few inches. The pleats mean that it can easily be lifted. I have tucked the blouse in, but my lack of bra is making me feel as though I'm completely naked.

On top of everything else, my panties are wet from my arousal. There is a knot in my belly too. It's like I'm wound extremely tight and nothing is going to relieve the pressure for as long as I'm dressed like this. It will get worse when I leave the room.

I close my eyes and force myself to take several slow, deep breaths. Master Roman is right. I've never been more aroused. I need this type of submission. I'm already restless from the idea of role-playing as a young girl.

The only part I don't think I can tolerate is the lack of bra. Everything else is fine. But with my breasts hanging loose and brushing against the stiff material, I'm going to feel exposed and unable to concentrate on anything.

I glance at the clock. I've taken so much time worrying about my outfit that it's already ten minutes until seven. I need to head to Master Roman's office. I can't imagine how this day is going to go, but it's time to face it.

CHAPTER 24

Master Roman

When Lucy steps into my office, she shuts the door before slowly shuffling toward me. I haven't instructed her to shut the door, so I'm fighting a grin already.

I barely glance up at her and then lift a finger so that she will know I want her to wait until I'm finished concentrating on the work on my computer screen.

There is no work open on my computer, but I need to compose myself. My dick has gone from stiff to out of control at the one glance.

Lucy is as divine as I knew she would be. She is dressed in exactly what I picked out for her. She also looks like the young girl she is meant to portray. I have just one addition I'm going to add…

When I think I can focus without giving away how damn affected I am, I lift my gaze and motion for her to come to my side.

She rounds the desk, her hands clasped in front of her. Her

gaze is toward the floor, or maybe her chest. I can't be sure. But because her attention is not on my face, I lower my gaze to take her in more thoroughly.

My God she is perfect. Her tits are fucking amazing. Small, but pert and high. I can see not only the outline, but also the faint darker area where her nipples are. She's trying to hide them with her arms by pressing her blouse forward. I'll be putting a stop to that in a heartbeat. This is the first time I've seen her without a bra, and I realize she hardly needs one. Her tits are indeed proportionately small, like the rest of her.

The skirt is exactly how I wanted it. Short but not too short. It's covering her butt, but I could easily slide a hand under it to inspect what's mine. I gulp at that thought.

My gaze scans down her sexy legs to her feet. The little girl shoes and socks cement the outfit. She even has her toes turned in a bit as she stands before me.

"Did you sleep well, cherry blossom?"

She nods. "Yes, Sir," she murmurs before tucking her lower lip between her teeth. Sexy as fuck.

I wonder if she has any idea how damn turned on I am. I need to rein it in a bit. She is way too innocent for me to bend her over my desk and fuck her senseless. "Don't slouch, Lucy. Hands at your sides."

She slowly straightens her spine and drops her hands, her fists curling at her sides. "Nancy didn't provide a bra, Sir." Her voice is soft. "I feel weird."

I fight the urge to grin. God she is precious. "Nancy wasn't supposed to provide you with a bra, Lucy. It wasn't an accident. I'm the one choosing your clothes. You're twelve. You're playing a role. I want you to fully immerse yourself in the age. For the time being, until I say otherwise, don't break from the role. Understood?"

"Yes, Sir," she whispers. She draws her heels closer together and clenches her thighs.

My dick jumps.

"For this entire week, you're twelve. It's the oldest age bracket we're going to explore. When I think you're ready, I will switch to a younger age. At no point will you wear a bra."

She tips her head lower. Her hair falls over her shoulder. The lack of bra is making her very self-conscious. I'll watch to make sure she handles it okay, but squirming isn't going to make me let up on that issue. It tells me she's turned on, even if she's self-conscious. She'll get used to having her tits free in a few days.

And my God her breasts are amazing. I want to slow down and back up a pace, but I can't stop myself from stroking one finger from each hand down her cheeks, over her neck and shoulders, and then along the sides of her tits.

She jumps, a soft gasp escaping her lips. She also arches her chest slightly toward me as her lips part. Yeah, she's fine.

I drop my hands. "Turn around, little blossom."

She slowly does as I've requested, and I reach up and remove the clip from her hair. I open my desk drawer and reach inside for a comb. Standing, I part her hair down the center and then set one side over her left shoulder. With practiced ease, I divide the right side into three sections and quickly braid her thick long hair, starting behind her ear.

She stands very still while I work, but her breathing is labored.

I reach back into the drawer for the pink ribbon and tie off the end. When I drop the braid over her shoulder, it falls across her breast and reaches down to her belly. Her curly hair is even longer braided. I love it.

I repeat the process on her left side and then take her shoulders and turn her back to face me. "Look at me," I demand.

She lifts her gaze. Her face is flushed. She's biting that lip. I find it suits her, and I'm not going to say anything about it. It makes her look young.

I hope she's ready for what I'm about to do. "You need a safeword. How about jacks?"

She smiles. "Jacks?"

"Yep. It's a toy I haven't provided you. If there are any childhood toys you would like to have, let me know, and I'll get them so you can make the most out of this role, but jacks will infuriate me if I step on them, so you won't have any."

She giggles, the sound racing to my cock. My balls are going to be blue before lunch. "Okay, Sir."

"The only time you're permitted to break this role is to stop me with the word jacks."

She nods.

I lift a brow.

She clears her throat. "Yes, Sir."

"Now, I'm not going to go easy on you, not even from the start. So, I'm going to spank you now for two reasons."

She shudders, her face going white. Her teeth sink into that bottom lip harder.

"One, you won't decide when the door to my office is open or closed. I will. If I want it closed, I will do it myself or ask you to shut it."

"Yes, Sir," she whispers.

"And two, don't question what Nancy sets out for you to wear again. And if I ever hear that you question my staff about anything, you won't be able to sit down. Have I made myself clear?"

"Yes, Sir." A tear escapes one watery eye to run down her cheek. It's expected. She's uncertain.

I watch her expression. "Has anyone ever spanked you before?"

"No, Sir." She lifts a hand and swipes at the tear. Another one falls to replace it.

"It will hurt because it's meant to deter you from being disobedient, but I will never strike you hard enough to harm you or draw blood."

She nods. I let it slide.

I take her hand and bring her trembling body to my right side. When I press on her lower back, she leans over my thighs. A soft sob escapes. I know she's nervous. After this first spanking, she will relax a bit more into the role.

I gently pull her hands to her lower back and clasp both wrists with my left hand. When I lift her skirt and tuck it under her wrists, she squirms. Another small sob makes it difficult for me to concentrate.

The panties I provided her are so fucking sexy covering her bottom. I can't resist smoothing my palm over the pink, cotton material covered with teddy bears. I'm dragging this out, and I know it.

Finally, I tuck my fingers under the elastic at her waist and drag the panties down over her bottom, leaving them tangled tightly on her upper thighs.

She breathes heavily, wiggling on my lap.

I stroke her bare cheeks for the first time, admiring how damn smooth they are. Her skin is so tender. "I want you to count while I spank you, Lucy."

She lets out a slight moan.

I watch as I continue to caress her bottom. She is so petite that my hand nearly covers both her cheeks. My palm is going to cover a lot of skin, leaving most of her bottom bright pink with just a few swats.

I close my eyes. *Jesus.* I lift my hand and spank her right in the center, hard enough that she flinches, low enough that I know I have her attention. She moans.

"Count, Lucy," I admonish.

"One," she whimpers.

I strike her again in the same spot.

"Two," she murmurs.

Another spank slightly higher.

It takes her a few seconds to react. She's breathing heavily. "Three."

I don't stop. I'm afraid if I drag this out, she will come on my thighs. She's that aroused. The next swat lands palm open on her right cheek.

"Four." Her voice is so low.

Another on her left cheek.

"Five." She's panting. Her body is stiff. Her toes are digging into the floor. Her skin is pink and hot. I decide she's had enough. I smooth my palm over her bottom, staring at my perfect little girl.

I can't resist the temptation to check her pussy, so without warning I slip my fingers between her thighs and drag them through her folds.

She is soaked. And she moans so loud it shocks me. "Sir..." It's almost a question.

I don't want her to come right now. I want her to spend the day aroused. Wanting. Needy. Consumed with desire.

I release her wrists and lift her to standing with my hands on her waist. I position her between my legs. Her knees will not hold her up, so I don't release her as she sways.

Her face is red and she's blinking. I can tell by her expression she was close to coming. The angels are on my side.

She licks her dry lips.

When it seems she can stand on her own, I slide my hands up to hold her at the sides of her breasts, stretching her blouse so that her tits rub hard against the starched material.

Her eyelids lower until they are almost closed. Her mouth is open. I watch her face as I drag my thumbs over and flick her nipples.

She slumps toward me, gasping.

I have her though, and I quickly turn her to set her on my knee between my legs. I pull her against my chest and palm the side of her head.

She is shaking and whimpering.

"Shh. You're okay, cherry blossom."

Her bottom is still exposed and the warmth seeps through my slacks. When I smooth my other hand up her thigh, I encounter her bunched-up panties. The crotch is soaked. I know she will shoot off like a rocket if I touch her folds again, so I resist. Instead I tug at the tangled panties around her thighs until she squirms in my hold.

I should talk to her about what she's feeling, but I decide to push her further. "I want you to shave your pussy in the bath tonight and every night from now on."

She stiffens.

"Little girls do not have hair on their pussies, blossom," I point out.

"Yes, Sir." Her voice is barely audible. As is often the case.

I like her slightly off kilter, so I don't give her quite enough time to regroup before standing her between my legs again. "Hold your skirt up," I demand.

She lifts it a few inches with trembling fingers.

"Higher, Lucy," I admonish.

She pulls the hem up to her chest finally. She is shaking.

I give a tug to her pubic hair. "This. I want it gone. All of it. When I tuck you in tonight, I will inspect to make sure you were thorough. If you can get yourself completely smooth, I'll let you handle it from now on. If not, I'll spread you open every night and shave you myself." I lift an eyebrow.

Her face grows even redder. "Yes, Sir."

I reach for the tangled mess of her panties and right them, pulling them up over her bottom. "You can let go of your skirt now."

She drops it.

I slide my hands up her middle again, and this time I cup her small breasts. Perfection. I give her nipples a quick pinch between my thumbs and forefingers before releasing them. I straighten her shirt and tuck it back into her skirt, ensuring it is tight across her amazing tits.

She grits her teeth and hunches her shoulders forward.

I know she feels exposed, but she isn't really. Women all over the country wear far less than what she has on to go to the grocery store. She's only embarrassed because it feels awkward right now not wearing a bra. She'll get used to it.

I reassure her. "Lucy, my staff is fully aware of my lifestyle. They've seen naked women roaming this house for as long as they've been working here."

She flinches.

I realize I've given her the wrong impression. "Not mine, mind you. But my father and his father liked their submissives naked at all times. My father sometimes had several women in the house at once. None of my staff is going to bat an eye at a girl not wearing a bra under her blouse."

She chewed on her lower lip. It was trembling.

"I enjoy seeing your tits free. I prefer to be able to fondle them whenever I want. I especially like that you're uncomfortable this way, *and* that it's making your pussy wet. Embrace the discomfort."

"Yes, Sir."

"All day your nipples are going to rub against your blouse. If I catch you trying to keep it from happening, I will remove this blouse and make you stand in the corner in a very long timeout with your tits to the wall. Understood?"

"Yes, Sir." Her trembling is precious. The way she shifts her weight from one leg to the other before clamping them together is almost my undoing.

"I have another rule for today."

She purses her lips.

"Keep your thighs parted. Don't let them touch. Not even when you're walking. When you're seated, spread your knees to the edges of the chair. When you're walking, learn to do it with your feet parted wider than natural. It will feel awkward at first, but you'll get used to it."

She nods and then stiffens. "Yes, Sir."

"Am I asking too much of you?"

"No, Sir," she murmurs.

"Safeword?"

"Jacks, Sir."

"You should go eat your breakfast now. I'm sure it's been ready a while." I swat her bottom.

"Yes, Sir," she says as she steps away from me.

"Tell Evelyn I'll be in shortly."

"Yes, Sir." She spins around. Her hands are fisted at her sides as she walks slowly toward the door, feet parted slightly. I've made her uncomfortable.

And I smile as she leaves.

CHAPTER 25

Lucy

I have never been so out of my body in my life. Every nerve ending is on fire. Desire consumes me. I don't breathe until I've stepped into the hallway and out of Master Roman's line of sight.

I have to stop and catch my breath. I'm shaking. I have been nearly constantly since I got up this morning. It's only been two hours. My bottom is hot and sensitive. My panties feel tight against my warm skin. They are soaked with my arousal.

My nipples are tight, hard buds rubbing against the front of my blouse. No matter what Master Roman has told me, I'm self-conscious about people noticing them. It's absurd since Nancy knows perfectly well she didn't give me a bra, Evelyn is the sweetest woman I've ever met who would never glance twice, and I rarely see Weston. Besides, he's older. He won't notice.

I notice. That's all that matters. And it's odd that of all the things I'm dealing with today, my boobs would stand out the most. For heaven's sake, I'm dressed as a twelve-year-old girl. I have on shoes a child would wear. My socks are folded down. My legs seem gangly and exposed. My panties are high on my stomach and covered with teddy bears.

I almost laugh at my plight as I continue walking toward the kitchen, careful to keep my legs slightly parted. It's awkward and difficult, but I don't trust Master Roman not to have cameras on me in the hallway.

"Good morning, Lucy," Evelyn beams when I enter the kitchen. "I've made you scrambled eggs and some Mickey Mouse waffles." She taps my nose with one finger as I reach the table where she has just set my plate.

I feel twelve. She's been instructed to treat me as a little girl. My stomach clenches. Embarrassment consumes me as I pull out my chair.

"Sit, little one. Eat before it gets cold." She rushes across the room and then returns with a tall glass of milk.

The second my butt hits the chair, I flinch. It burns slightly, and I realize for the first time that my skirt is too short to tuck under my thighs. My little girl panties are against the chair. I'm trying to remember everything I've been told, and I jerk my knees apart as I recall that instruction. I spread them slowly wide until they are obscenely open under the table.

I pick up my fork and glance around, realizing for the first time that this table really is smaller than a normal table. So is the chair. Because Master Roman intended for me to be his little from the moment I took this job?

I'm not sure how that makes me feel. It's unnerving.

I'm a child in this house. It was always the plan.

No. Not a child exactly, but a grown woman pretending to be a little girl because it makes me horny and apparently does the same for my Master. Am I out of my mind?

I tremble, unable to take a bite. My mind is racing. Master Roman has left me books about this role I've assumed. I'm aware that there are many women in the world who enjoy age play. I've seen it. I've read about it. But is it normal to feel this way?

"Is something wrong with your food, Lucy?" The deep voice makes me jump. I lift my gaze to find Master Roman leaning casually against the counter, sipping his coffee.

"No, Sir. I'm just... My stomach is fluttering."

He smiles. "I understand. Take your time. I want you to eat everything, but you don't have to rush." He remains in that spot when I think he will return to his office.

I lift the glass of milk and take a long drink, holding my breath. I won't be able to down it as quickly as I normally do today, but I hope it will help me find my appetite.

As I set the half-empty glass down and wipe my mouth on my napkin, he speaks again. "Wrap your ankles around the legs of the chair, Lucy. It will help you remember my rule."

Wetness floods my panties. Evelyn is standing just yards away as he orders me to spread my knees. My heart is racing. I'm so aroused again that it hurts. A literal ache is growing in my belly.

It's the taboo I suppose. The fact that I'm in a man's home pretending to be a child. The cook knows it. His butler knows it. His headmistress knows it. Yeah, I'm thinking of Nancy as the headmistress at a boarding school. I can't shake the visual. It's stuck.

And who is Master Roman in this picture? My father?

I shudder as I stare at my food again, poking it with my fork. I don't want him to be my father. It makes me feel icky.

Every time I breathe, my nipples brush against my blouse.

"I chose well," Master Roman continues. "Those clothes suit you perfectly. I like how the skirt fits." He is staring at how it is spread out over the tops of my thighs and flared behind me on the seat. "Sit up straighter. Use your manners when you eat. Take your time. Come to my office after you're finished."

He finally shoves off the counter and leaves me in peace. Relative peace. I don't think there will be any actual peace for as long as I live in this home.

I take a deep breath and find the will to eat. After a few bites of scrambled eggs, I perk up enough to swallow without difficulty. I switch back and forth between the eggs and the Mickey Mouse waffles. When I'm done, I drain the rest of my milk. It still tastes horrible, but I've been drinking it for two weeks now. I'm getting used to the necessity. It's not optional.

I'm beginning to realize Master Roman has picked an age before puberty so that nothing is optional. I'm not old enough to make my own decisions. I'm also not old enough to have pubic hair. I shudder at the memory, knowing I will worry all day about shaving myself to his satisfaction. I've never shaved down there before. I've never had cause to.

Tonight will be challenging. On so many levels.

I finally rise from the table and carry my dishes to the sink.

I turn toward Evelyn. "Thank you, ma'am."

"You're welcome," Evelyn says. Her hands are buried in dough she is kneading on the island. "Have a good morning. I'll see you at lunch."

I leave the room. It's not until I'm in the hallway that I remember my thighs and spread my feet wider. I head for the bathroom I've used for two weeks, brush my teeth, use the toilet, and then return to Master Roman.

He's on the phone, but he holds up a book and nods toward my office.

I assume he intends for me to read it, so I carry it to my office, settle myself at my desk, and then glance down. It's the same book I intended to read last night but never started. *Being the Best Me: A Little's Guide to a Happy Life.*

I open it and start with chapter one, wondering if I'll still be given the jobs of an assistant, or if my new role is replacing my old one. And if that's the case, will Master Roman hire someone else? I hate that idea. Hopefully, just because he has assigned me to read this book doesn't mean I've been demoted.

I spread my knees apart and tuck my ankles under the swivel chair. It doesn't have legs, but I improvise. Sitting up straight, I set my gaze on the pages. I've been given a task. I'm meant to complete it. There's a good chance Master Roman will question my reading later.

CHAPTER 26

Lucy

I'm fully engrossed in my reading when I sense Master Roman at my side. He leans over my shoulder, setting his hand on the desk. "Have you learned anything?"

I flinch and sit up straighter. "Yes. I mean, uh, yes, Sir."

He smiles. "Take a break and go have lunch. It's noon."

I glance at the time on the computer, shocked. Have I been reading that long? "Okay. Thank you, Sir." I push to standing, hyperaware of Master Roman in my space. He is inches away from me. I glance at the desk, thinking he must have something else to say. "Oh, I didn't do any work this morning. Did you mean for me to read for that long?"

He's smiling at me as he picks up one of my braids and twirls it around his fingers. "Yes. Relax. The world hasn't come to an end. I want you to focus on yourself right now. If I need something else done, I'll let you know." He drops my braid and his fingers come to my cheek. "You're so precious. Go eat before I change my mind." He releases me.

I back up a few paces, needing the space so I can breathe.

He nods toward the door. "Go on."

I scramble from the room. Flustered. What did he mean that he might change his mind? I flush when I consider the possibilities. He was staring at me like he wanted to eat me himself. I'm not sure that would be a bad thing. Maybe I should have balked.

Evelyn has prepared me grilled cheese and tomato soup. It's delicious, and I'm so grateful to have healthy food for the first time in years. Ramen noodles are fine to get by, but they're nothing compared to this.

I don't see Master Roman during lunch, though I'm careful to sit up straight and keep my knees spread. It's my second meal in this outfit. I'm still unnerved, but not as bad as earlier.

Not until Weston walks through the back door. He nods at me in greeting. "Lucy."

I lift my sandwich as a way to hide my breasts. "Sir."

"I trust you slept well in your new room?"

"Yes, Sir. Thank you."

He smiles at me. I think it's the first time I've seen him smile. He's usually rather serious. When he drove me to and from work, we often sat in silence. I don't think he's a very social man. "I'll let you finish your lunch then." He finally walks away, saying something to Evelyn as he passes.

I lower my arm. This situation with not wearing a bra is the hardest part. It's weirder than any other aspect of my submission. The thought that I won't be permitted to wear a bra for a very long time makes me even more self-aware.

After lunch as I'm heading back to Master Roman's office, he pops into the hallway and stops me. "Why don't you go outside for a while. You need some fresh air. I never think to let you out during the day." He takes my arm, gently guiding me back through the kitchen, only this time he leads me to the far side of the large room where floor-to-ceiling windows lead out to the enormous patio I've only seen from inside.

He opens a glass door and leads me out onto the deck. It's nice out. The weather can be unpredictable in Seattle, but today there are few clouds in the sky and it's not raining.

The sound of the waterfall cascading down into the hot tub is soothing. There is steam coming off the surface of the water. Inviting. I've never been in a hot tub. I wander closer, aware that Master Roman is at my back.

"I'll order you a bathing suit so you can use the hot tub. Sorry I didn't think of that before," he states.

I turn toward him. "Thank you, Sir. I feel weird about you always buying me things. You've done too much already."

He steps close to me and takes my chin, tipping my head back. "If you haven't noticed, I make plenty of money. It's nothing for me to purchase a few outfits and a swimsuit, Lucy."

"It's more than that, and you know it." I roll my eyes.

He grips my chin tighter. "Don't get sassy. You may express your feelings, but don't forget to remain respectful."

"Sorry, Sir," I murmur.

He drops my chin. "Come on. Let me show you around the gardens. My gardeners keep the property in excellent shape. It's even magical in winter, especially when it snows."

Will I still be here in the winter? It seems so far off in the future. I can barely imagine what is going to happen to me later tonight, let alone months from now. Will it get easier? This submitting?

Master Roman takes my hand and leads me to a path off the back deck. His garden is truly beautiful. People would pay admission to see it if they knew about it.

We wander down a winding path between the plants and flowers. Eventually, we come to a bench, and Master Roman sits. He's still holding my hand, and he pulls me between his legs and sets me on his knee just like he did earlier in the day.

I'm acutely aware of my bottom—covered only in underwear—against his slacks. They are black. He also has on a perfectly ironed white shirt and a dark blue tie. I've never seen him in any other clothing. Not even at the club.

He rests one hand on my hip around my waist and sets the other on my thigh. He can nearly reach all the way around me, and the hand on my leg covers the majority of my sensitive skin. "Tell me what you learned this morning."

"In the book, Sir?" My body is alert now with him touching me in so many places.

His fingers stroke back and forth over my inner thigh. There is no way to ignore what he's doing to me. I'm instantly aroused. My nipples jump to attention. "Yes, blossom. The book. What did you learn?" He squeezes my thigh.

I lift my fingers to my mouth and subconsciously chew on my thumb nail.

Master Roman lifts his hand from my thigh and tugs my finger from my mouth. "Stop doing that. It's a horrible habit."

"Yes, Sir."

He pulls my hand down and clasps it with his other one at my waist. When he sets his palm back on my thigh, he keeps my wrist pressed to my side. "The book, Lucy."

I try to think. It's hard with him staring at me like this. With me on his lap. With him holding my wrist. With his fingers stroking the skin between my thighs. With my nipples hard points he can easily see.

I press against the sides of my breasts with my biceps, hoping to push my blouse off the tips so that I can think.

Master Roman narrows his gaze. He suddenly lifts me off his lap and sets me on my feet in front of him. His hands go to the front of my blouse, and he rapidly unbuttons it.

I'm shocked. I glance around. People could be watching.

He tugs it from my skirt and pulls it down my arms and off my body so fast I can't gather the wherewithal to stop him. I'm naked from the waist up. My nipples are so hard, and I'm chilled. It's a nice day in Seattle, but not nice enough to go without a shirt. I cross my arms before I can stop myself.

He points at the grass next to the bench. "On your knees, cherry blossom."

I shuffle to the grass and lower myself to my knees. I'm shivering and nervous, but I love the pet name he's given me. It makes my cheeks warm every time. It's endearing.

"Back straight. Hands clasped behind you. Knees wider. You've done this a dozen times. You know how to kneel in front of me, Lucy."

I glance around again. Someone is going to see me. I don't want to disappoint Master Roman, but he's pushing me further than I'm comfortable with.

His voice is deeper when he reprimands me. "Lucy, now."

I obey because I can't not. A shudder wracks my entire body as my boobs lift higher on my chest. I lower my gaze, shocked by what I see. Who is this woman on her knees in the grass in clothing meant for a young girl and no shirt?

Master Roman leans forward, his elbows on his knees. "No one is going to come out here. Relax."

Relax? Is he crazy?

He reaches out a hand and gently strokes my breast, sending goose bumps across the surface. His fingers are warm against my bare skin. His thumb brushes over my nipple, making me whimper. "Your tits are amazing, Lucy." His voice is lower now. Calm. He is not angry. "I want you to stop worrying about them all the time. Some days I'm going to make you spend time with nothing covering them at all until you stop fretting over not wearing a bra under your shirt."

I gulp. The idea is unimaginable to me. I don't know why I didn't consider the ramifications of committing to this odd arrangement with him. He's a Dom. He owns his own club for God's sake. Of course he likes his submissives naked. But am I up for this? I don't know.

He picks up my braid and toys with the ends before using it to tickle the skin on my breast. When he flicks it over my nipple, I let out a soft cry.

"That's my girl. I'm going to love worshiping these tits. And you're going to learn to love exposing them to me."

I shiver. Is that possible? Am I too modest for this lifestyle?

"I'm not asking you to strip naked in front of other people, Lucy. Baby steps here. But I'm going to push your boundaries hard. These little titties are mine. If I want to see them, you'll show them to me."

"Yes, Sir," I murmur.

He continues teasing my nipples with my braid, dancing the ends of my hair across my puckered skin. "So gorgeous. Your skin is flawless. Your nipples are perfection. I can't wait to wrap my lips around them." He's speaking out loud, but it's as if he's talking to himself.

The chill begins to recede as my skin heats. The way he looks at me makes me feel pretty. I've never had a bad body image, but I've also never been naked with a man before. Today I have had both my breasts and my genitals exposed to my new Master. I'm both nervous and excited by the prospect of taking things further.

He drops my braid, and it sways back and forth over my nipple. He leans back on the bench and casually crosses his legs. "Now, tell me about the book. You're going to kneel there with your sweet tits exposed until I'm satisfied."

I swallow. The book...

He lifts a brow. "My staff knows not to follow us into my

156

garden. But eventually they will send out a search party if we don't return."

I nod. "Okay. So, the book. I was reading about the different types of littles." I force myself to ignore my exposure and concentrate on what I've read. I go into my head.

"And? Did you discover anything insightful about yourself?"

"Not yet. I read about the dynamic between littles or middles and their Masters. Most of them don't have arrangements like ours it seems. Most of them role-play for a few hours at a time."

"This is true. I can't say what the long run will look like for either of us yet. This is a unique arrangement born from a unique set of circumstances. Most people don't have the ability to drop everything and move into a 24/7 situation so they can figure things out."

I watch him as he speaks. He's sitting so casually in front of me while I kneel before him with my breasts hanging free. It's unnerving.

"Did you read about the various ages people like to assume?"

"Yes, Sir. But I don't know what suits me yet. I think I like this one though." I *know* I do. Other than the bra thing, I have enjoyed the freedom I've experienced from turning over every decision to a Master while my only job was to do as I'm told. Even kneeling in the lawn like this is refreshing in a way. I didn't make this choice. I simply obeyed.

Another reason I like this age is because it's not so young that I can't exercise rational thought. Twelve-year-old girls have had enough education to know about the world. They can read at an adult level for example.

Master Roman is watching me, so I decide to share. "I'm not sure I would enjoy pretending to be an age where I can't

157

read or I'm expected to play with toys all day. It wouldn't be enough to keep my mind occupied."

He nods. "Understandable. What about the actual baby stage? Did you read about that?"

I shudder. "If you're asking if I want to drink from a bottle and wear a diaper, hell no."

He lifts a brow. "Watch your language, Lucy."

I rarely cuss, and I don't think I have since I met Master Roman. At least not in front of him. I'm surprised by his admonishment. But then again, I remind myself, I'm twelve. "Sorry, Sir."

He reaches out a hand. "Come here, blossom."

I rise to my feet and shuffle to him.

He lifts my blouse from his lap and holds it up for me to slip my arms into it. He then proceeds to button it and tuck it into my skirt once again. "There. Now do you feel naked?"

"Not as much, Sir, but it's still weird having my breasts loose. I'm constantly conscious of them swaying and my nipples grazing against the material."

He gives my hips a squeeze. "That's the idea, blossom."

"I'm not sure I will get used to it, Sir," I add. I'm concerned. He wanted me to share my concerns. So, I am.

"Mind over matter. If I catch you fidgeting tomorrow, I will remove your clothes and make you sit in your office all day in just your panties. Understood?"

"Yes, Sir." My mouth is dry again. I'm not sure how I feel about his demand. On the one hand, I'm mortified by the prospect. That's twice he has suggested making me spend time without my shirt. It should horrify me. And it does. Right? Except it also doesn't. At the same time, I'm aroused by the idea.

It seems apparent that Master Roman is not going to expose me to his staff. At least not at this stage in our play. He knows I'm not ready for that. The idea of being forced to sit topless in my office makes me aroused. It has just enough edge to it to make me worry I might be seen mixed with a knowledge that is incredibly unlikely. The combination is titillating.

I don't share my thoughts with Master Roman.

CHAPTER 27

Lucy

I spend a few more hours in the afternoon reading the book. I'm almost finished with it when Master Roman fills my doorway. "We're going to have dinner together tonight, Lucy."

I twist my head to look at him. "We are, Sir?" I have eaten all my meals alone in the kitchen since I started working here. I usually have no idea where or when Master Roman eats. I assume there's a dining room someplace, but I've never seen it.

"Yes. You remember Master Julius?"

"Yes, Sir. He's the manager of Surrender, right?"

"He is. He's also my closest friend. We've known each other for many years. He owns a part of Surrender. In addition, we have several other businesses we own together."

I have no idea what specifically Master Roman owns or what he does. He has clients. I'm pretty sure he manages their portfolios. That's all I know.

"He and his two housemates, Levi and Beck, are coming to

dinner tonight. Another friend of mine named Claudia will also be here. I expect you to join us. I've instructed Nancy to set out clothes for you. I want you to go ahead upstairs now and have your bath early and then dress for dinner."

I stare at Master Roman. This is the first time I've felt unsure about our arrangement. It's one thing to pretend to be twelve alone with Master Roman. It's stressful enough knowing that his staff is aware of my odd choices in lifestyle. But he's going to have friends over? Four of them? And what does he mean by "housemates"? That's an odd description. I've met Claudia at Surrender. In addition, I've noticed her speaking with Julius. I wondered if they were a couple.

"Leave your hair the way it is, blossom. You don't need to take it down or wash it. But I do expect you to shave your pussy. By the time dinner is over, it will be your bedtime. You won't have time to take your bath then."

I swallow, needing to understand better. I can't stand up for fear my knees will buckle. "Is Claudia Master Julius's girlfriend?"

"No." Master Roman shakes his head, chuckling. "Though I've always wondered how the two of them would be if they ever got together. But no. Claudia is an old friend too. Julius and I met her in college. She's a Domme—a female Dominant —and she's been in the lifestyle for many years.

"If you're worried about what people might think, put it out of your mind. Nothing can shock any of them. They're friends who have been in the lifestyle for years. I expect you to be on your best behavior and impress my friends with what you've learned and what a sweet little girl you are. I specifically picked the four of them to introduce you to society because they will not judge you or us."

"Yes, Sir." I somehow manage to stand. I was wrong earlier. There is something more challenging than not wearing a bra all day. It's entertaining guests when I'm so new to this lifestyle.

Master Roman dismisses me by spinning around and returning to his desk. He is seated, intently studying something in front of him, as I pass. I have to concentrate hard to keep my feet spread apart enough so that my thighs don't rub. It's been difficult all day, but it requires extra concentration when my brain is occupied with concerns.

As soon as I'm free of Master Roman's gaze, I rush down the hallway and then take the back stairs at a near run. When I reach the landing, I nearly collide with Nancy.

She steadies me with both hands. "Lucy, slow down. It's not ladylike to run through the house."

"Yes, ma'am," I mumble. "I'm sorry, ma'am." I'm privately praying she doesn't rat me out to Master Roman.

"No harm done. But in the future, you should walk. I've set clothes out for you for the evening. You'll find them on your chair. I assume Master Roman has instructed you to take your bath now?"

"Yes, ma'am."

"Good. You have an hour to get ready. That should be plenty of time."

"Yes, ma'am. Thank you."

She steps out of my way and I walk as calmly as I can to my bedroom, shutting the door behind me. I'm out of breath. The idea of having dinner with four people I don't know is daunting. Beyond daunting. And before I even get to that unnerving event, I'm faced with the task of shaving off all my pubic hair.

I'm so worried about getting it right and not cutting myself that I hurry to the bathroom where I kick off my shoes and then quickly remove the rest of my clothes. I glance through the open bathroom door toward the wicker chair. I can't tell for sure what's on the chair, but something is. It's pink. It's enough to ensure me it's okay to drop my clothes down the chute.

No matter how long I live in this house and occupy this room, it will forever stress me out to release my clothes like that. I certainly can't retrieve them.

I turn the water on in the tub and find a hair clip in the bathroom drawer. I use it to pin my braids up on top of my head so they won't get wet. While I'm waiting for the water to heat and the tub to begin to fill, I stare at myself in the mirror. I look so young with these braids, my face void of all makeup. I've never worn a lot of makeup to begin with but seeing myself with no mascara and not even lip gloss adds to my youthful appearance.

You're twelve, I remind myself. No one's dad lets them wear makeup at twelve. I gasp. Dad? Yikes. No. I don't want to think of him like that.

I jerk my gaze from the mirror and step into the tub. I decide to quickly wash my body with the cherry-vanilla body soap first, and then I consider how I'm going to accomplish this monumental task. It might have been better if I'd asked Master Roman to do it for me, but I shake that plan out of my head. It would be humiliating.

I stand and lift one foot to set it on the edge of the tub. With one hand filled with soap, I use it to get a good lather between my legs. And then I take the razor and start shaving.

I start at the top. My hair is thick, and it's never been cut. It takes me a while and several passes to get the top of my mound smooth. And then I move lower, spreading my lips apart and trying hard to slide the razor over my skin without cutting myself.

I'm stressed. My hand is unsteady. I keep pausing to take a breath, wondering if most women do this every day? I've never had girlfriends who were close enough to share this kind of information.

I sit down and rinse my skin and then stand back up and start all over again, certain I have missed a great deal on the first pass. It takes forever, and I'm not convinced it's good enough to pass Master Roman's inspection later, but it's the best I can do, and I'm relieved I haven't cut my clit off in the process.

After rinsing and re-rinsing, I let the water run down the drain and then turn it back on to ensure none of my hair gets left stuck in the tub. I would be mortified if Nancy called me out on something like that.

Finally, I dry off with my towel and hang it back up. I'm worried about the time and grateful that I don't need to dry and style my hair. I remove the clip, letting the braids fall, and then rush back to the bedroom.

A glance at the clock tells me I still have twenty minutes. Plenty of time. I pick up the pile of clothes and carry them to the bathroom, shutting the door behind me. I'm thinking this will become a routine. The thought of someone walking in on me naked is too stressful. At least if I'm in the bathroom, I have another layer of protection.

I set the pink pile on the vanity and then lift the top item. It's a dress. I hold it in front of me. It's exactly the kind of dress I wish I could have owned when I was twelve. It's cut to fit an older me though. I'm both giddy and concerned.

I'm not sure I'll ever get used to thinking this fetish of mine is sane. Why would I want to put on this dress and pretend to be a child for the evening with my master's friends? Have I lost my mind?

I set the dress aside and confirm there are only two things left for me to put on. White cotton panties with a pink bow at the top and frilly white socks that fold at the ankles. The dress might be a bit younger than what some twelve-year-olds would wear, but I love it.

I step into the panties first, biting my lip when I realize

how odd it feels to have my bare sex against the cotton material. Next, I lift the dress and let it slide over my head. The top part is dainty with thin spaghetti straps holding up the satin bodice. It's meant to be flat against a girl's chest, so it's pressing against my breasts after I zip up the side. The satin is thin, and my nipples make obvious bumps underneath. They are so prominent that I'm already squirming.

The fitted waistline is higher than my actual waist. It sits snuggly against my body a few inches below my breasts. And from there the skirt flairs out. It's full and light with layers and layers of ruffles. If I twirl, it would flow all around me. It lands a few inches below my butt just as my skirt from earlier did.

It's very pretty, and I would be excited to wear it for Master Roman. I'm hesitant about his guests though. I grab the socks and return to the wicker chair to sit down and put them on. The ruffles are very babyish when I fold them over, but that's when I notice the pair of shoes under the chair.

Pink flats that are very similar to the pair I already own that are now in some mysterious storage. The toes are rounded; the shoes are patent leather and shiny. I stand, feeling free and nervous at the same time.

It's ten minutes until I'm supposed to be downstairs somewhere. I rush back into the bathroom and look at myself in the mirror. I look so young. Younger than twelve. Since I'm also a petite woman, I could almost pass for twelve. There are girls that age who are taller than me. There are probably girls that age with bigger breasts too.

I turn from the mirror, take a breath, and head toward the hallway.

CHAPTER 28

Lucy

I'm nowhere near in the same rush to get downstairs as I was to hurry upstairs, so I step slowly, listening for people.

When I arrive on the first floor, I decide to head for the kitchen. I assume Evelyn will be in there. She can direct me where to go next, I hope.

As soon as I step inside, I find I was correct. Evelyn is rushing around the room. Weston is also in the kitchen; he's sitting on a bar stool. Both of them turn as I enter.

Evelyn beams at me. "Oh, sweetie, don't you look pretty?"

"Thank you, ma'am."

"You do. Prettiest girl I've seen," Weston comments.

"Master Roman is in the library with his guests," Evelyn adds. "Weston will show you where it is."

"Thank you, sir." I wait for him as he stands and then joins me at the door. It's strange that I don't know my way around this house, but I've only had the pleasure of entering the few rooms that I've needed. Even though I've moved in and slept here last night, I still have only seen a small fraction of the mansion.

I hear voices as I follow Weston toward the front door I entered when I came for my interview. He leads me past the entrance to a set of double doors that are standing open to reveal a large room that is most definitely a library.

Weston clears his throat. "Miss Lucy has arrived, sir," he announces.

"Ah, thank you, Weston." Master Roman strides across the room to meet me. He holds out a hand as he approaches. His face is lit up.

I'm well aware there are four other people in the room, but I haven't had the nerve to look their direction yet. My gaze is on Master Roman.

When he reaches me, he lifts my chin with his fingers. "You look beautiful, blossom. That dress is lovely on you."

"Thank you, Sir." My cheeks flame.

He takes my hand and leads me farther into the room.

I shuffle my feet, feeling reluctant. This seems like the worst idea ever. But I'm determined not to disappoint my Master. With my gaze down, I feel decidedly ridiculous all of a sudden. My patent leather shoes and frilly socks are laughable. The fact that my dress is poofy and too short and my nipples are visible makes me almost run from the room.

I don't though. Somehow I manage, reminding myself that Master Julius, his housemates, and Mistress Claudia are in the lifestyle.

"Master Julius, you remember Lucy," Master Roman says by way of introduction.

"Of course. Don't you look stunning tonight."

I see his hand in front of me and lift my gaze slowly to meet his as I take his hand. He shakes mine firmly and then releases me, angling toward the two men to his left. "These are my housemates, Beck and Levi."

I swallow as they each shake my hand.

"So nice to finally meet you," the dark-skinned man who I realize is Levi states.

"Yes. We've heard a lot about you," the pale blond, who is Beck, adds.

I'm unnerved. They've all heard about me before today.

The only female in the group steps forward from Julius's right. She is wearing a long gown in deep green that hugs her perfect curves and looks extremely elegant.

Even if I were dressed in my best clothes and had every sort of makeup I own in place and had my hair tamed to the smallest poof possible, I would still look twelve next to this woman.

Master Julius introduces her. "Lucy, this is Mistress Claudia."

Mistress Claudia holds out her graceful hand with her recently manicured fingernails that have white tips and pink nailbeds. She has on several rings and a gorgeous diamond bracelet. I take her hand in my childish one and murmur, "Nice to meet you, ma'am."

"Oh, Roman, she's so sweet. I love her," Mistress Claudia exclaims. She gives my hand a squeeze before she releases it.

I can't breathe. I think I'm going to hyperventilate. She loves me. She is playing the role I'm in. For the millionth time, I'm both horrified and aroused.

I glance down at my blunt nails, ragged from nervously biting them. They are nothing like Claudia's.

"I'll make you a Shirley Temple, blossom," Master Roman announces before he leaves me standing there with these adults and heads across the room toward a bar.

This is when I notice that Julius is holding a tumbler with a brown liquid in it. Probably whiskey. Beck and Levi each have a beer. Mistress Claudia has a glass of white wine. I

168

lower my gaze and shuffle my feet, knowing they are both watching me.

I'm not a drinker. I've never had alcohol in my life. I wouldn't have waisted money on it, nor do I like to feel out of control. But I feel decidedly ridiculous when Master Roman hands me a glass filled with what I assume is Sprite with a splash of grenadine. He's also placed a cherry in it. And a straw.

I take a sip. It's really good. I've never had a Shirley Temple. It's been ages since I've had soda. The only drinks I'm ever offered in this house are milk and water.

"Shall we sit down?" Master Roman suggests. "Evelyn will have dinner ready soon." He leads us across the room, and I take the time to look around, trailing behind everyone. The room is done in the same dark paneling as nearly the entire house. Floor-to-ceiling bookshelves line the walls. In the center of the rear wall is an enormous fireplace, ornately carved and inviting. A fire is burning in it now.

As we approach, I observe the furniture arranged in front of the fireplace. There are two high-back maroon leather armchairs and a matching sofa. Master Julius sits on the sofa, Beck and Levi joining him. Mistress Claudia perches on one of the armchairs. She crosses her ankles and sits as though she's a trained model. She could be for all I know.

Master Roman lowers himself into the other armchair, and then he reaches out for me to join him. I'm not sure if I'm comforted when he parts his legs for me to perch on his thigh between them or if I'm further mortified.

The dress poofs out behind me, leaving my bottom against his suit pants. Tonight he is wearing a dark gray suit with a light blue shirt and black tie. He has on the matching jacket. If I saw him on a crowded street, I would stop and drool over him.

He wraps his hand around my hips, holding me close as

he's done before. His other hand holds his drink. I'm grateful he isn't able to stroke my thigh. The distraction would make me squirm more than I'm already fighting.

"I've heard so much about you, Lucy," Mistress Claudia declares. "Roman tells me this is your first day living here."

"Yes, ma'am." I'm confused by everyone's admission that they've heard about me. I lift my gaze to fully take Claudia in. She is stunning. Her blond hair is cut in a bob that frames her face. She has blue eyes and sexy dimples when she smiles. Her skin is tanned, perhaps from a lotion. She is smiling at me indulgently. It's not condescending. It's exactly appropriate for the role I'm playing.

"Well, I can tell you you're in good hands. Roman is the best Master I know. He'll ensure you reach your fullest potential."

Julius chuckles. "Who's the best Dom you know?"

She laughs and sips her wine. "You all can fight for the title later. How about you come to the club and perform together. I'll be happy to direct the scene," she jokes.

Master Roman laughs, making my body jiggle. "I'd like to see this."

"It will never happen," Julius jokes while Beck and Levi groan and roll their eyes.

I squirm on Master Roman's leg.

"Sit still, blossom," he admonishes.

I finish my drink, and he takes the glass from me to set it on the end table next to the chair. "Enough sugar for you. You'll be bouncing off the walls."

I flush. I'm obviously capable of handling my sugar, but I realize twelve-year-old Lucy might not be.

"Dinner is ready, sir." Weston's voice, coming from the double doors, draws my attention. I'm not sorry that we are moving this party into the dining room. I want to get this evening over with and go back to my own room to ponder what I've experienced alone.

I'm a long way from that happening, however. I still have to get through dinner.

The formal dining room is located on the same side of the house as the library. I follow Master Roman and his guests, watching them from behind. Five grown adults who are about forty years old. Even if I weren't playing the role of a twelve-year-old, I would still be half their age. I'm young in this group by any standards.

Should this bother me? For some reason it does not. I would see Master Roman as a figure of authority in my life no matter how old either of us was. He carries himself with an air of dominance that I'm certain has always been a part of him. It's what I'm attracted to. It's the reason I went to his club in the first place.

I'm drawn to powerful figures. I crave the attention I've gotten from Master Roman like a dying man in the desert craves water.

Maybe it really is because I never had a father who even looked my direction, let alone raised me or disciplined me or cared about me. I glance up at Master Roman as he takes my hand and leads me into the dining room. He's smiling at me. He's proud of me.

CHAPTER 29

Lucy

I glance around the dining room, taking in the long table that would hold at least twenty, but is set for six on one end. The room is elegant, as I would expect. The focal point, and what catches my eye, is the chandelier. It's enormous with hundreds of dangling crystals.

Master Roman pulls a chair out for me—the one next to the head of the table. He slides it in after I've sat down. I'm beyond acutely aware of my panties, which are the only thing between me and the plush velvet maroon cushion. He even tugs the hem of my dress out from under my bottom and spreads it out around me.

He's smiling when he leans down and whispers in my ear. "You look precious, blossom." He takes a seat at the end of the table.

I blush. "Thank you, Sir."

Claudia sits to my right. Julius, Beck, and Levi take seats across from us. Master Roman sits at the head of the table.

Evelyn scurries into the room and sets a salad at each place setting.

"Thank you, Evelyn. That looks delicious," Claudia praises. "I had the most horrible fast food for lunch. I really needed to see some fresh vegetables this evening."

Evelyn nods. "Enjoy." And then she's gone.

I pick up my fork with everyone else and survey the contents of my plate, praying Evelyn doesn't serve anything I can't recognize. I don't consider myself a picky eater. The problem is that I haven't been exposed to many things. This makes me nervous every day, but so far Evelyn has proven that I love nearly all foods.

"Eat your salad, Lucy."

I glance at Master Roman to find him staring at me with one brow lifted. When I shift my gaze, I find Claudia smiling at me. Encouraging me with a look.

I stab my fork into some spinach and bring it to my mouth, realizing Master Roman's demand is part of our play. Everyone at the table is going along.

"Good girl." He turns to face Julius. "Luckily Lucy isn't a picky eater. I'm glad I don't have to spend half of every day coercing her to eat. Kids are so wasteful these days. They have no appreciation for their good fortune."

I chew my second bite while he speaks of me as if I'm not there. My belly clenches. He had just praised me, but on the other hand, I've heard a warning in there too. I hope he doesn't think I'm not appreciative of everything he's done for me. I feel like Orphan Annie most of the time. Beyond grateful. Not only do I have a job and food and clothing and a roof, but also someone who's fulfilling a deep-seated fetish at the same time.

I don't want to let Master Roman down. I don't want to disappoint him. I will do my best to be exactly the little girl he's asking me to be.

Julius says something business related, and the five of them begin to discuss clients and numbers. Everyone is well-educated. Though I know I'm intelligent, and I made good grades in high school, I never went to college. I've never even considered the possibility.

"What do you want to be when you grow up, Lucy?" Claudia interrupts my thoughts to ask.

I set my fork down and sit up straighter. The question takes me off guard. I don't have an answer.

Evelyn removes the salad plates while Claudia smiles at me indulgently again.

"Don't rush her, Claudia," Master Roman responds. "She's still young. She has plenty of time to figure out what she wants to be." He grabs my hand under the table and squeezes it. "I want to let her be a princess for a while."

I love his answer. It's perfect, and I tip my gaze to him, grinning wide. I start to swing my feet under the chair too.

When he releases my hand and sets his palm on my bare thigh, I suck in a breath. Arousal slams into me. Wetness leaks onto my panties. His fingers stroke too close to my sex, idly.

He finally removes his hand as Evelyn sets our main course in front of us. By then my nipples are stiff again, and I know everyone can see them pressing against the silk of my dress.

I breathe out slowly when I take in the lasagna on my plate. It looks and smells delicious, and I no longer have to worry about what I might be expected to eat. I also notice my portion is significantly smaller than Master Roman's, for which I'm grateful. He can't expect me to clean my plate if I'm served more than I could possibly eat. So far, this has never been an issue. It's as if Evelyn knows exactly how much I can handle.

While Master Roman speaks to his guests, I eat. It's a relief actually. I don't want to be included in their conversation. I would feel inadequate. I'm glad they all see me as a child who doesn't understand.

I glance around at them, wondering if I might ever be as knowledgeable about any particular subject as they are. Age. Experience. Maybe even some schooling? It seems like a pipe dream right now, but considering how different my life is from just a few weeks ago, anything is possible.

As Evelyn clears the table, Master Roman tugs on one of my braids. "Would you like some ice cream, blossom? It's almost your bedtime."

I perk up. Ice cream sounds divine. I haven't had any for a long time. "Yes, Sir."

It turns out Evelyn serves everyone a scoop of vanilla. I eat mine slowly, enjoying every bite. When I'm finished, Master Roman meets my gaze. "You need to go on up and get ready for bed. I'll come tuck you in soon."

"Yes, Sir." I push my chair out and stand. My damn nipples are hard again. Every time he speaks to me, they stiffen. I can't stop my reaction to him. Do other girls react so sexually during age play? "Nice to meet you all," I say to everyone.

"You too, honey. Sleep well. I'm sure we'll see you again soon." Claudia is so kind to me. I see no judgment in her eyes. In fact, I feel that she approves of this arrangement.

Master Roman wraps an arm around my torso and pulls me against his side to kiss the top of my head. His hand slides down to my thighs and runs up under my skirt. He strokes my bottom through my panties.

I can't breathe with him touching me like that. I'm going to have trouble walking. My legs turn to rubber as he squeezes my butt cheek. Finally, he gives me one last pat on the bottom and releases me.

I say nothing as I scurry from the room. I'm completely aroused. Every inch of my skin is tingling. I miss his touch immediately. I wish no one else had been in the room and he would have ordered me to kneel before him naked. My thoughts run wild.

It's difficult, but I force myself to walk down the hallway and up the back stairs to my room. No one is around, and I'm grateful I don't have to face Nancy as I shut my bedroom door and make my way to the bathroom. I don't want anything to interrupt my high. My arousal.

I stare at myself in the mirror for several minutes, admiring the dress, wondering if I'll get to wear it again someday. I can see that my breasts are still obscene under it. Pressing against the thin silk that wasn't cut to contain breasts. It's intentional. It flattened me. It forced my nipples to be obvious.

It's odd that of all the things I've consented to, I'm bothered by my chest. I just spent the evening with five grown adults in a frilly, little-girl dress that barely covers my butt and flouncy socks and pink patent shoes with little buckles, and I'm still obsessing over my uncontained boobs.

Maybe it's because that's the part I know everyone can easily notice. Especially after we sat down at the table. No one else was watching what happened under the table. They couldn't readily see that I was sitting on my panties. That my legs were swinging. That I felt so natural under the table. But my chest was a different story.

I jerk my gaze away, hoping it will get easier every day. I need to get ready for bed before Master Roman comes to tuck me in. I haven't forgotten for a minute that he specifically told me he would inspect my shaving. It's had me in knots all evening.

I quickly unzip the side of my dress and tug it over my head, leaving me standing in the bathroom in my panties and shoes and socks. Should I put the dress down the chute? It seems like it should go on a hanger. I don't have access to the closet though, and no one has suggested otherwise, so I open the chute and drop it in.

I set my shoes on the floor, and remove my panties and socks next. I certainly wasn't given permission to keep either of them. After grabbing the thin white nightgown off the counter, I shrug it over my head. It's like a baby doll lingerie. Thin. See-through. Lacy. Extravagant. I feel like Cinderella.

The gossamer material is so light, it's like cotton candy. Delicate lace lines the neck, the short, poofy sleeves, and the hem. It lands just barely under my bottom, and it teases my nipples instantly.

I rush to use the toilet and then brush my teeth, deciding to leave my braids for now. I'm not sure what Master Roman wants me to do with my hair. It doesn't need to be washed. In fact, if I washed it every day, it would be a disaster of poof.

With a deep breath, I scamper to the bed and slide under the covers. A glance at the clock tells me it's nine thirty. The lights will go out in half an hour. There is no way I can concentrate on reading, so I fold my hands over the covers and try to still my racing heart.

I pray Master Roman will indeed come tuck me in.

I pray he will also inspect my sex.

I pray he will do so much more than that.

I'm also freaking out with worry.

CHAPTER 30

Lucy

Several minutes go by before a knock at the door makes me jumpy. I've begun to worry he might not show up. "Come in." My voice squeaks.

Master Roman enters, shutting the door behind him. I've come to consider that a sign that he intends for us to be alone.

I scoot over a bit so he can sit on the side of my bed. He sets his hand on my hip. "Did you have a nice evening, blossom?"

"I did. Thank you, Sir. Your friends were nice."

"They were impressed with you too. You were very well-behaved. I was proud of you. I know that was hard."

"Thank you, Sir." I'm blushing.

"Did you do as I asked and shave the hair off your pussy earlier?" He wastes no time.

My stomach knots. "Yes, Sir. I did my best."

He tugs the covers down my body slowly until they are wadded up at my shins. His gaze roams over me.

I have my legs clamped together, an ache between them making it hard to think. I'm also aware my nightie is not covering my sex. The hem is resting on my belly. This is the first time he's fully seeing me down there. I'm both nervous and excited. I want him to touch me.

He reaches for my nightie and pushes it up over my breasts. For a moment, he stares at them as if mesmerized. He makes me feel cherished. Precious. When he traces a finger around my nipple in the lightest circle, I gasp.

He smiles. "My little blossom is so responsive. I love these little titties." He flicks his thumb over the distended nipple.

I whimper. I feel restless. Like something wants to come out of me. It's indescribable. He's turned me inside out.

"They looked so perfect in your dress, blossom. With your petite size, the only thing that stands out to make you look erotic in my dresses is these sweet little titties." He cups them both. "I love how you blush because you're worried about them. I love that I can see them bouncing under your dress or blouse, and I love that the tips get hard whenever you're aroused. It tells me everything I need to know."

He sits back, still dancing his fingers around my breasts. "I bet your panties get wet at the same time. Do they, blossom? Do your panties get wet during the day when your little titties are tight points?"

I can't breathe. Did he ask me a question?

"Never mind. Tomorrow I'll start checking. I bet I can drive you crazy if I stroke my fingers over your panties throughout the day."

That's an understatement. I'm pretty sure I would faint.

He's smiling at me, but not in a mocking way. He's pleased. "Bend your knees for me, blossom. Spread your legs open wide." He smooths his hands down my torso and thighs. When he reaches my knees, he guides them up and then pushes them open.

It's obscene. My entire sex is now visible, and without any hair, I feel beyond exposed. I'm panting. I fist my hands in the sheet at my sides.

"So pretty," he murmurs. He releases my one knee to smooth his hand down my inner thigh until the tips of his fingers touch my sex.

I gasp, flinching.

He ignores me. His finger strokes over my outer lips. "You did a good job, blossom. I'm proud of you. I know that was hard. I expect you to keep this pussy bare. Shave it every night. I want it naked so that your sensitive skin rubs against your little panties during the day."

My arousal is through the roof now.

His gaze is on my sex. My *pussy*. His finger is trailing everywhere, the smooth sensitive skin engorged.

I start to draw my knee inward. Instinctively. Unable to take another second of this torture. My belly is so tight. I've sucked it in. I'm shivering. I'm going to explode from the inside out.

Master Roman lifts his fingers and shocks me by swatting my sex. "Grab your knees and hold them open for me."

I'm stunned. My body is on fire. My sex is pulsing from the little spank.

"Knees, Lucy." He lifts my wrists and sets my hands on the insides of my knees.

I'm shaking so badly, and my ears are ringing.

"Wider. Hold yourself open for me," he murmurs. He's not mad. He's simply issuing a command like any other command.

I try to do as he's asking, pressing on my thighs.

"That's a good girl." He resumes stroking my folds.

Wetness leaks to run down my crack. I'm going to leave a spot on the sheets. I squirm at the sensation.

"Stay still, blossom," he demands.

I stiffen, sucking in a breath, wondering how much more of this I can take before I implode. I've never felt like this before. Aroused to the point of pain.

Does he know what he's doing to me? Is he going to leave me like this?

I whimper.

He lifts his gaze and smiles at me. "Don't worry, sweet, sweet blossom. I'm going to make the ache go away."

I lick my lips. How is he going to do that?

He shifts slightly on the bed, and then uses both hands to spread my lips open.

I squeeze my eyes shut against the mortification and the pleasure. The air hits my wetness, making me shiver again.

"So pretty. You have the prettiest little pussy I've ever seen." He strokes a finger through the wetness, dragging it slowly up until he flicks it over the sensitive little nub I know is my clitoris.

I jump, grasping my knees harder and biting into my lower lip.

"That's a good girl. Let me make you feel better." He dips the tip of his finger just a fraction into me and then swirls my arousal around my clit, circling it over and over until I think I might die from the growing pressure.

My entire body is tight with anticipation. I'm not sure how it's ever going to subside, but he must know what he's doing.

More circles. The tension increases. I'm holding my body tight. Every ounce of my attention is on how his finger is making me feel and the desire to have him touch my clit again.

Suddenly, he adds a second finger, flattens them below my swollen nub and rubs them over the tip. At the pressure, something snaps. I cry out as I unravel. My clit pulses against his fingers, over and over.

I can't see. I can't think. I'm lost. Falling. Falling. Coming apart under his touch.

When I land, it's on a fluffy cloud. Pure bliss.

I sigh as he lifts his fingers. My body that has been nothing but a tight ball of nerves for hours or days or weeks relaxes into the mattress. I'm no longer holding my knees open. My fingers don't work. But my thighs are wide and resting against the mattress.

I blink several times until I meet Master Roman's gaze.

He's smiling. His expression warms me. He's pleased. "Feel better now, blossom?"

I try to nod. "Yes, Sir." My voice cracks.

"Was that your first orgasm, little blossom?" His fingers trail down to stroke between my lower lips again.

I shudder. "Yes, Sir," I whisper, assuming that was indeed an orgasm. I've been missing out. That was the best moment of my life.

"I'm so pleased. You have no idea how happy that makes me." He pushes his finger partway into my tight channel, and I buck, lifting my hips off the bed, shocked by my body's reaction. It's like the bliss just disintegrated and I'm aroused again. Only this time I need more.

He withdraws his finger and taps my pussy. "You're so precious. I'm going to thoroughly enjoy teaching you everything you've been missing out on."

"Are you going to have sex with me now, Sir?" I ask. I realize I'm still needing more. Something else. Probably his erection inside me. I crave it.

He shakes his head. "Not tonight, cherry blossom. You've had enough firsts." He cups my knees and eases them back to center so my legs rest on the bed. "You have to earn that kind of pleasure, Lucy. I'll give it to you every time I think you deserve it." He tugs my nightie back over my breasts and then lifts the covers up to my waist.

I swallow. I'm shaking with a need that hasn't dissipated enough. I loved what he did to me, but I want more. I crave it deep inside.

He gives a slight chuckle. "You're so precious." He pats my thigh. "That's all you get tonight. But now you know. Now you know what I can do to you. What I *will* do to you. Often." He leans over me and kisses my forehead. "If you're a good girl tomorrow, maybe I'll give you that kind of reward again."

"I will be, Sir."

His smile melts me. I love when he's pleased and happy instead of stern. I find I'm getting more and more of that side of him as the days go by. Maybe I'm making him happy. I hope so.

He taps my nose, his expression going serious. "What you may not do, Lucy, is take that pleasure for yourself. You know that, right? You're only permitted to come like that under my direction. Do not touch yourself without permission, and certainly not in the night."

"Yes, Sir," I whisper. Now that I know how good it feels, it will be much harder to obey this rule.

"I will know because you won't be able to look me in the eye and lie to me."

I nod. He's right.

"Do you want me to strap your wrists to the bedposts?"

"No, Sir." I shake my head. "I won't touch myself, Sir. I promise." Though this conversation is making me almost as aroused as I was before he came into the room.

"If you break that trust, your life will be challenging for a long time. I won't hesitate to install a camera in the corner of your room and take away your comforter so that you're left nearly naked in bed at night with your wrists strapped to the bedposts and your nightie riding high so your pussy is exposed." His warning makes me tremble. Even though he's told me this before, it's like he knows what it will do to my body to say it again now. Now that I'm living in a new universe. Now that I've experienced ecstasy. Now that he's made me come.

He's good. He's brilliant.

I'm wet and swollen and needy. My nipples ache. It's going to be a long night.

He pats my leg again and stands. "I'm going to spend some more time with my friends. You need your sleep. I'll see you in the morning." He pads to the door, opens it, and reaches his hand outside.

The room goes dark, and this is when I realize the light switch is just outside of the room. "Sleep tight, cherry blossom."

"Thank you, Sir."

CHAPTER 31

Lucy

The door shuts, and I'm alone. Alone in my little girl bedroom. Panting and restless for release. It wasn't as hard before I knew what that release would feel like. Now I'm a mess.

I try to remain still. It's difficult.

My heart is pounding.

I take a slow, deep breath and let it out just like Master Roman tells me to do when I kneel before him. I'm a long way from calm though.

I keep my hands on top of the covers, fisting my comforter to keep from doing what I've been expressly commanded not to do. Touch myself.

Now that I know what it's like, I'm confident I can do it to myself. I had no idea before now. It had been an elusive concept that other people spoke of or wrote about.

Orgasms aren't just a blip on the radar. They are amazing. Beautiful. So wonderful.

I'm aware of every inch of my skin. My nightie is bunched up under my breasts, rubbing against them with every breath. I would probably be less aroused if I pulled it off and only had to contend with the soft sheets instead of the tulle.

My bottom is exposed. It makes me so very aware of the wetness that's increasing instead of dissipating and the fact that my sex is swollen and sensitive.

I squeeze my eyes shut, remembering in detail that moment when Master Roman pressed his fingers against my clitoris, shattering me into a million pieces. My sex pulses now at the memory, and I jerk my eyes open, clench my thighs together, and hold my breath, afraid I might come again without even touching myself.

It wouldn't be my fault, but somehow, I don't think Master Roman would understand. And I'm certain he will ask me point blank in the morning if I came without permission. I will never be able to look him in the eye and lie. Never. It's not in my disposition, and besides, it would destroy what we have.

He trusts me. I must maintain that trust or I will lose everything I have here. This is my new life. My place. My perfect world. I won't do anything to upset the balance.

I've been here only twenty-six hours, and it seems like a lifetime. I'm not the same woman I was when I arrived last night. I'm not even a woman. I'm a little girl. I'm cherished and cared for. I have everything I need. I don't have to worry about anything.

I don't have to make decisions. I'm free to just be a little girl. The little girl I never got to be when I should have been.

A tear runs down my cheek, shocking me. I swipe at it and let another one fall and then another. They are welcome. They are tears of joy and release.

I'm where I belong. I have a Master who will take care of me.

My only concern in life right now is ensuring that I please him all the time so that he won't grow bored of me and make me leave. That would kill me. I think I love him.

It's too soon, and that's ridiculous, but my heart swells at the thought.

I can't know if this arrangement will always work for me. I can't know how long I might enjoy being twelve. I don't even know how long Master Roman might leave me in this age before changing me to another. He said we would explore others.

I'm not sure how I feel about that. It's too overwhelming. And it doesn't matter. I won't be involved in the decision. Master Roman will decide when and if he wants me to switch to another age. My job will be to obey his decisions. And I will do so. Eagerly.

My breathing evens out as I calm. The arousal finally simmers down to something manageable. I ignore the tiny part of my brain that contains my only worry—that Master Roman might grow tired of this arrangement. As long as I can keep that fear jammed to the dark corner of my head, I'll be fine.

CHAPTER 32

Master Roman

"Is she asleep?" Julius asks me with a smirk as I catch up with them in the library. He hands me a tumbler of scotch.

I take a sip before glancing at Claudia. She's holding a glass of wine, perched on the sofa, legs elegantly crosses, spine straight, expression as mischievous as Julius's. Beck and Levi are beside her.

I growl as I plop down in the armchair and lean back. I'm exhausted, and my dick is hard. "Doubt it," I respond. "I'm betting she'll be tossing and turning for a while."

Julius chuckles as he sits in the armchair.

"She's not a brat, is she?" Claudia inquires.

"No." I shake my head. "Not even close. And I'm glad. The thought of handling a brat makes me cringe. They are a lot of work. She's a pleaser. She hates making mistakes or upsetting me."

"I'm impressed with how quickly she slid into the role. This is her first full day with you. It seemed almost natural."

"Yeah. Granted, I've been grooming her for two weeks. I didn't blindside her. I explained everything before she left on Friday. She had the weekend to internalize what I would be expecting."

Julius glances at Claudia. "Keep in mind, Roman's been watching her closely for weeks. He has a good intuition when it comes to submissives."

"Yeah. I know that. I get it. I like to think we all do. But it's so rare to find someone who so easily slides into a specific role, exactly the sort of submissive Roman has craved for years. I just...want you to be careful." She meets my gaze.

I tug at my tie, loosening it. "I will. And I'll be honest, I'm in deep. Careful flew out the window weeks ago. If she walked out the door even right now, I would be in bad shape."

"I'm worried she has craved this for so long that she doesn't realize fully what she's getting into," Claudia adds. "You need to ensure she doesn't get restless. She's twenty-two. She should be in school. You can't expect her to stay under your roof with no outside interaction for the rest of her life. It wouldn't be healthy."

I nod. "I've thought of that. It's hard for me to consider letting her out of my sight right now, but I'll watch her closely for signs of restlessness. As badly as I'd love to have her near me at all times for fifty years and never share her with the world, I know it's not reasonable. When she needs more, I'll do my best to give it to her."

"You sure you can do that?" Julius asks. He knows me better than anyone alive. "You're so into her that you're blinded."

"I agree," Levi adds. "I've never seen you like this."

Beck nods also. Even though I've known him for years, he rarely comes to the club. He prefers to play at home. I see him less often. Usually, when the three of them meet a submissive

189

requesting their training at Surrender, they move their show to Julius's home.

He's right. Again. Thank God I have these amazing friends to keep me straight and help me see past my own lust. "I have to. She's everything. I'd do anything for her."

"It's so soon to feel that way, Roman," Claudia murmurs. "We're just worried about you."

I sip my scotch. "I know, and I appreciate it. One of these days, you all will find the perfect submissives, and then you'll know. Every day I grow more certain she's mine. I'll do anything to keep her."

Claudia leans back with a sigh. "It's a beautiful thing. I wish you the best."

"Thank you."

CHAPTER 33

Lucy

"It's a Small World" yanks me out of a deep sleep as the lights come on and make me squint into the room. I reach over and slam my hand down on the Hello Kitty clock as a knock sounds on the door. "Come in," I grumble into the pillow. I'm on my belly. Warm. Comfortable. Trying not to be awake.

I've never slept so long in my life until the past two nights. I don't know if it's the fact that the room is so dark or that the bed is so comfortable, or if it has something to do with not having the weight of the world pressing in on me all the time.

I don't have to come up with the rent or scrape together enough money for off-brand mac and cheese or figure out if I have enough fare for the bus. It's refreshing. It's not something I've ever experienced.

"Good morning, Lucy," Nancy chirps. "I'll set your clothes on the chair, dear. You better get up." She leaves just as fast as she entered. I hear the snick of the door.

I'm too cozy. The last thing I want to do is get out of bed. But I must. Right now. The fear of falling back to sleep propels me.

I groan as I slide out from under the covers and cross the room to grab the pile of clothes. I shut myself in the bathroom next and proceed to go through the morning ritual. Toilet. Wash my hands and face. Brush my teeth. Pull the nightie over my head. Drop it in the chute.

I wonder what today's mystery outfit might be. I haven't picked out my own clothes now for two weeks except on the weekends. Those days are over too. I won't be choosing my clothing this coming weekend. I smile as I lift the lavender dress. It's a cotton knit. The upper section is a tank top with no sleeves except the few inches that will land on my shoulders. The skirt part is short, of course. It flares out slightly. It's a tank dress. For a girl. For me.

I set it aside and pick up the panties. They are white today with a lavender bow at the belly. I step into them and then shrug the dress over my head. It covers my bottom, but just barely. It's shorter than anything I've worn yet. Intentional? It's not pleated or full, but it flares out enough to make me aware nothing is touching my panties.

I'm suddenly very aroused. The combination of the dress and the panties and my shaved sex and my messy braids and even the fact that I'm staring at my blunt cut fingernails. I've always bitten them too often for them to grow.

I take a breath, trying to ignore the pulsing need between my legs. I separate my thighs, but my panties are pressing against my naked labia. My breasts are hugged tight by the body of the dress, making my nipples prominent. More than ever. The dress has a high waist that is tucked under my chest.

Honestly, my breasts look amazing. If I were the sort of person who would ever go out in public without a bra, I would be proud. But I'm too modest for that. Master Roman's words ring in my ears. *You're twelve, Lucy. Little girls don't wear bras.*

I shiver. My nipples are traitorous. Everyone, and I do mean everyone, who sees me today will know I'm aroused. I hope I don't see Weston. My most embarrassing moments are when he sees me.

I can almost handle Nancy and Evelyn. But Weston is a man, and he's older. My bottom is almost visible. It's too much.

I look in the mirror again, ignoring my chest. I can hear Master Roman's voice again, soft and gentle. *These little titties are mine. If I want to see them, you'll show them to me.* Every time he says titties, my belly flips over. It yanks me into the role instantly. It also makes me wet.

My hands are shaking as I unravel one of my braids, comb out the hair starting at my scalp, and re-braid it. I assume Master Roman will want my hair braided. I also assume he will appreciate it if I tidy it up so it's not messy.

After I fix the other side to match, I grab my socks from the counter and my Mary Janes from the floor, and head for the bedroom. I sit on the wicker chair and put on my shoes and socks, carefully folding them over so that the lace ruffle is at my ankles.

I've taken too long again. I need to stop spending so much time in my head in the mornings or I'm going to be late.

I rush from the room and down the stairs, slowing to a reasonable walk as I make my way down the hallway.

Master Roman's office door is open, and I step inside, instantly feeling very young at the sight of him behind his desk. Just being in his presence drags me deeper into the role.

I shuffle forward, lifting my hand to my mouth.

Before he lifts his face, he admonishes me. It's like he has eyes on top of his head. "Stop biting your nails, Lucy."

I drop my hand and clasp my wrist behind my back. The

act lifts my chest and possibly even the front of my dress. When I reach his desk, I wait for him to finish whatever he's working on.

Finally, he sets his pen down and smiles at me. "Good morning, blossom." He motions for me to round the desk, and then he sets his hands on my hips and draws me closer. "Did you sleep well?"

"Yes, Sir."

"Did you keep your hands to yourself?"

"Yes, Sir." I hold his gaze and decide to admit what almost happened so that I can free myself of the possible guilt. "It was hard, and I couldn't stop thinking about you touching me... down there." My voice drops to a whisper. "I almost came without touching myself. I tried real hard and held my breath and everything to stop it." I hear myself and realize I even sound like a child now. I've even adapted some speech patterns.

He pats my bottom. "Good girl. The important thing is you stopped it. You need to learn to control your urges. I know it's difficult, but you don't want to disappoint me."

"Yes, Sir." I'm flushed now from this conversation and the way I have slipped further into the role. I bite my lip.

His hands slide to my thighs and then up over my panties, rising until they push my dress up and he's cupping my breasts.

I gasp and glance at the door. It's standing open.

"Eyes on me," he demands. He's never exposed me like this or fondled me or even dominated me with the door open.

I'm nervous. I take a step back, trying to free myself. It's too much. I remember my safeword. *Jacks.*

He grips one breast and slides the other hand to my lower back, keeping me from escaping. "Lucy," he warns. His word is sharp.

I'm frantic, but I meet his gaze.

"I know where my staff is."

I swallow.

"Evelyn is in the kitchen. Nancy is in your room. Weston is in the security room."

"Okay, Sir." I try to stop fighting him. I assume he's right.

He nods toward the computer on his desk. Sure enough there are three screens open. One shows Evelyn at the sink. One shows Weston looking at a row of monitors. One shows my open bedroom door. He must have seen Nancy go inside. Which also means there is a camera in the hallway outside my room. Good to know.

I relax marginally.

"Good girl." He pinches my nipple and then releases me entirely, his hands coming out from under my dress. "You'll be assigned some chores today, Lucy. It's part of growing up."

"Yes, Sir." I clasp my hands again, rocking back and forth on my toes. I'm so aroused. I'm sure he knows it.

"I know you didn't make your bed yesterday, and I assume you didn't this morning either." He's staring at me, his hands on his thighs.

"No, Sir," I mumble.

"Speak clearer, Lucy. The mumbling needs to stop."

"Sorry, Sir," I try to say louder.

"It's not Nancy's job to keep your room clean. You'll put your books and toys away at night, your clothes down the chute, and make your bed in the morning. Is that too much?"

"No, Sir." I feel the heat rising on my face.

"You'll put your dishes in the sink, wipe off the bathroom counter when you use it, and keep your playroom tidy." He nods over his shoulder, and I realize my "playroom" is my office.

"Yes, Sir."

"I put a new shelf in your playroom this morning. It's low enough for you to reach. A place where you can keep your things. Go have a look. I'll call you when it's time for breakfast."

I'm excited. He's put some things for me in my office? I hesitate though, wondering if I'm still expected to work for him. It bothers me. If I don't work for him, who will? I don't want him to hire someone else to take my place. I want to feel needed. I want to be necessary to his life. It's important to me. It gives me a sense of security.

He lifts a brow.

I decide not to question him right now. Instead I turn and run across the room, partly to escape this conversation, partly because I'm excited to see what he's arranged for me, and partly because it seems appropriate. It feels natural to run toward my new things. It's what I would do. It's what I do because I'm twelve.

I know my dress blows around me as I skip away. I'm sure my panties peek out from under my skirt. I'm not concerned. Instead I'm aroused that a glimpse of my panties might make Master Roman want to touch me like he did last night.

I round the corner to my office/playroom and find a white bookshelf against the far wall next to the filing cabinets. In front of it is a fluffy, pink beanbag chair and an oval rug in pastels. The shelves are covered with books and toys.

I giggle out loud when I see no jacks. I don't care. I never really had any interest in jacks. I squat down and peruse the books first. Most are actually adult books about the little lifestyle. Some are self-help books about finding oneself, eating healthy, and meditation. There are some novels too, including a new YA series I've never heard of.

I switch my gaze to the lower shelf and grin. There is a kit for making glittery nails. Another kit for beaded bracelets. And lastly, a Disney coloring book with a set of two dozen markers. I've never had any of these things before. I'm so excited that I plop down on my bottom on the rug and pick up the nail kit. It has pink and purple and green and yellow polish as well as gems to decorate my nails with.

I twist my head to see Master Roman leaning in the doorway, smiling. "You're only allowed to use that if you stop biting your nails."

"Yes, Sir. I will." I set the kit down and pick up the markers. Does he realize I've never had a set of markers in my life? Not ones that were new and had all the colors and weren't dried up.

I set them down and pick up the bracelet kit. It has instructions to make friendship bracelets, like the braided ones all the girls had in school. Well, not all the girls. I never had one. I never even had a friend who would make me one.

I'm sitting cross-legged on my pretty rug with my dress flared around my thighs, feeling like it's Christmas morning. I don't know where I want to begin.

"You can open the boxes after breakfast. Put them back on the shelf for now, Lucy. You need to go eat."

"Yes, Sir." My voice comes out unintentionally as a groan, shocking me. I've slid so far into the role that I feel like I'm seriously twelve. I've lost myself for a moment. I've been lost since I got dressed. I really would rather skip breakfast and rip open the markers. That's where I'll start.

"Lucy…" he warns from the doorway.

I shove the boxes back on the shelf and scramble to stand up, not caring that he can see my panties as I do so. I might even be taunting him.

When I turn to face Master Roman, I flatten my skirt and clasp my hands behind my back, shuffling slowly toward him. My face is tipped toward the floor.

He takes my chin and lifts my face, meeting my gaze. His brows are lifted. "Did you just whine?"

"Sorry, Sir," I mumble.

"I think the new toys can stay where they are for the morning. After breakfast, you can do some educational reading instead."

"Yes, Sir." I flush at the reprimand, a mixture of remorse and arousal twirling around in my belly. It's an odd sensation. I'm disappointed that I won't be permitted to play this morning, but shockingly my panties have grown wet at the way he speaks to me. It's confusing.

He glances at my chest. A flicker of a smile crosses his lips. "Your titties are hard." He pulls me closer with just the two fingers gripping my chin until his face is inches from me. "I need to tell you something, and it's important."

"Yes, Sir." I can smell his breath, minty from his toothpaste.

"There is a type of little known as a brat. Do you know what a brat is?"

"Yes, Sir. I think so."

"A brat is a little who likes attention from acting up. They are exhausting. I see them at my club. I don't like that kind of behavior, and I won't tolerate it. So, if that thought enters your mind, wipe it away. You'll be an obedient little girl, or you'll find yourself standing alone in this room in the dark with your nose to the corner for hours on end. I'll only have to do that once. Do you understand me?"

"Yes, Sir."

"Good. I'm not saying I'm upset that you were whining. It happens. You aren't perfect. You'll make mistakes. All little girls make poor decisions sometimes. It's my job to discipline you and make sure you're the best you can be. It's done. You won't get to play with your toys until after lunch. I won't mention it again. But watch that you don't become a brat."

"Yes, Sir." I would never want to be a brat. I don't like to be in trouble. I don't like disappointing anyone, especially not Master Roman.

He releases my chin and then surprises me by setting his fingers along the sides of my breasts and then flicking his thumbs over my already distended nipples.

I gasp and rise onto my toes, leaning closer to him, trying not to fall forward. He has a way of sending me into the stratosphere in just seconds.

Without a word, he lowers his hands, tugs my dress up above my panties, and then holds it there with one hand while reaching between my legs with the other. I moan when his fingers drag slowly over my private parts.

He releases my dress just as quickly and removes his hand. "I'm going to check your panties often because I'm curious if they are wet every time I see your sweet little titties puckered." For emphasis, he flicks them one more time, and I nearly stumble.

He brings his fingers to his nose and inhales my scent. "Mmm." He smiles. "You're going to scream so loud the neighbors will hear the first time I suck your pussy into my mouth."

My jaw drops as I take one step back and plant my foot. *Suck my...pussy?* I know characters do it in books. I get the concept. But in real life? Master Roman intends to put his mouth on me down there? I swallow.

He chuckles and cups my face with one hand. "You are precious. Your innocence is so refreshing. I'm going to take my time defiling you just to drag out the reactions I'll get every time I do something new."

I can't respond. I don't think he expects me to.

He steps back. "Go eat, Lucy, before I change my mind and flatten you on the floor."

I hesitate, partly because I'm too shocked to move and partly because I'd rather he toss me on the floor. I want him to have sex with me so badly. I want to know what it feels like. I want to get it over with. I don't want to be a virgin anymore. Not after I got a taste of paradise last night.

Instead, I rush past him and jog from the room. I don't slow down until I'm in the hallway. Master Roman hasn't chastised me for rushing around in his presence yet, but Nancy has.

CHAPTER 34

Master Roman

Jesus. I'm so fucked. Either that or so lucky. Both I think. Lucy has my head spinning. As I watch her romp across my office, I can't stop smiling. I run my hand through my hair and wander back to my desk. I need to sit down. Think. Regroup. I ordered all that stuff on a whim yesterday, had it delivered last night, assembled it after everyone left. I wasn't sure how she would react. She blew my mind. I even love that she whined about stopping for breakfast. I'm not seriously concerned about her being a brat. But it didn't hurt to point that out to her.

I buzz Nancy and ask her to bring me a cup of coffee, thanking her profusely when she strides in moments later with a steaming mug. I need a few minutes to regroup without breathing down Lucy's neck in the kitchen.

I'll let her read for the morning, and then play in the afternoon. It made my chest hurt when I saw how excited she was. Now that I understand the reason for her exuberance is that she never had many things growing up, I hurt for the little girl she never got to be.

I can't believe my luck. Fate must have put her in my club that first night. It's incredible that I happened to be there and happened to notice her and happened to do a double take, recognizing her potential and my attraction.

My cock is permanently hard. No matter how many times I jerk off, it's not satisfied, and it won't be until I have her under me. But she isn't ready. Her reactions to sex are so pure it's as if she isn't even play acting as a twelve-year-old. She's literally that innocent.

I know she's well-read. I know she isn't ignorant about sex. It's as if she didn't really consider kinky things happening to her. As if they only belong on paper in books.

No matter what, I need to take it slowly with her, give her a little more each day, enlighten her. Part of my reasoning is that I love watching her blossom and grow. I don't want to ruin that by rushing to the finish line. I can take care of my cock when she isn't around. It will be worth it.

I watch her shuffle past my office after breakfast and then she returns a few minutes later from the bathroom. She comes in with her head level, uncertainty on her face.

"How was your breakfast?"

"It was good. Miss Evelyn made me pancakes again. With chocolate chips." Her face lights up.

"Good." I pick up a book from my desk and hold it out. "I want you to read this for a few hours. You can sit on your beanbag."

She takes it from me without looking. "Yes, Sir." And then she pads toward her office. I lose sight of her as she turns toward the play area. From my desk, when the office door is open, I can see her desk and chair straight through to the other side of the room in front of the wall of windows. I can't see deeper into her space.

It's intentional. I would be horribly distracted if I could watch her on that beanbag chair. I'm already distracted just picturing it, wondering how she has arranged her dress around her legs. How much of her thighs would I see if I stepped into the room? Would I get a glimpse of her panties?

I take a deep breath as my mind wanders to my past. I've played with littles before. Role-played. For an hour or two. Several different women and even a few men. About half of them included sexual feelings in their role. The other half simply liked to slide into an age where they're comfortable and don't associate age play with sex.

It could have gone either way with Lucy.

No. That's not true. I watched her for five days. It couldn't have gone another way. She was clearly aroused when she watched littles play. Well, not the babies, but the older age players.

I knew. And now it's confirmed. In addition, the dynamic is smooth. I'm pleased. Ecstatic actually.

I take a few hours to get some actual work done and then I push from my chair and head to check on her. I haven't heard a peep from the other room.

As I approach, my throat catches. Lucy is curled on her side on her beanbag chair fast asleep. The book has fallen to the floor. Her hands are clasped together under her face. Her dress has risen up to reveal her panties. Almost entirely.

I stare at her perfect bottom for a moment, wanting to run my hands over it. Wanting to strip those panties down her sweet little legs and bury my face between her thighs. That would wake her up.

Instead I kneel beside her and stroke my hand over her hip and then her arm.

She moans slightly in her sleep and then rolls toward me. Her eyes pop open, and she glances around before they widen. "I fell asleep," she exclaims.

I smile. "I see that. Were you awake too late last night?"

She pushes partially upright, smoothing her hands down her dress to cover her panties. The hem was bunched up nearly to her waist. "No, Sir. I don't think so. I guess I was too comfortable here."

"Apparently." I cup her face and hold her gaze. "I don't want you staying up late at night. You need your rest."

She nods. "Yes, Sir."

I fight the urge to grin. I'm certain any trouble she had falling asleep was my fault for leaving her hot and bothered. It probably took her a long while to control her body so she could rest. I know it took me hours after leaving her with her scent on my fingers and the vision of her coming apart in my mind.

My hand is on her thigh. I have a constant need to touch her. It's getting worse. When she's near me, I want my hands on her. She doesn't seem to mind. She has never flinched or pulled away.

In fact, as I'm staring at my hand on her leg, she sets her smaller one on top of mine. "Your hands are so big," she tells me.

I chuckle and then a crazy sudden urge overtakes me. I grab her small hand with my free one, circle her wrist, capture the other hand in the same grip, and pull them over her head. Before she has any idea what I'm thinking, I reach for her waist and tickle her.

Her eyes go wide with shock and she squirms wildly, laughing as she tries to escape my fingers. I tickle her mercilessly, up and down her sides and across her belly.

Her tits jiggle as she struggles to escape. Her dress rides up above her panties, revealing the little purple bow at the top. She digs her feet into the floor, her knees jerking around until I begin to fear for my safety.

I plant one knee between her legs, trapping her while she

continues to giggle and squirm. It's the sweetest sound I've ever heard.

"Sir…" She can't catch her breath.

Finally, I stop, flattening my palm on her belly to hold her steady. I don't release her wrists. "You awake now?" I tease.

"Yes, Sir." She stares at me, breathing heavily. Her face is beet red. Tears have escaped her eyes to run toward her braids. Her chest rises and falls, and I lower my gaze to watch as her nipples stiffen. I love how damn lovely her tits are. Perfection.

She squirms again. "Sir…" The word is breathy, and she's gripping my thigh between her knees. She's aroused.

I lower my hand to her panties, set my palm flat on her pubic bone above her clit, and stroke my fingers over her cotton-covered pussy.

She moans as her head falls back.

She is soaked. Clean through the cotton.

I stroke her again, dragging my finger across her lower lips and then over her clit.

She tugs on her arms, but I grip them tighter. "Don't fight me, blossom."

She stops her struggle and blinks up at me.

"Just relax into the beanbag. Let me make you feel good."

She swallows, nodding.

I want to make her come without touching her directly, and I know I can. She's that aroused.

She stares at me while I drive her crazy with one finger, over and over between her soaked mons and across her clit. I can feel the swollen bundle of nerves that is no longer hidden by the hood but pressed against her cotton panties.

When she whimpers, her eyes glazing over, I remove my hand and tug her dress up over her tits. I want to see them. I want to watch them rise and fall while I make her come. The rosy pink tips are so hard.

She's squirming again.

"Stay still, little blossom," I command. "If you can stay really still for me, I'll make you feel good."

She bites her bottom lip. I know it's hard for her. I can see how much effort it takes in the set of her jaw and how stiff her neck is. Her eyes are wild.

I pinch a nipple, making her drop her lip and moan. While her mouth is hanging open, I pinch the other one. The matching set is now even more distended. I blow across them as I lower my hand back to her pussy, settling it in the same location, using just the one maddening finger to drive her to new heights.

She's so damn wet. It makes me rock hard. I love knowing what I can do to her.

I pick up my pace, flicking my finger over her clit rapidly.

She gasps, her mouth falling open.

I keep up the pace, working her little clitty to a frenzy, watching her expression so that I know the exact moment when she can't hold back anymore.

She cries out as she comes, her pussy pulsing hard against my touch.

I continue to flick her until the pulses slow, and then I flatten my palm to cup her pussy. Warm. Wet. Greedy.

Like last night, she sucks in a long breath and then goes limp. Her eyes close and she turns her head to one side. Embarrassed? Adorable.

I release her wrists, stroke her forehead with my fingers, and then bend down and plant a soft kiss on her lips. It's the first time I've kissed her on the mouth.

She turns toward me, kissing me back. It's a sweet kiss. Chaste. Perfect.

When I draw back, it's with great reluctance. I know myself though. If I were to keep kissing her, I would end up mauling her, and I don't want that yet.

Finally, I rise to my knees and then to my feet, still squatting next to her. I reach for her dress and gently pull it down over her tits.

She shivers and grabs the material to tug it as low as she can, lifting her bottom to get under it. Her sudden modesty is cute.

I stand and reach out a hand. When she takes it, I pull her to her feet. I can't resist hauling her into my arms and hugging her tight. Her head is under my chin. I've never felt so good in my life.

I give a silent prayer to whatever god might be listening to not let this bubble burst.

Lucy is mine.

I'll do anything to make sure she remains happy and carefree.

CHAPTER 35

Lucy

I'm a ball of nerves during lunch. Frazzled from what Master Roman just did to me. My legs are jelly. My belly is flipping around. My panties are soaked. Beyond soaked. When I sit at the table, my skirt not long enough to tuck under me, I worry I'll leave a wet spot.

Maybe Evelyn knows this. Maybe she's used to it. Maybe Master Roman has had other girls here before. I lose my appetite before taking a bite, worrying that I'm not the first, worrying about how long he usually keeps his littles, worrying about what I might do when he's done with me. How will I go on with my life?

"Eat your lunch, sweetie," Evelyn states from across the room.

I flinch and pick up my fork. I haven't even looked at the plate yet. I smirk. Chicken nuggets and fries. A little cup of ketchup is next to my plate. I set the fork down and use my fingers, hoping no one expects me to eat with a knife and fork. A bowl of applesauce sits next to my glass of water.

After forcing myself to take the first bite, chew, and swallow, I gain my appetite. I've learned this trick. It's not the first time I've sat down at this table with no ability to swallow. I manage to eat everything, grateful once again that Evelyn is spot on, always providing me with the exact right amount of food. I hear Master Roman's voice as he enters the kitchen. Nancy is with him. She heads to the island and hands Evelyn a folder. "I printed those recipes you were looking for."

"Thank you." Evelyn sets the file on the counter.

Master Roman saunters closer to me. I watch him. His face is unreadable, but he is up to something. Finally, he speaks to the room at large. "Lucy is going to start taking a nap after lunch. She's not getting enough sleep at night. I'll see her upstairs today. Nancy, will you wake her in an hour?"

"Of course, sir." Nancy nods.

I'm frozen. Mortified. I feel ridiculous. A nap? I don't need a nap. I couldn't sleep if I wanted to. Especially since I just slept half the morning on the beanbag. He's making a point.

He reaches my side and sets a hand on my head, ruffling it. "You finished eating, blossom?"

I swallow the lump in my throat. "Yes, Sir," I murmur.

He lifts a brow.

I clear my throat this time. "I'm finished, Sir," I say in a slightly louder, squeaky voice.

He steps back, making room for me to rise.

I do so slowly, reluctantly, feeling like I've been chastised in front of everyone. I stack up my dishes and carry them to the sink, setting them in gently.

Evelyn smiles at me warmly. "Have a nice nap, sweetie. I'm sure you'll feel better if you get some rest."

I nod at her and dip my face as I follow Master Roman from the room. His enormous form looms ahead of me as I rush to keep up on the way down the hall and then up the back stairs.

When we reach my room, he opens the door and lifts his arm for me to pass under it. He shuts the door. "Do you need to go potty first?"

I flush a deep red and shake my head. "No, Sir."

He heads over to my bed, pulls the covers back, and turns toward me. I haven't moved. "Lucy, don't make a big deal out of this. Lots of little girls need naps. You'll feel refreshed afterward."

"I slept all morning." I try not to whine. I'm embarrassed that he told Nancy and Evelyn I haven't been getting enough sleep. What must they think I've been doing in my room for eight hours a night?

"Lucy." His tone is sharp. I've pushed his buttons.

I rush over to him. Why am I arguing? The embarrassing part is done. All I have to do is lie in bed for an hour.

"Take off your shoes, blossom." His voice is softer now.

I bend and remove them.

When I stand, he grabs the hem of my dress. "Arms up."

It takes a second for his intention to register, and I'm shaking as I lift my arms for him to pull my dress over my head. He turns and drapes it over the chair, leaving me in my little girl panties and socks. "We don't want your dress to wrinkle while you nap, do we?"

It's not a question. I fight the urge to cover my breasts. There are times when I long to be naked with him. Now is not one of them.

He holds the covers up. "Climb in."

I crawl onto the bed and lie on my back.

He tucks the comforter under my chin and then sits on the side of the bed, stroking my thigh. "You're not in trouble, blossom. I'm just taking my cue from you. If you can't stay awake with eight hours of sleep, then you need more. You'll take a nap after lunch for the rest of the week. If you seem to be more awake, we can renegotiate.

"I don't have time to tuck you in and wake you up in the middle of the day, though. Just this once. Nancy will see you to your room. I'll expect you to set your clothes carefully on the chair and nap in your panties so your clothes don't wrinkle. Understood?"

"Yes, Sir." My voice is weak.

"Good girl." He pats my leg and then stands. "Nancy will stick her head in when you're allowed to get up."

"Yes, Sir."

He bends down and kisses my forehead, and then he leaves.

I stare at the door for a moment, and then the light goes out. The room is not completely dark, though, because it's the middle of the day. Sunlight seeps in through the shutters. I can still see.

I close my eyes and steady my breathing. I should definitely read the books Master Roman has on meditation. I should probably not read while sitting on that beanbag chair. Not unless I want to be sent to my room for a nap for the rest of my life.

Resigned, I roll to my side and snuggle in. It's weird not having a shirt on. I think my naked boobs feel stranger than my naked bottom at night. Odd how I'm expected to sleep without panties at night and only in panties in the day.

If nothing else, at least I have a reprieve from submission. It's stressful. Everything I do all day keeps me on edge, making me think. Worry. Ponder. Maybe a nap is a good idea...

CHAPTER 36

Lucy

I can't believe I actually slept. I might have spent half the time with my mind wandering, but I did fall asleep. Nancy pulled me out of my rest with a knock at the door.

I spent a few minutes using the bathroom and putting my clothes back on, and now I'm standing in front of Master Roman. I have a concern. It was the last thought I had before I fell asleep and the first thought when I woke up.

"You look rested, blossom," he states as he pushes his chair back and motions for me to join him on his side of the desk.

I do, and then I take a deep breath. "I haven't done any work for you for two days, Sir."

He smiles and pulls me between his legs, his hand landing on my bottom under my skirt. He brushes a loose hair away from my face. "Don't worry about work right now. It's more important that you find yourself and settle in."

"But it will pile up. You didn't hire me to be your little girl. You hired me to be your assistant." My lip is trembling. I'm worried. He doesn't know how worried I am about this situation.

He hesitates, glancing away oddly for a moment. I don't understand, but then he speaks, his face too...controlled. "I don't want you to worry about the job, blossom. Let's give this new role some time. You can take things slow. If it turns out we decide it's not reasonable for you to be my assistant, I'll hire someone else."

I flinch, sucking in a sharp breath and then wrapping my arms around my middle. I don't even care what that does to my breasts or that my dress rises too high and my panties are visible underneath.

"What's the matter, blossom?" He rubs my bottom with his palm. His expression is filled with concern.

I watch his Adam's apple rise and fall as he swallows. Why is *he* worried? I'm the one freaking out here. "Sir, I don't want you to hire someone else. I want to do the job." I purse my lips, worried about his response. I have not challenged him like this before.

He frowns. "Why? What are you upset about? It's just a job. Your arrangement with me can be renegotiated. Are you worried you won't have enough money if things don't work out between us? Because I promise you, I would never let you leave me without substantial savings." He tugs me closer, his finger going under my chin in that way he does to get me to look at him.

I chew on my bottom lip.

"We can draft another contract right now. Or I can deposit enough money in your bank account to ensure you stop worrying about the future. Or my lawyer can come over and work up a settlement. Anything you want. The last thing I want is for you to feel stressed about your future finances."

I swallow. "What I want is to do my job, Sir."

He holds my gaze. His hand clenches on my bottom. "I

think I'm asking a lot of you right now. Exploring age play is draining. I want you to concentrate on that side of you for a while."

I shake my head, knowing I need to stick up for myself. "I don't feel right living in your house, eating your food, wearing your clothes...without earning my keep." That's not entirely true, but the truth might not go over well.

"And I've told you before that providing you with room and board in my home is a drop in the bucket. I make a lot of money, Lucy. You're not making a dent in it. A substantial deposit to your account won't either."

I'm losing this battle. And I just can't. It's too important to me. I have to get my point across.

"Blossom..." His voice is soothing now. "Please... I want you to let me take care of you. At least for a while. I don't want you to be overburdened. You might get overwhelmed and decide to leave. I'm trying so hard to make everything perfect for you."

I suck in a breath. He's trying to make things perfect for *me*? There is a desperation in his voice. Is he as worried about losing me as I am about losing him? I hadn't considered that. But it changes nothing. I still don't want him to replace me. It's personal.

"If you're worried about the work, let me hire someone else right now. Put it out of your mind."

I can't stop the tear that runs down my cheek.

"Lucy?" His voice rises.

I shake my head, trying to stop the emotional outburst.

"Blossom, talk to me." He pulls me the rest of the way into his embrace, his one large hand flat on my bottom and lower back under my skirt, his other cupping my face, stroking my cheek, wiping away my stupid tears.

I take a breath. "I don't want you to hire someone else. I don't want you to replace me. I don't want someone else to come in here and join us. I'm not ready for that. I might never be."

He wipes my cheeks with his fingers. "Blossom... Honey..."

"Please," I beg. "I'm struggling with how your current employees see me. It's awkward. It's going to take me some time to let myself truly relax and be whoever I am in front of other people. I don't want you to add a stranger. And I don't want you to need that person more than you need me." I finish on a whisper.

He doesn't say anything for a moment. Just keeps stroking my face and my bottom with his thumbs.

"I think it would actually be easier on me if I spend at least a few hours every day helping take care of your needs instead of you taking care of mine."

Finally, he nods. "Okay, blossom. I understand." He wipes another tear. "Shh. Don't cry. It's okay. We'll figure this out together. Sometimes we just have to stop and renegotiate."

I hiccup. "You won't get mad?"

"No, Lucy, I won't get mad. I'll never get mad at you for coming to me with a concern. I want you to be able to tell me anything. If we don't have open communication, we have nothing."

"Okay," I murmur. I wipe my face with both hands. "Will you let me work this afternoon?"

He nods. "Sure. Tell me what it looks like to you. Are you going to stay in the role? Or do you want out for a few hours?"

I chew on my lip. I'm not sure until I do it. "I don't know. Can we try it like this first? I'll stay halfway in the role, still dressed as your little girl, but maybe after you give me a to-do list, you leave me be to get it done. Would that work?"

He smiles. "I think so."

"Then afterward, can I maybe play with my nail polish, Sir?" I ask to soften the blow.

His grin widens. "Absolutely."

Good. He likes the idea of me being his little girl. It lights up his face. But he's also willing to let me take a break from the stress of submitting to help him get his office in order. Win win.

I hope.

CHAPTER 37

Lucy

Hands land on my shoulders, and I about jump out of my skin. I didn't hear Master Roman come up behind me. I twist around to face him.

He takes the pile of folders from my arms and sets them on my desk. He pushes my chair in next. "That's enough, blossom. You've been working for four hours. I'll let you do that every afternoon after your nap if you promise to stop when I tell you and return to your role-playing." He lifts a brow.

"Yes, Sir."

He points at the desk. "The work won't go anywhere. It'll be there tomorrow. The grownup desk will be for when you're working. When you're done, the chair gets pushed in and you go back to your play area." He's telling me, not asking.

"Yes, Sir." I smooth my hands down my dress. I've ignored it for four hours. I've ignored my role entirely, separating my mind. Compartmentalizing. I paid no attention to my dress length, my panties, or my lack of bra.

I realize I feel energized. Refreshed. I smile. "I think that arrangement will work perfectly."

"Good." He swats my bottom. "Now, go check out your new things."

I spin around and rush across the room, a totally different person from two minutes ago. A twelve-year-old. A child. With new toys to play with.

"Lucy," he calls from the doorway as he's leaving.

"Yes, Sir?"

"Don't spill anything on the rug."

"Okay, Sir." I watch him leave and stare at the space. A weight has been lifted. I'm giddy with this new arrangement. Master Roman isn't going to replace me. Nor is he going to bring someone else into our space. That idea had made me crazy. I can do both. I'll show him.

I plop down on my new rug, my panties the only thing between me and the soft material. My skirt flares out around me as I sit cross-legged and reach for the nail kit to tear into it.

I haven't owned nail polish in a few years. I'm dying to paint my short nails pink and put glitter on them. I won't spill it. I'll be careful. Maybe if Master Roman lets me keep them painted, I will stop biting them and let them grow longer.

Maybe.

CHAPTER 38

Master Roman

I can't stop smiling as I watch Lucy in the hot tub. I have declined to enter with her, preferring to watch her enjoy herself. Instead, I sit nearby in a lounge chair, leaning my chin on my palm.

It's Saturday. She's been my middle for two weeks. She's not a little. Or at least we haven't tried that yet. She's so content at this age that I hate to rock the boat. Maybe one day soon I will suggest it.

I've purchased her a mermaid swimsuit which made her giggle when she opened it. It's a one piece. Mostly pink. She looks so fucking delicious in it that I knew the moment I pulled it up her body and over her shoulders there was no way I could get in the hot tub with her.

I have brought her to orgasm every day at least once, usually at night when I tuck her in. She's so pliant at night. Something about putting on her skimpy little nighties and climbing into her little-girl bed with no panties over her pussy makes her horny.

I greatly enjoy tugging her comforter down, spreading her legs, and stroking her folds until she comes for me. I usually make her keep her arms above her head. I've only penetrated her with one finger so far. She's so damn tight.

On two occasions she pointed at my cock and asked if she could touch it.

I've turned her down so far, but it's time. I need to at least let her hold it and see it. Warm her up to the idea. I know it will still be a while before I penetrate her, but it's time to stretch her tight pussy and prepare her for the nirvana she is unaware will blow my simple little orgasms out of the water.

She giggles, splashing in the water.

I keep smiling. Her swimsuit has sucked against her skin, and when she stands up, I can see her nipples poking the thin fabric near the mermaid's head. It's comical since the suit was meant for a girl with no tits yet.

Lucy is so small that I don't have to work too hard to find her clothes. Some Doms have to have their little's clothes custom made. In Lucy's case, most of her things can just be ordered in the largest girl size and slightly altered. The chest is often too tight, but I like it that way. It still unnerves her after two weeks. She especially flushes when Weston comes in the room. I've seen her try to hide her tits and check to make sure her bottom is covered.

It's adorable. I don't mind it. Her embarrassment is part of her role. I secretly hope she never loses this innocence. It's possible she will keep it forever. It might be imbedded in the way she sees herself in the role.

As if thinking about her reaction to Weston conjured him, the man is suddenly walking toward me. He's holding an envelope. "Sir, I went by Lucy's apartment today to make sure everything was cleared out and to get her mail. Most of it was junk, but this letter was in the pile."

"Thank you." I glance at Lucy as I take it from him. She's facing the other way, paying no attention. Or more likely she noticed Weston and turned away from him intentionally.

As Weston returns to the house, I flip the envelope over a few times and then open it. The return address means nothing to me. It has come from Missouri. Inside is a single sheet of regular notebook paper. It's a letter. Handwritten in pencil. I glance again at Lucy. She's sitting peacefully in the hot tub, head tipped back, eyes closed, smile on her lips.

For a moment, I consider putting the letter back in the envelope and giving it to her. I'm invading her privacy. But my curiosity is too strong. She's told me she has no one, so who would be writing to her?

Dear Lucy,

My name is Daven Neill. I have no idea if you've ever heard of me or know who I am, but I'm your half brother. I only recently found out about you. We have the same father. I found your information in my mother's things after she died last month. I was hoping we could meet someday. I realize our father died years ago, but I never met him. Maybe you could tell me what he was like. Perhaps you have pictures. I hope I'm not upsetting your life by writing. I tried to find you on social media, but didn't succeed. Please forgive me if this is the case. If you don't mind connecting, I'm including my phone number below.

Daven

I'm too stunned to move a muscle for several moments. Lucy has a brother? For a second I wonder if she's lied to me, and then I dismiss that thought. She had no idea she has a brother. He must be older. From a marriage or relationship her father had before she was born.

221

I fold the paper back up and return it to the envelope, my gaze lifting to find Lucy still relaxing in the water. I consider my options. I should tell her about this presumed brother. Now. But I won't. She's fragile. She's only been with me a few weeks. She's still finding herself. I don't want to upset that balance. Besides, it's possible this Daven guy is a liar. Maybe he's some guy she once knew who has found out she's living with me and decided to capitalize on my wealth.

No. I won't tell her just yet. I'll call my PI and have him dig deeper into this man. I want to have more proof he is who he says he is before I tell Lucy. Yes. That's the best course of action.

I run a hand over my face and tuck the letter in my pocket. I need to put on a poker face and put the weird correspondence out of my mind for a while.

I sit forward. "It's time to get out, blossom." I hold up the matching mermaid towel that came with the swimsuit.

"Ah, already?" She stands and looks at me. "The water feels so good."

I lift a brow.

She grumbles as she gets out. I don't mind this kind of disobedience. In fact, I like it. She doesn't throw tantrums or refuse to do things, but she does balk when I ask her to stop playing. It's appropriate for her age. It's part of the roles we've assumed.

She frowns as she shuffles toward me. "Five more minutes?" she pleads.

We've added this to our game too.

I shake my head. "Not today, blossom. I have work to do this afternoon, and you know you can't be in the hot tub alone. It's not safe."

Her shoulders droop. "I'm a big girl, Sir. I won't drown in the hot tub."

"That's right." I tap her nose after I've gotten her wrapped up in the towel. "You won't drown because you won't go near the water without supervision. Understood?"

She groans. "Yes, Sir."

"Good." I stand and take her hand. "Let's get you changed. You can play with your toys for a few hours while I work. Julius is coming over. We need to discuss some business."

"Okay, Sir."

I lead her into the house through the glass doors off the kitchen. She follows me through the kitchen, down the hallway, and up to her room. I've decided I enjoy dressing her myself. She's a bit old for that, but she hasn't resisted. I don't do it in the mornings, but sometimes I help dress her after her nap or come into her room before she gets out of her bath.

The first time I did that, she nearly hit her head on the tub before she saw it was me. I leaned against the vanity and watched her bathe. When she was finished, I dried her off and helped her into her nightie.

Now, I do that every chance I can get.

We return to her bedroom. "Let's get you dressed before you catch a chill." I pull the towel from her body and finish drying her. After setting it on the arm of the chair, I reach for the top of her swimsuit and lower it down her body. Next, I pick up her panties. She puts her hands on my shoulders. Her nails are green today with little jewels on them.

She doesn't lift her foot to step into her panties.

I tap her ankle. "Lucy."

"Maybe we could have sex first?" Her voice is soft, cracking. She takes me by surprise. It's been a while since she's asked me to have sex with her.

I lift my gaze. She's slightly above me since I'm crouched in front of her naked body. My dick just got harder than it already was. "Is my little girl needy this afternoon?"

She nods eagerly, as if I've offered her ice cream.

I set her panties down for a moment and slide my hands

up her legs and torso until I'm cupping her tits. "I have to work right now, blossom. Julius will be here any minute. But if you're a really good girl while I meet with him, I'll see about making you writhe after dinner. Deal?"

"Will you use your penis?"

I smile. She doesn't have to work hard to use appropriate language for her age play because she's so inexperienced that it's hardly different from what she would say if she were twenty-two. "I promise my cock will be involved. I don't think you're ready for me to put it inside you, blossom, but I'll let you explore. Okay?"

She beams. "Yes, Sir."

"Good. Now let's get you dressed quickly before Julius gets here." She steps into her panties and I pull them up too high, yanking the cotton against her pussy hard enough that it separates her folds.

She sucks in a breath but says nothing.

I pull her Hello Kitty T-shirt over her head next. It's too small. It's just right. It barely covers her tits and flattens them. I know it drives her crazy that her belly is exposed below the hem and she has to tug on it often to ensure the bottom of her tits don't show. They don't, but she worries. She fussed with it all morning. Her nipples were stiff the entire time. I loved it.

Next, I tap her leg so I can put her jean skirt back on. It's also too small. It fits around her waist, but her bottom is bigger than a twelve-year-old's so the pleated skirt doesn't hang flat against her. It barely covers her panties at the top and the bottom. In fact, right now, her lime green panties are sticking out above the skirt. I leave them.

I haven't given her shoes today. It's Saturday. A little girl wouldn't put on shoes to run around the house on a Saturday.

Her braids are damp, but we'll take them out tonight when she bathes. I'm looking forward to it. I might even get her pliant enough that she lets me bathe her myself. I've been wanting to do that for days. Wash her. Set her in the tub and dump water over her head. Run my hands over her body and across her pussy. I want this. It's younger than her age. Some of the games we play are. She never balks.

I know we're blurring the age play a bit at times. Until I see signs that she doesn't like it, I won't change my plans. We've discussed it in vague terms a few times. She has hard limits when it comes to ages less than five. She shudders at the thought of baby food or bottles or even highchairs and finger foods. The mention of diapers almost had her running from the room. She shook her head so hard it had to hurt.

I'm fine with that. I don't care what age she prefers, really. I just want her to be happy and fulfilled.

I know I'm growing more and more possessive of her. Part of the reason I haven't had sex with her yet is because it will strip me bare. Bring me to my knees. Make it impossible for me to let her go.

Mentally my legs have been knocked out from under me because of her. My soul is no longer my own. I live with a certain amount of fear that she might one day change her mind and leave me. It would slay me. So I try to pretend I'm more aloof than that.

I take a deep breath and shake my maudlin thoughts from my head as we enter my office. I'm holding her hand.

CHAPTER 39

Lucy

Julius is already in Master Roman's office when we enter, leaning casually back in a chair across from his desk. "About time you showed up, slacker," he jokes, aiming his barb at Master Roman.

I grip Master Roman's hand, self-conscious about my clothes. It's something that hasn't changed in two weeks. Part of me worries I will never get over my embarrassment, even in front of people I know to be Doms themselves who have seen it all. Nothing can shock Julius. I'm aware of this.

I've analyzed and over-analyzed my predicament, and mostly decided that I like the way I get on edge. It might be confusing if I tried to explain it out loud, but the truth is that when I get embarrassed, my heart starts racing and my body comes alive at the same time. The embarrassment is part of my arousal.

Like now.

Julius glances up and down my body, making me aware

that my breasts are absurdly flattened under the cotton T-shirt and that my panties are sticking out of the top of my skirt because that's how Master Roman put them and I wasn't about to adjust my clothes. He might have swatted my hand away. I've learned that lesson more than once. If he puts something on me crooked, I keep my mouth shut and leave it. It's probably intentional.

My panties are also up in my butt crack and wedged between my labia. I know for a fact *that* was intentional. He jerked them up that high. It's the reason they are sticking out of my skirt too. They are lime green and incredibly obvious.

I fidget, recognizing the symptoms I get every time we are in this position. I'm mortified that someone is seeing me dressed like this, and I'm also aroused. The familiar tight knot in my belly is back. It started to build when Master Roman told me Julius was coming over, and it's now full on clenching my stomach.

I've learned I like that feeling. I've also read enough to know that I'm some kind of exhibitionist. Not the normal kind. I really don't want anyone but Master Roman to see me naked. But I do like people to stare at me in my flouncy childish outfits that don't fit my actual age.

I haven't been exposed to anyone who isn't in the lifestyle, of course, nor do I have any interest in something like that yet, but having Claudia, Julius, Beck, Levi, Nancy, Evelyn, and Weston all play along and pretend I'm twelve pushes me to this special place that I secretly love. A place where I'm a combination of embarrassed and aroused because of it. It's odd. It works for me.

There's a certain level of humiliation that I get off on. A perfect balance that makes me thrive.

I'm experiencing that right now. I'm smiling inside while I shuffle my bare feet on the hardwood floor, lowering my gaze.

Master Roman squeezes my hand. "I had a hard time

getting Lucy out of the hot tub. She thinks she's old enough to be out there alone." He lifts my chin with one finger and then taps my nose. "Invincible."

"I'm a big girl," I remind him to keep the banter going.

"Yes, you are, blossom. But you still won't be permitted in the back yard alone. It's not safe. If I catch you out there without supervision, I'll spank your bottom so hard you won't be able to sit for a week." He narrows his gaze.

"Yes, Sir," I murmur.

"Good. Now go find something to play with while Julius and I work. If you're good and don't interrupt us, I'll get you some ice cream after."

I giggle. "Okay." And then I race off to my playroom. It's something I started doing on about the second day. I only do it with Master Roman still. I don't want Nancy to admonish me in the hallway. Master Roman must not mind. He hasn't said a word about me rushing around him.

I plop down on my bottom in my usual position with my legs crossed and my panties on the carpet. I'm used to this now. It's soothing. It's part of a routine.

I don't work on weekends. Master Roman made that abundantly clear last weekend. I haven't argued with him, and I won't.

I can hear the men talking in the other room, and I grab my Disney coloring book and markers. I've used them several times, but I keep them in order in their package so they always look new.

I carefully select a pink one and then I swing around to lie on my belly and start to color. It's calming. I'm aware that my panties are showing from behind. If Julius comes in, he will see them. My breasts are also hanging almost out from under my shirt.

I block out the discomfort and focus on my picture for a long time. When I'm finished, I sit up, putting the last marker back in the package. It's pretty. I've stayed in the lines. I tear it out of the book carefully, planning to give it to Master Roman later.

I reach for a book next, closing my eyes so that I'm forced to select a random one. And then I flounce onto my beanbag, cross my legs at the ankles, and open the front cover.

The book is one of a dozen I have on that shelf about littles, middles, and babies. I usually skip around to the parts that interest me. I personally was a late bloomer, so the truth is that if I had the means, I might very well have dressed like this when I was twelve. I hadn't even started my period.

It's okay that Master Roman often treats me younger. I don't mind. I like it actually. It keeps me on my toes. Like when he dresses me or imposes strict rules that wouldn't be reasonable for a girl that old. Like going outside alone. Or even sitting in the hot tub.

He gets overprotective. I suppose some parents might actually be that overprotective of their young girls too. I thrive on his attentiveness. It works for me.

How long will I be able to play this role though? I'm glad that he's letting me work four hours a day. I work hard and efficiently, blocking out my clothing for the duration. I'll do anything it takes to keep him from hiring someone else. The thought makes my stomach hurt.

I'm getting more comfortable in this role every day. It's scary. If he changes his mind, I might be lost out in the real world. And the longer I stay, the harder it will be to even leave the house. I'm not sure after two weeks as a child and two weeks before that as a submissive that I'm equipped to leave and behave as a grown up.

I'm nervous about that, and not sure I want to completely lose myself in this role. It would leave me vulnerable. Unprepared to function in the real world. It's a dangerous game.

I open the book to the section about middles and start reading. I get so involved in a chapter that truly speaks to me personally that I don't hear Master Roman come in the room. He's standing over me before I notice him.

I lower the book.

He's smiling. "It must be good."

"It is, Sir. I'm learning a lot."

"Good. I like to see you putting your mind to work. You're a bright girl."

I love it when he praises me. "Thank you, Sir."

"I even have some ideas on that subject." He holds out a hand. "For another time. Come say goodbye to Julius."

I follow Master Roman into his office, my bare feet padding along behind him.

Julius is still seated in the same spot. "You were quiet as a mouse, Lucy. I forgot you were even in there."

"I was coloring mostly," I tell him as I set one foot on top of the other, fidgeting under his gaze again.

"Roman tells me you've got quite the playroom in there."

"Yes." I wrap my arm around Roman's enormous one and half hide behind his biceps.

Julius stands, chuckling. He reaches out a hand to shake Master Roman's. "I'll let you two enjoy the rest of your Saturday. It's getting late. I need to be at the club."

I continue to hold on to Master Roman's arm as we slowly follow Julius to the office door. "Let me know if there's anything else you need. I'll talk to you Monday."

"Sounds good. See you later, Lucy." Julius dips his head to meet my gaze.

I nod.

Master Roman extricates his arm and wraps it around me, angling us toward the loveseat situated by his bookshelves. He sighs as he plops down and pulls me onto his lap. He tucks his hand around my hip and strokes my arm with the other one.

"You were a very good girl today, blossom. Thank you for not interrupting us while we worked. It went much faster that way."

I beam.

"How about we order a pizza tonight and snuggle in the media room with a movie. Would you like that?"

I sit up straighter, my eyes going wide. "Really?" I've never seen the media room. I know it's at the end of the hallway past the dining room, but I've never walked that far. I still don't wander around Master Roman's home without permission. I've never been anywhere on the second floor other than the distance between the back steps and my bedroom. I've never set foot on the winding staircase at the front of the house.

"Yes." He chuckles. "I must be a very bad workaholic if you're this surprised to hear that I can relax and have fun."

He is a workaholic. I know this for sure. Though he did leave me with lots of free time last weekend, he never suggested a movie.

"Can we have popcorn?"

He laughs again. "I think that can be arranged." He glances at his watch. "It's already six. Do you think if I let you stay up past your bedtime you can keep from being cranky tomorrow? I won't be inclined to let you stay up late again for a long time if I have to spend the day tomorrow with a whiny child on my hands."

I flush. "I can do it. I promise." I nearly bounce on his lap. "I won't whine a bit. I'll be really good."

He lifts a brow. "I'll make you a deal. We'll eat, watch a movie, and spend some time together. But if you can't get out of bed or you talk back to me in the morning, I will put you in timeout for so long your legs will hurt. Understood?"

"Yes, Sir."

"Good." He grabs my hips and lifts me off his lap, setting

me on the floor between his legs. "Why don't you go get your nightgown on. You'll be ready for bed when we're done."

"What about my bath?" I ask. Maybe he forgot. He never lets me skip my bath.

"You can skip it this once."

I smile, nearly bouncing on my feet. My boobs bob up and down. My shirt rises too high. I stop when I realize this and tug my T-shirt over them. My nipples are hard.

Master Roman's gaze lowers to them. He smooths his hands up from my hips to my breasts and squeezes them in that way that always makes me wet.

"Is your pussy wet, blossom?"

"Yes, Sir," I whisper, butterflies gathering in my belly.

He lowers a hand, nudges my legs apart, and drags his fingers over my panties. He smiles. "I like that, little blossom." He's done this so often to me that I should be used to it. I'm not though. It drives me just as crazy today as it did the first time he did it.

He sets me aside and rises, spinning me around to face the door. With a swat on my bottom, he says, "Go get your nightie on. Meet me in the media room."

I scamper from the room, my jean skirt flaring up as I go. It's not until I slow my pace in the hallway that I begin to worry about the nightgown Nancy has probably left me. Every one so far has been completely too indecent to wear out of my bedroom.

I'm nearly shaking as I enter my room and close the door. I rush to grab the pink article of clothing I see on the chair, relieved to see it's a cotton nightgown. It's not long, but it's longer than many others I've worn. It will cover my bottom at least.

I head for the bathroom, considering the idea of leaving my panties on. I've never been permitted to do so before, but I've also never left the room in my nightgown.

As I remove my shirt and then my skirt, I chew on my bottom lip. I stand in my lime green panties for a while, thinking. Pondering. Making a list of pros and cons.

Finally, I pick up the nightgown and shrug into it. When it settles over me, I notice the front also has a mermaid on it. Today must be mermaid day.

The neckline is elastic, loose, and wide. It dips low all the way around. The sleeves are puffy with another elastic cinching them on my biceps. The hem has a ruffle, and I decide it's at least a few inches below my bottom. No one will know I'm not wearing panties if I'm careful. It's better to take them off and put them down the chute than risk getting in trouble and ruining what should be a fun night.

I'm still hopeful that Master Roman will let me see his penis tonight. I've begun to worry about this subject lately. The fact that he touches me so intimately but won't let me even see him makes me fear that he doesn't enjoy having sex with littles.

If that's the case, I'm going to be very disappointed because I really really really want to have sex with him. And I'm not at all sure he'd be willing to negotiate coming out of the age play to do it.

Does he expect our life to settle into a routine where he fondles me and tickles me and makes me come but never joins? I don't like that idea. I want to see his penis. I want to hold it. I even want to take it in my mouth. I need to find the courage to tell him.

Maybe tonight.

CHAPTER 40

Lucy

The pizza is delicious. I'm stuffing the second slice in my mouth while Master Roman chooses the movie. I have no idea what he picks. He says I will like it.

"Slow down before you choke, blossom. There's plenty of pizza. Don't make me tell you again."

I chew slower. I even wipe my face with my napkin.

We are settled in the media room now. Master Roman has been sitting on the gigantic black leather sofa. I've been sitting on the floor with my legs folded under me, nervous about my naked bottom. He hasn't mentioned it.

I finish my last slice and pick up my lemon-lime soda. It's a luxury, both because I rarely ever bought soda before I moved in with Master Roman and because he doesn't let me have sugary soda very often. This is only the third time. And he never offers me cola, only lemon-lime. He says the caffeine would keep me up at night.

I finish it slowly, enjoying the treat, and then I set the can on the end table.

Master Roman dims the lights and reaches for me. "Come here, blossom."

I stand and come to him, nervous. I don't care about the movie at all. If I had a choice, I would tell him to leave it off and take his pants off instead. We're closed in the room. I know he locked the door because I watched him. It's a good sign.

He pulls me between his legs, hands on my hips. "You're having a mermaid day," he says.

"Yes." I giggle as I pinch the front of my nightgown and hold it away from my body. "Watch out that you don't get swatted by her pectoral fins." I shrug so that the left sleeve of my nightie will go back onto my shoulder. It has slid down to my arm.

He rubs my arms. "Big words. Pectoral fins," he mimics. "Where did you learn that?"

"At school," I respond. It's a reasonable answer. And true. It just didn't happen yesterday, but rather a decade ago.

"You're good at school, aren't you, blossom?"

I nod. Where is he going with this?

His expression changes slightly. "Have you ever thought about going to college, Lucy?" he asks. He has stepped slightly out of the role. He obviously has an agenda.

I'm curious. "No. I've always been too pragmatic to even buy soft drinks. It would have been stupid to dream that big." I'm being honest.

He glances at my empty soda can on the end table. "I tend to forget you haven't had that kind of luxury. Does it bother you that I limit you on things like that?"

I shake my head. We are definitely having a serious conversation. "No. Not really. I'm happy, Sir." I add that last part, hoping he will let whatever is on his mind go. I'm worried I won't get the opportunity to explore his body if we get too serious.

"I want you to be happy, Lucy. That's the most important thing. If setting boundaries and enforcing strict rules makes you feel loved, then that's what you will get from me."

I shiver in his grasp, my hands hanging at my sides. "I like our arrangement, Sir."

He smiles. "What if it could be more?"

I frown. "More how?"

"I've been thinking you might like to go to school."

I lick my lips. "School?"

"College. There's a university nearby. You could look into it. You're so smart. You made straight A's in high school. You're quick and sharp and I know you're being held back without an education."

"I can't afford it, Sir."

"I can." His expression is even more serious.

I don't move.

He sighs. "It's just something to think about, Lucy. I want you to have the world. I can afford it. I started thinking about it after you made me see why you need to work a few hours a day. I love having you as a middle. So much it's frightening. I wouldn't care if you stayed in the role 24/7 forever if it made you happy. But I worry you're going to get restless and want more from life."

I start to cry for some reason that's inexplicable. He's rocking the boat. It scares me.

He slides his hands up to my face and wipes my tears with his thumbs. "Don't cry, blossom. I hate it when you cry." It's the first time he's said that. "I'm only asking you to think about it. Think about what you want in your future. If it makes you nervous not to work, then imagine how much more empowered you would be if you had a degree?"

I try to nod slightly.

236

"Trust me. It's hard for me to make this suggestion because I'm growing extremely possessive of you. If I had my way, I'd never let you leave the house. I'd never share you with anyone outside of our little bubble. But that's not fair of me, and eventually you will resent me and feel trapped. You'd suffocate."

I swallow past the lump in my throat.

"Does it scare me to let you leave the house without me? Hell, yes. Will I do it because it's the right thing for you, absolutely. Granted, I'd prefer you took some online classes first, but I'll bite my tongue if you want to go to the campus."

I'm stuck on his irrational fear. "It scares you for me to leave the house? Why? Do you have anxiety about me getting injured or something?"

He blushes. *Blushes!* I've said something that has embarrassed him. I have no idea what.

He lowers his hand to my shoulders and pulls me closer. When he sets his forehead against mine, I nearly panic. This is important to him. Whatever it is. "Lucy, my greatest fear is losing you."

"I'm not going to get hit by a car, Master Roman. I'll be careful. I promise."

He shakes his head. "I don't mean losing you in an accident. I mean losing you to someone who is not me."

I stop breathing. "You think if I go to college, I'll meet someone my age and want to leave you?"

"Yes."

I'm shocked. Especially because I've been irrationally scared that I'm the one too deeply involved. I never thought that he was just as interested in me. "I wouldn't, Sir," I whisper. "There is no way I'll ever meet someone who can dominate me precisely the way you can. It's exactly perfect for me. In every way. I know it's only been two weeks since I moved in and became your little girl, but it's what I feel destined to be. Yours. Not someone else's. There isn't a single boy on any college campus who could make me an offer better than this, and even if he could, my heart already belongs to you."

Master Roman closes his eyes, smiling. "I'm so lucky. You make me so happy."

I need to say more. I need to share what's on my mind. "I have a concern though."

"Let's hear it."

"Do you not see me as someone you want to make love to?" I hold my breath.

He flinches, his eyes narrowing. "What gives you that idea? Of course I want to make love to you, blossom. So badly it hurts."

"Then why haven't you?" I'm blushing now. Heat rises up my neck and cheeks.

He stares at my chest as he responds. "Because I want you to have time. I want to ease you in slowly. I don't want you to be rushed. I want you to savor the sexual side of our relationship so that you look back on it with the best memories. Sweet and slow and perfect."

I'm not buying his speech, especially because he isn't looking me in the eye as he delivers it, and his hands are rubbing my arms at an awkward pace. He's done this before. The only other time we had a misunderstanding when he didn't want me to work, and I put my foot down.

I call him out again now. "You're full of shit."

He jerks his gaze to mine. "Language, Lucy. I don't care if we have stepped out of the role for a while, I still don't want you to cuss. It's totally unacceptable for a little girl and equally crude coming from the woman who is your real age too."

"I'm sorry, Sir. I won't do it again."

"You will. But I'll spank your bottom next time," he assures me. "Hard rule. In or out of the role. Understood?"

"Yes, Sir. But you changed the subject. Why haven't you had sex with me?" I ask him point blank. He needs to be honest. I want a real answer.

He hesitates and then blows out a long breath. "A number of reasons. Nothing I just said was a lie. I do want to go slow with you. It's a joy watching you grow and learn. I want to slow time down because I get to see the look of pure bliss on your face from the first time I enter you only once."

"I think you're going to be disappointed. Everything I've read has suggested it's going to hurt." I glare at him. He owes me more of an explanation.

"You might be right. But if I work your pussy for several days with my fingers though, I can stretch you out and make the first time more enjoyable."

I shake my head. "There won't be any several days. We're having sex tonight," I insist.

He smirks. "Bossy girl. I don't think you're strong enough to take me on like that."

I roll my eyes.

"Sassy too. I'm going to spank your ass in a few minutes."

"Looking forward to it," I challenge. There is a good chance I'm going to regret this entire conversation. Master Roman has threatened to put me in timeout for far less than the sassiness I'm tossing at him now. In or out of the role, I know I'm in trouble. Too late now. Might as well keep pushing.

I set one hand on my hip and cock it out to the side.

He laughs. "Tomorrow is going to be a very long day for one naughty little girl."

I don't move. It's worth it.

He shakes his head. "I'm not sure how I feel about this demanding side of you but simmer down. I'm getting there. Let me finish."

I wait.

"You're right. I've been stalling. For those reasons and more. It's not completely altruistic. The reality is that I've known I wanted you in my life and in my bed from the moment I set eyes on you. Every day that I spend with you not only solidifies that fact but scares me to death."

"Why?" I ask gently.

"Because after I put my cock in you, you'll be so totally mine that I will never want to let you go. I need to know that you're sure about staying with me before we make love. Because you're it for me. It would destroy me if we have sex and then you walk away. I don't want to rush you on that issue. I need you to be committed. Even if my balls are blue all day every day." His effort to lighten the severity of his story fails.

I'm humbled. I reach out and touch his face. "I just told you how deeply I feel about you. You can stop worrying. I'm sure about us." My heart is beating so hard. Master Roman is in love with me. He hasn't said it in those words, but I can see it in his eyes. He really believes he would be devastated if I left him. I know how hard it is for him to make himself vulnerable by saying that.

He tips his cheek into my palm, kissing the sensitive skin.

I need to be sure of something. "So, no part of you is squicked out by the age play? Because it's a problem if you feel like you're molesting me or something. I don't feel that way. I don't want you to either."

He shakes his head. "God no. It's not that at all. I'm hard all the time around you, blossom." His expression grows serious. "I get aroused every time I see you and even more so when you slide deeper into the role. It's a role. Nothing more. I'm completely aware under the act is a grown woman with grown body parts that are going to explode under my touch in a grown-up way."

I giggle. I'm so happy.

He continues. His explanation is so clinical, but he's making sense. "Millions of people enjoy some form of kink that involves pretending to be something or someone they are not. People dress as pets or vampires or naughty schoolgirls. The luckiest thing in the world is to find someone who enjoys the same kink you enjoy.

"I get rock hard when you walk into a room dressed as a young girl. When you act like one, it makes my cock even more anxious. The fact that you get off on dressing the part of a younger age too is icing on the cake. It definitely has nothing to do with me being attracted to actual children." He shudders. "I'm looking at a grown woman playing the part of a child. Huge difference."

I nod. "Good. I was worried you saw me as a child instead and maybe you were only interested in nurturing me to fulfill some deep need to have a kid around or something."

"Not even close. I get aroused by the game. Nothing more."

It's time to end this serious conversation. "Settled then. We're having sex tonight. Now." I lower my hands and my gaze to the bulge in his jeans. This is only the second time I've seen him this casual. He so rarely wears jeans. I wrap my palm around his length before he can stop me.

He groans and grabs my wrist. "I'll set the pace. You'll do as you're told."

"Yes, Sir." I bounce on my feet once. My nightgown rises, reminding me I'm naked under it. "I'm not wearing panties, Sir."

"I'm well aware of that, blossom." He rolls his eyes as he inhales deeply. His fingers are tight on my arms.

I tip my head to stare at the connection and lower my voice as I find myself sliding back into the role. I need to tell him something else. "Even though it's role play, it doesn't hurt that you are so ridiculously large and I'm so petite. When your hands are on me, I feel small and childlike."

He slides his hands to my neck, cupping my cheeks as well. "I agree. You are incredibly small. But you're also proportionate. And when you're naked in front of me, you are all woman." His hands smooth down to cup my breasts. He jiggles them. "These are so perfect and sexy. You have no idea." His hands slide lower to my waist. "And your waist dips in a very womanly way. You may be tiny, but you're proportionate. The clothes I buy you often don't fit right over your tits or your bottom, but that just makes me hornier."

I shiver now. "I'm glad, Sir," I whisper.

CHAPTER 41

Master Roman

I hold her gaze for long seconds, letting time put her back into the age of twelve. We've had a very serious discussion, and it went better than I could have anticipated, but now she needs me to show her how much she matters to me. And I need her to resume her place in our relationship.

I decide to set a new standard. "Lucy, I want you to be free to discuss anything with me at any time. If you need to stop role-playing to talk to me, just say so. Let's give those times their own safeword of sorts. How about marbles."

She giggles. "Marbles?" And then she smiles. "Ah, because you hate them for the same reason. You think you'll step on them and break a leg. You aren't going to buy me any marbles, are you?"

"Exactly." I smile at her, pleased she got my meaning. "So, if you need to break through the age play, just say 'marbles.' You won't be in trouble. You're permitted to do so any time. It will put you in a headspace similar to the one you use when you're working."

She beams. "I like it."

"However, there's a catch. You may bring any concern to me you want, but you still have to be respectful when doing so. You don't have to call me Sir, but you also can't cuss or sass me or roll your eyes or toss out that hip." I tap her hip for emphasis.

"Yes, Sir."

"I'm going to spank you now for three reasons. One, you kind of knew you would be punished for those things when you did them already."

"Yes, Sir." Her voice is barely audible.

"Two, taking you over my knee and swatting your bottom right now will help you fall back into the role."

She shudders. I knew she would. She gets fidgety every time I use the word spank or even bottom. I love it.

"And three, you'll be so aroused when I'm finished that your body will easily relax for me to take you out of this world with what comes next."

She flushes spectacularly. Gorgeous.

I angle her around to my side and lower her over my lap. Like the first time I spanked her, I clasp her wrists at the small of her back. I know she relaxes more when I take away her ability to squirm as effectively.

I slide my hand up her thigh and over her bare bottom, pushing her nightgown up to tuck it under her wrists. Her butt is so smooth. Every time I see it, I get hard. Right now, I'm about to bust the zipper of my jeans.

I take my time, knowing with every passing second she is getting more and more aroused.

She whimpers as I stroke her skin.

"Spread your legs, blossom." I reach between her thighs

and hike her closest knee up, forcing her pussy to be exposed. I settle her bent knee on the sofa near my hip.

Her breath hitches, and she squirms.

"Are you wet, little blossom?"

"Yes, Sir."

"Good girl. You look so pretty in this pink nightgown. So sweet and innocent and young. I think half my attraction is the innocence, and with you it's not even pretend." I keep touching her. Everywhere. Up and down her back and thighs. Smooth perfect skin that is going to be pink in a minute. Pinkened for me. Pink because she trusts me to discipline her when I see fit.

She moans. I close my eyes for a minute, savoring the sound. Memorizing it. A sound she's making before I've done anything. A gift she gives me for nurturing her.

When I finally lift my palm and spank her sweet bottom, she doesn't stiffen. Instead, she relaxes. Her body is slack on my lap. I swat her four more times, rapidly, watching her skin grow darker. So sexy.

With her leg hitched up at my side, her pussy is spread open. I know it will be wet, but I don't touch it. I rub her warm bottom again now. "Good girl. I'm proud of you."

She whimpers, a shiver racing down her body.

I don't release her yet because I'm not ready. I love seeing her over my knee like this, her nightgown bunched up around her waist, her braids hanging down to the floor, her bottom pink and hot from my punishment.

Finally, I stand her in front of me and meet her gaze, wanting to repeat myself because it will solidify the roles we're in. I put her in her place, and she slides into that twelve-year-old girl mindset that drives both of us to a heightened level of arousal. The deeper she goes into the age play, the more alert her body becomes to my touch and my voice.

I know how to get her there. She knows it too. And it has to come from me.

I hold her shoulders, giving her a slight shake and a stern look. "Should I expect to hear naughty words from your mouth again?"

"No, Sir." She lowers her gaze, her body trembling.

"Is it okay for you to sass me?"

"No, Sir." Her voice dips as her head tips farther at the same time.

"I know twelve is a difficult age. You're confused. Your body is changing. You have trouble concentrating. But I won't have you copping an attitude with me. If I see you toss that hip out and plant your hand on it, rolling those eyes at me again, you'll be grounded for a week. No hot tub. No nail polish. No coloring books. You can spend your days sitting on the floor on the hardwood next to my desk bored out of your mind. Have I made myself clear?"

She nods. "Yes, Sir." Her voice shakes this time. She has fully slid into the role. It's almost a subspace. And her physical reaction is just as precious. I can see her beaded nipples through the nightgown. She has shifted her weight several times and then stepped her feet together too. If I were to stroke through her pussy right now, I would find it wet. Soaked.

She sniffles.

I lift her chin with one finger. "It's done, blossom. Your punishment is over. Take a breath."

She inhales deeply, watery eyes on mine. On a sob, she says, "I won't be sassy again. Promise."

It's time. She's ready for more. I won't deny her any longer. A plan comes to mind of how we might work through this next step. "Now, I know you're starting to have sexual feelings. It's normal. All girls reach an age where they're curious about sex. I know you're feeling things and experiencing things that are confusing. Your titties are probably tender, and sometimes you get wet between your legs."

"Yes, Sir." She nods, solemnly.

I'm taking my cues from her. I want our dynamic in bed to be special. I need to go slow and play my cards right to set the vibe. "It's normal for you to have sexual thoughts and natural for your pussy to get really wet when you think about touching it or putting something inside it."

She nods.

"I want you to come to me if you have any questions, but I also want your information to come from me. Not your friends."

"Yes, Sir."

"I'll satisfy your curiosity. I've probably put it off too long because I wanted you to remain innocent as long as possible, blossom. But it's time for you to understand what the male body looks like and how it works."

"Okay, Sir." She licks her lips. It's almost hard for me to separate the role-playing girl from the woman because I know the adult Lucy has also not touched a cock before. Her innocence is not feigned. Not this time. She might choose to pretend scenes like this in the future. It's hard to say. I can't predict our dynamic. But for tonight, she is totally as innocent as I'm implying.

"Lower to your knees, blossom." I want her in a submissive position, but I decide not to take her nightgown off yet. I know she reacts strongly to wearing the age clothing. I grab a pillow from the couch and set it on the floor between my legs.

She is shaking, but her gaze is wide as she drops to her knees.

I cup the back of her head. "It's okay to be nervous. Perfectly natural. Open my jeans now, blossom."

She reaches with her fantastic hands and manages to push

the button through the hole and then lower the zipper, but her hands tremble.

I'm not wearing underwear tonight, and I'm sure it shocks her. It's intentional.

She lifts her gaze as my cock pops free. Her eyes are wide, her mouth open.

I smile and reassure her with my hand on the back of her neck. "Go ahead, blossom. Touch me."

With tentative fingers, she touches the tip of my engorged dick.

This is going to be the hardest thing I ever do. One of the most important also. I'm setting the groundwork for our future dynamic. I know this deep in my soul. We may alter things along the way and shake things up to keep it spicy, but the next hour is everything.

I release her and lift my hips to tug my jeans down my legs.

She leans back for a moment while I pull them over my bare feet, and then I tug my T-shirt over my head. I'm completely naked now. For the first time with my girl.

I want to freeze this moment. The look of fear and concern and awe and excitement all over her face is mostly genuine. Another day, it will be for play. But not tonight. Tonight she really feels all the sensations.

"It's so big," she whispers as she strokes a finger down the length.

My cock bobs against my belly at her touch. I'm going to come prematurely from her fucking sexy words. She doesn't even have to touch me. But the fact that she is currently stroking my shaft is almost my undoing.

I'm not going to lie to her about my size. I am larger than most men. My entire frame is. It's going to hurt when I press into her tight little cunt. I'll do everything I can to stretch her first.

I haven't pushed more than one finger into her before tonight. I've never needed to. My little blossom's eyes roll back into her head and she loses her mind every time I slide just my pointer into her pussy. I wish we had more time. But I know I can't put her off any longer.

She needs encouragement, and I need to think about something other than how sweet it's going to be to fuck her so that I don't come too fast. Or better yet, maybe it would be better if I come right now. I might stand a better chance of lasting a bit longer if I've already had an orgasm.

"You don't have to be gentle, blossom. Wrap your hand around my cock. Feel the strength." I stroke my fingers up her arm.

She wraps her much smaller hand around my dick, gingerly. "What should I do?" she asks, her face rosy as she lifts her gaze.

"Whatever you want, blossom." I cup her neck again. "Two rules. Be careful with my balls." I grab them with my free hand so she knows what I'm talking about. "And don't sink your teeth into me."

She flinches. "My teeth?" Her eyes are wide.

I know some of this is role-playing. She obviously knows what a blow job is. "Yes, little blossom. You're going to wrap your lips around my cock and suck it into your mouth. That would make me happy."

The red on her cheeks deepens, making my dick jerk in her hand.

"It will take some time for you to learn how I like it, but I'll teach you to suck it deep into your mouth until my come squirts out and runs down your throat."

She swallows. Precious.

"Go ahead. Lick the tip. I'll tell you what to do."

She hesitates, and then she leans down and drags her tongue across the tip.

The urge to groan is strong. I grit my teeth. Damn, she is sexy. And that nightgown. Hanging from her left shoulder. Fuck me. I'm so glad I left it on.

"Swirl your tongue around the head, blossom."

She does as I instruct, driving me insane. I want to thrust into her greedy little mouth and take her hard. But she isn't ready for that.

"It's salty." She giggles as she releases me.

"It is. You'll learn to love the taste. You'll crave it. And I'll expect you to swallow it often." I tip her head back with my hand at her neck and lift my brows. "I know you're nervous, but you're a big girl now, and it's time for you to learn how I expect you to take care of my cock. Understood?"

She nods.

I'm totally going to come. Lucy is so deep in the role that I'm literally going to shoot my wad on her face in a second. She'll probably like it.

When she licks her lips, I know the dynamic is set. I don't have to feel her out anymore. She's got this.

"Good girl. Now open your mouth wide, little blossom, and take my cock in as deep as you can. Slide your hand down the shaft at the same time."

"Okay, Sir." She lowers her face, her braids falling forward to slap against my thighs. That alone is my undoing. Jesus.

When her lips wrap around my erection, I close my eyes. My hand is on the back of her head, guiding her, but I tip my face to the ceiling and lean back against the cushions. I do nothing but concentrate on the way her mouth feels around my cock.

I let her experiment for a few moments, and then I grip her neck. "Look at me, blossom." I manage to lift my head to meet her gaze.

Her wide eyes are so genuine.

"You see that little slit on the tip of my dick?"

She glances down. "Uh huh. It's got white stuff coming out of it."

Fuck me seven ways to Sunday. Her word choice is perfect.

"That's my come. The next time you suck my length into your mouth, a bunch of that white stuff is going to squirt into your throat, and you're going to swallow it. You ready for that? It's a big step. Once you do it, you can't go back. You'll crave it often, and I'll expect you to drain it for me also."

"Do you have to like, uh, empty it every day?"

"Yes, blossom. Several times. Usually I do it in the shower. It gets so hard when you're around, and the only way to release the pressure is to empty the come. You're old enough to do it yourself now."

"I'm going to swallow it every day?"

"Yep. More than once. But sometimes you can take the come into your little pussy or even your bottom."

Wide eyes again. She squirms on her knees. Her hands fly to her tits and squeeze them. That isn't part of the role. It's a visceral reaction to the picture I painted. Her tits ache. I'm sure they feel heavy swaying behind the mermaid nightie. I'd bet money her juices are running down the insides of her thighs.

My words are so filthy, and she's thriving on them.

She licks her lips, totally unaware that she is now pinching her nipples.

I glance down. "Let go of your titties, Lucy. I've told you before you aren't permitted to touch them."

She gasps, releasing her grip. Her body sways back and forth.

I stroke her cheek again. "I know it will be hard for you, but it's part of growing up. Having sex feels good, but you won't be allowed to break the rules. There's a reason girls crave cock. It will make your body feel so good every time you service me. It's a natural reaction.

"After you've swallowed my come the first time, you won't be able to forget. You'll think about how it made you feel all the time, even in the middle of the night. Sometimes it will drive you crazy how badly you want more. It's normal to want to please me like that. It's also normal that your titties will swell and ache when you think about me. Your pussy will also pulse and throb and your juices will run down your legs. Your panties will be wet all the time now. But you mustn't touch yourself without permission. You aren't allowed to give in to that temptation. You'll save your desires for when I need you to service me. When you take my come into your mouth or pussy or bottom, that's when I'll permit you to feel all the good feelings I've been slowly showing you the past few weeks. If you're a good girl, sometimes I will let you come without taking my cock. But you will never do so without permission. Understood?"

"Yes, Sir." She's flushed now.

This is filthier than I ever could have imagined. And so sexy and so perfect and so natural between us. I'm the luckiest man on earth. "You ready to swallow my come, blossom?"

"Yes, Sir." She nods rapidly.

"Go ahead." I release her neck, hoping I can keep my hands off her this first time so she can set the pace and not feel pressured. For as filthy as my words are, I still would never insist she suck me when she doesn't want to.

She lowers her face again, sucks me into her mouth, and clasps her hand around the base of my dick.

I'm in so much trouble. I may have been improvising during that speech, but if she's going to suck me like this, I probably will ask her to do it every day. I'm going to need to up my game to keep up with her. She's liable to be insatiable starting now.

So far, I've doled out an orgasm a day, sparingly. Teasing her. Tempting her in so many ways. After this, I'm thinking I'll strap her to my desk top tomorrow and make her come over and over until she can't breathe and has no intention of ever leaving me.

She sucks me deeper on the next slow pass, and then she hollows her cheeks and I'm done for. The second I'm in as far as she can take me, I come, just like I warned her, hot streams of my orgasm hitting the back of her throat.

She swallows me as if she were born knowing how to do so.

When I'm finally spent, blinking to focus, she lifts her gaze.

She's smiling, knowing she did well.

"That was perfect, blossom," I manage to say between breaths.

"Thank you, Sir. Now can we have sex?"

I will never get tired of this persona. The eager young girl who speaks out of turn and begs for things she should not have.

"As soon as I recover, little blossom." I smile at her. My dick is already growing stiff. It's not stupid. It knows it's going to get more tonight.

CHAPTER 42

Lucy

Oh. My. God.

I know Master Roman is turning this into a dirty game, but I love it. Every second of it. Every filthy word makes me hotter. He made me want to put my mouth on his penis with his words.

And he was proud of me. He liked it. I mean he wouldn't have come if he didn't like it, I assume.

I'm sure he was exaggerating when he said he would want me to suck him several times a day, but after that heady experience, he might not be wrong. I already crave more. I thoroughly enjoyed the weird power I had over him for just a moment.

Master Roman is always in control. Of everything. Even me. He dictates nearly every aspect of my life. He's even dictated what he expects from me sexually. I'm soaked. My lower lips are swollen. I have my knees spread open to help with the pressure, but I'm going to collapse soon. I'm surprised I didn't come without permission the moment he moaned.

The control was intoxicating. He was mine. He didn't even know what his hands were doing while I sucked him. All he knew was his release. Now I understand better the power he must feel over me when he makes me come. He just left his body the same way I do every time I orgasm.

I crave having him inside my sex now more than ever. I want to know the rest. I want to know the last piece I'm missing.

I shudder when I remember something else he said. He fully intends to put his penis in my bottom too. That makes me nervous. I hope he doesn't do it today. I might have to tell him I don't think I'm ready for that.

"What are you thinking about, blossom?"

I jerk my gaze to his, flushed.

He smiles. "Don't even try to come up with a lie. I watched your face. It went from total bliss to nervous horror. Tell me."

I bite my lip and then release it. "Uh, I was thinking about how you said that you would empty your penis in my, uh, private parts, which I really really want you to do," I start, eagerly. "But you also said you would put it in my bottom. Did you mean that?" I squirm and not entirely what the role calls for.

He leans forward and kisses my nose. "Yes. You'll learn to take my cock in every one of your holes, little blossom, but you don't have to worry about that today. Or even this week. It will take a while to stretch out your tight little bottom before I can fit in there. We'll work on it. Soon. Not today."

I'm speechless. Truly speechless this time. Not from my little-girl role but from my grown-adult self. I've never considered anal sex. It seems taboo. I squirm at the idea.

255

I realize how ridiculous my thoughts are. Everything about this arrangement is taboo. Taking his erection into me doesn't even make the short list. I shake away my concerns. He's assured me he won't do that tonight.

He leans back on the sofa and reaches for me. "Come here, blossom. Straddle my lap."

I stand, leaning to one side before I grab his lap and scramble up onto him. It's awkward, but I manage to tug my nightie over my hips and straddle him. My legs are pushed very wide in this position, and I gasp out loud.

Master Roman chuckles as his hands go to my bottom and then run up and down my back. He tugs me closer until his penis taps my belly. It's already almost as big as it was before I swallowed his come.

I shiver. I can't believe I just swallowed Master Roman's come. In my mouth. It seems like such a naughty thing to do. I feel like a naughty little girl, but not the kind of naughty that will get my bottom spanked.

Master Roman continues to caress my back under my nightgown. It feels good. Soothing. But it's hard for me to concentrate on anything except my swollen needy sex.

I'm embarrassed that my body always has obvious signs that tell my Master I'm horny. It's humiliating that I can't hide my desire for him. I know that he's right that after tonight I will crave his touch more often and want his big penis inside me. He will tease me more than he already does about my hard nipples and my wet pussy. He can easily check how naughty I am by touching my panties. They are always wet. Does he know that?

I can't know when Master is aroused like he knows. His only symptom would be his penis growing big. But he usually hides it under his desk. I've only been able to discern a tent in his pants a few times when I dared to look or when he didn't hide his erection.

I purse my lips as I realize I'm going to drip my juices on Master Roman's thighs.

He tucks his big hands under my bottom again and shifts me forward even closer. Now his penis is totally hard and rubbing against my little clit.

I moan when he lifts me a few inches and sets me back down, dragging his velvety skin over my sensitive nub. "Sir..." I'm desperate.

"Shh. Be my good girl now. Let me get you ready."

I whimper. My hands are on his shoulders, but I can't hold myself up.

He brings his palms around to my front and pushes my nightie up until he cups my breasts. He drives me crazy squeezing and pulling on them, pinching the tips over and over until I cry out.

"Such a good girl. I'm so proud of you, blossom." He removes his hands and brings them to my face. "I'm going to teach you how I expect you to kiss me now, Lucy."

I lick my lips. He has only kissed me a few times. Always a quick peck that leaves me wanting more.

He angles my head to one side and holds both my braids in one hand at the nape of my neck. "Open your mouth. I'll guide you."

I do as I'm told, my juices running out, dripping. I know I'm getting his thighs wet. I'm embarrassed again that he does that to me. I'm so naughty. Will he be disappointed in me that I'm so naughty?

His mouth descends until his soft lips are on mine. He starts slow, but then drags his tongue along my bottom lip. When he slides his tongue into my mouth, I touch mine against his. It's so intimate. I feel like I'm going to faint. He deepens the kiss, pressing harder, angling slightly more to the side. His tongue dances with mine, teaching me, taking from me, draining me of brain cells.

I love how he kisses me. So much that I know this will be my new favorite. Every time I look at his mouth, I will think of him kissing me. I hope he does it often.

He doesn't stop until I'm moaning into his mouth. My nipples are so sensitive from him tugging on them that they ache every time they touch my nightie. Every stroke of the fabric reminds me of my age. Has he left my nightie on so I won't forget my role?

When he breaks free, I'm panting.

He smiles. "Did you like that?"

"So much, Sir."

"Good. That's how you'll kiss me from now on."

I nod. I want nothing less.

"Are you ready for more, little blossom?"

"Yes, Sir." I'm past ready for more.

"Hold my shoulders, Lucy."

I grab them, and he sets his hands on my bottom, inching it forward until he's prodding my opening. My wetness coats his fingers.

"My girl is very very naughty, isn't she? So greedy. Her pussy is desperate to be filled."

I'm red again. My muscles clench down there.

He teases my soaked, swollen folds with the tips of his fingers, and then without warning he thrusts one finger up into me.

I cry out.

He's smiling at me. Not looking away. "That's a good girl. Can you take more?"

"Yes, Sir," I breathe out.

He adds a second finger and thrusts the two in together. So much pressure. It's so tight. And it feels like heaven. "Sir..." I moan. I'm going to come.

With his other hand, he strokes my swollen clit. "Come for me, blossom. Get the first one out of the way so I can really stretch this sweet cunt." He thrusts deeper, so fast that my breath leaves my lungs as I come all over his fingers. Wetness runs out of my channel. He thrusts those fingers in and out of me while I pulse around them.

"Sweet sweet cherry blossom. You are angelic when you shatter on my fingers. This greedy little cunt is insatiable."

He's right. I'm mortified, but he's telling the truth. His hands disappear, and I watch in horror as he sucks my juices from his fingers. Slowly. One at a time. While my channel tightens all over again at the erotic scene.

When he's done, he reaches back around, drags one finger through my folds again, and then brings it to my mouth. "Taste yourself, blossom. Taste how sweet you are."

I suck his finger into my mouth, tasting my come. It is sweeter than his come, that's for sure. When he's satisfied that I've cleaned his finger off, he reaches for my nightgown and pulls it up. "Lift your arms, little blossom."

I hold them above my head, and he whisks my nightie off. Instead of tossing it aside, he hands it to me. "Hold on to it. Press the soft cotton against your face. It will help you remember who you are and soothe you while I work your pussy open farther."

I grip it with one arm against my cheek like a child would a blankie. He's right. It calms me. My mermaid nightie. Pink and sweet and young. A nightgown meant for a little girl. Me. My Master's little blossom.

He taps my nose. "Good girl."

I hug it tighter, tipping my head into the warm cotton.

He lifts me slowly off his lap and turns to lay me on my back on the sofa. The leather is cool against my heated skin as his gaze scans up and down my body. "Open your legs for me, Lucy. Pull your knee up to the couch cushion so I can see your pussy."

I drag my leg up high and press my knee into the cushion.

The other heel is resting on the edge of the sofa. I glance around. It's bright in the room. I wish Master Roman would dim the lights. I feel so exposed. Even though he's seen me naked lots of times, never like this.

His large hand lands on my thigh and presses to widen me more. As he spins to more fully face me, he uses his other fingers to tap my nipples each several times and then tease my still sensitive labia. "This little pussy is desperate to be filled, isn't it, blossom?"

I nod, grateful for the nightie he's given me to hug. I'm squeezing it tight now with both hands, rubbing my cheeks and lips against the cotton. It takes my mind off the bright lights and the way Master Roman is staring at my private parts.

He pulls me open with his fingers again, and then he flips his hand over so his palm is up and pushes three fingers into me.

I arch my back and moan. It's tight, but it feels so good. So very good. His penis is thicker and longer than even those three fingers, but I know I can take it now. I want to. I want him to have sex with me so badly. "Sir…"

"You ready for my cock now?"

I nod. "Please…"

I watch as he reaches for his jeans on the floor, confused. And then I see the small square packet in his hand. A condom. He watches my face as he rolls it on. "We won't use these for long. But until you've had a chance to see my medical report, I want you to be safe."

His medical report? "Okay," I murmur.

He climbs over me, his erection poised at my entrance. His hand goes to my cheek again. "You sure you're ready?"

"Yes, Sir." I force myself to sound far more certain than I am. I'm ready to have sex. Yes. Definitely. But I'm also concerned about how it's going to hurt this first time.

"I know you're scared. I'll go slow. You tell me when you need me to stop. I promise it will only hurt for a moment, and then you'll never regret it."

"Okay, Sir."

He lines himself up and slowly pushes into me. The stretch is more than I expected. I pull my knee up higher as if that might help him fit.

He holds my gaze, but his jaw is tight, and I know this is hard for him. I fist my nightie in my palm as he continues to enter me. It doesn't seem possible. He's not going to fit. I bite down on my lip, trying to be brave.

"Fuck it. Your expression is making me hate myself. I'm going to thrust all the way in and get it over with." As soon as he warns me, he does just that, driving in all the way.

I gasp and then cry out at the sudden pain.

He grips my face and kisses me all over my cheeks and neck and shoulders and ears, distracting me from the pain.

"So sorry, little blossom," he murmurs in my ear. "It'll feel so much better in a minute."

I don't believe him. I have one hand on his hip, and I'm pushing him to get him off me. I can't breathe.

"Shh," he croons. "Stay still. Relax. Shhhh. You're okay. I promise."

I try to relax and take a breath. Gradually the pain dissipates. I'm fine. I'm okay. I lived. I don't want to do this again, but I'm okay. If he would just get it over with.

Instead of pulling out, he pushes one hand between our bodies and finds my clit. His fingers work the tight little nub, rapidly flicking and pinching and circling it until I can't think about anything else but his touch.

"That's a good girl. Concentrate on my fingers. Let the pressure build."

I'm consumed now. I need to come again. The muscles in

my channel clamp down on Master Roman. I need him to move.

He keeps stroking my clit until I'm so close to orgasm.

When my mouth falls open, he jerks his hand away, pulls his penis part way out, and slams back in.

I scream. Ohgodohgodohgod. That felt so good.

He does it again, and I scream louder, gripping his biceps with both hands, my nightgown still draped over my shoulder between us.

He lowers his body so that my nipples brush against the slight hair on his chest. His expression is a combination of lust, satisfaction, and bliss. As soon as he thrusts into me again though, I can't focus anymore. My eyes roll back as all the blood in my head rushes to my sex.

He's pulling in and out now. Over and over. Faster and harder.

The pressure is building. I'm going to come around his penis. I can't even speak. I can't stop it. I don't want to.

And then I shatter, my orgasm slamming into me, making every nerve ending inside my channel come alive.

Master Roman moans loudly as I scream a second time, my voice echoing in the room.

I close my eyes to savor every second. I wish it could last longer.

Finally, he stops moving. He's kissing me again, everywhere and then on the lips. I can hardly return the kiss, but I try. I'm a limp noodle. My hands have fallen to my sides, useless.

I don't know how he's able to hold himself over me. He would crush me if he didn't, but where is he getting the energy?

I'm shocked when he grabs me around the waist and flips us over so that he lands on his back and I'm draped over his chest. His penis has come out of me. I miss it already.

He palms my head and pulls it against his chest, stroking my back and my bottom with his other hand. "So proud of you, blossom. I'm sorry I caused you pain, but it's over, and now you know."

I certainly do know. I know a lot. I know I want to do that again. As soon as possible.

CHAPTER 43

Master Roman

I relish in the feeling of having Lucy's naked body on top of mine. Warm and sated and soft. She is so precious. I know I caused her some pain, but she was so brave, and in the end, I'm positive she didn't regret the brief discomfort.

I already need her again, but that's not going to happen. Right now, I need to take care of her.

She has relaxed so much that I think she might have fallen asleep, and the thought of her sleeping against me like this makes my heart rate pick up. I won't bring her to my bed of course. It's too risky. But I so wish I could. Thoughts of having her sweet little body curled against mine all night long make me nearly groan.

Finally, I shift, holding her against me as I push us to a sitting position, positioning her on my lap. She is groggy and curls into my chest. "Sir?"

"We need to get you cleaned up and ready for bed, blossom. It's past your bedtime."

She whimpers as I stand her on her feet in front of me. She sways slightly, making me smile.

"Arms up," I state, so I can tug her nightie over her head. Her hair is loose and messy and so sexy. She looks well-fucked, and I like it. I sit her on the couch next to me and then rummage for my jeans, standing to put them on. I'll come back down later and tidy up the room. For now, I need to get my sleepy girl to bed.

She makes a cute little sound when I lift her off the couch and cradle her against me, carrying her out of the room. The house is silent. I know my staff has all gone to bed, so I don't worry about the fact that her bottom is exposed. In fact, I cup her warm cheeks with my hand as I carry her.

She squirms in my arms, her cheek against my shoulder. So fucking adorable.

When I reach her room, I close the door and then continue into the bathroom, not setting her down until I reach the tub. "I'm gonna give you a bath, little blossom. Get you washed up."

I could just grab a washcloth and clean her up, but I'm not ready for our time to end yet. I want to pamper her a bit longer. Plus, her inner thighs are pink from the combination of her come and the remnants of her first time. She needs to soak for a bit or she'll be sore tomorrow.

I let the tub fill while I tug her nightie over her head, baring her sweet body to me once again. God, she is sexy. Every inch of her is perfect.

Mine in every single way now.

My possessiveness has tipped the scales now that I've been inside her. I will never let her go.

I reach for the bands at the ends of her braids and pull them free, unravelling her long hair slowly until it hangs in a wild mess of curls. While I admire the long locks, I grab a band out of her bathroom drawer and gather it on top of her head to keep it dry.

I lift her by the waist and set her in the water.

She whimpers.

"Shhh. Let's get you washed up and then tucked in bed," I croon.

I grab a washcloth, rub soap into it, and begin to wash my girl. She seems shocked for a second, but then she relaxes and lets me pamper her, only stiffening slightly when I wash between her legs.

After rinsing her off, I lift her from the tub, set her on her feet, and pat her dry. Finally, I reluctantly tug her nightie back over her head and lead her to the bedroom. "Climb in, blossom."

She crawls into the bed, but her eyes are wide. "Why can't I sleep in your bed, Sir?" she whispers.

I hope she doesn't notice my flinch. She's so tempting. It would be so easy to carry her to my wing of the house and tuck her into my bed. I'm certain I would sleep better than I have in years. But I won't go there.

I sit on the side of her bed and stroke her cheek. "Little girls need to sleep in their own beds, blossom. That's the rule."

Her bottom lip sticks out in the cutest pout. "I get lonely."

"You won't be lonely for long. You should be sleeping."

She curls onto her side and sighs.

I kiss her temple. "Sleep tight, blossom." It's so hard to leave her, but I do.

After I tidy up the media room downstairs, I head for my office. I can't bring myself to go to my bedroom yet. It will feel empty and too quiet. Half of me wants to bring her to my bed. I want her in my arms. The thought of sleeping alone doesn't seem appealing anymore. I've done so for forty years. Maybe it's time to change that policy?

I lower myself onto my desk chair and remind myself

there are no guarantees here. Just because I've had sex with Lucy doesn't mean she's truly mine. I shudder as I tip my head back and stare at the ceiling. I have secrets. Things that could greatly upset our perfect world if she found out. Eventually, I need to talk to her about the possibility that she might have a brother as well as the nefarious methods I used to get her in my life.

After a few moments, I open my middle desk drawer and pull out the file folder I keep buried under several other files. The tab says "Lucy Neill Private" on it. It's the same file Julius handed me the night Lucy applied to be my assistant. It's a lot thicker than it was that night, however. And today I added the letter that came from her presumed brother.

I read the letter again several times. How did this Daven, who claims to be her brother, find her? Since the letter went to her apartment, it's possible he knows nothing about me. He shouldn't, but I don't trust the situation at all.

I open my computer and send an email to my private investigator. If there's anything to be found about Daven Neill, if that's even his real name, Hersh Wilson will find it.

CHAPTER 44

Lucy

I wake up the following morning energized and happier than I've ever been. I'm no longer a virgin. Master Roman finally made love to me. He made it so perfect, and I vaguely remember him bathing me after he carried me to my room.

When my alarm goes off and I slide out of bed, I wince slightly. My sex is sore, but in a delicious way. A reminder of what we did and what doors are now open for the future. I hope Master Roman puts his penis in me again today. He said he would do so often and that I can also suck on it. He liked that. It made me feel so good when I made him moan and swallowed him.

I grab my pile of clothes and hurry to wash up in the bathroom. After I brush my teeth and wash my face and braid my hair, I put my nightgown down the chute and reach for my pile of clothes. It's Sunday. Master Roman said I won't be working on Sundays, so I'm not sure what he will have me do today, but I'm excited anyway.

I shrug into my panties—yellow with little ducks on them —and then I pick up the pale blue-and-white plaid dress. It's not until I hold it up that I realize it's for a younger girl. The top has intricate smocking with little bunnies embroidered around the rounded neckline. The sleeves are short and puffy with elastic that will circle my arms. It's an A-line cut with no waist. When I put it on, my breasts cause the front to stand out.

It's short, of course, barely covering my panties. I wonder how Master Roman always manages to get the hem exactly right so that I'm nervous but covered. As long as I don't lift my arms.

I stare at myself, concerned. For one thing, I'm worried Master Roman will push me to play at an age younger than I'm comfortable with.

But more importantly, I'm aroused. I'm more aware of my swollen private parts than usual today. And, of course, the smocking is rubbing against my nipples.

I put on the provided white socks and shoes, buckle the sides, and turn to head downstairs.

Footsteps behind me make me turn around to find Nancy heading down the stairs. "Good morning, Lucy. Don't you look pretty today."

"Thank you, ma'am."

"Master Roman is in the library. Why don't you go find him?"

"Yes, ma'am." I continue down the stairs and pad toward the library.

"There you are," Master Roman declares when I enter. "Shut the door, blossom."

I turn to shut the heavy wooden door, knowing this could mean anything, but will undoubtedly involve me exposing myself in the library. I shuffle toward him, my hands linked behind my back, which pushes the dress out in front of me.

He smiles from where he sits on the sofa, reaching out a hand so I'll come to him.

By the time I reach him, my panties are wet. I love the way he looks at me, and the twinkle in his eye is even more defined today. I hope that's because I pleased him last night.

He wraps an arm around my thighs and pulls me between his legs, his hand landing on my bottom under my dress in a way I've come to realize is intentional and something he very much enjoys. "Is your pussy sore this morning, blossom?"

I flush at his words, a little shocked he would go there already. "No, Sir. Not really."

He's holding a folder, and he hands it to me, nodding that I should open it.

I do, baffled. Inside is a single sheet of paper with the official logo of the doctor's office I visited before I started working for him. For a moment I worry that the letter is about me, and then I see it's addressed to Master Roman. I scan down the page. "What is this, Sir?"

"It's my medical record showing you that I've recently been cleared of all communicable diseases. I wanted you to see it before I take you bare."

I'm confused for a moment, and then I understand. He doesn't want to use condoms with me. I like that. I want to feel him bare inside me. "Thank you, Sir." My hands are shaking as I hand the folder to him.

He drops it on the floor, rises from his seat, and lifts me by the waist, hitching me up to carry me across the room.

I giggle as I wrap my legs around his hips and hold on to his neck.

When he reaches his desk, he sets me on top of it. It's extremely large, mahogany with a glass top. It's also devoid of any papers or books at the moment, so when Master Roman lowers me onto my back, nothing is in the way.

The glass top is cool against my arms and thighs.

Without a word, Master Roman hooks his fingers in my yellow panties and pulls them down my legs. I have to lift my bottom a bit for him to accomplish this task, but as soon as he sets them on the desk, he pushes my knees up and spreads them wide.

I know we had sex last night, and he's also seen every inch of me naked. Nevertheless, I feel obscenely exposed as he lowers his gaze to my private parts.

Instinctively, I lower my hand between my legs. Master Roman grabs my wrist and sets my hand above my head. He doesn't meet my gaze as he pushes my smocked dress up over my chest. And then he has both hands on my thighs, spreading my lower lips and prodding my tender, swollen skin.

I moan.

"Not sore, huh?" he asks.

"No, Sir," I murmur. I wouldn't tell him I was sore even if I were.

He keeps inspecting me, touching me everywhere, tapping my clit and dragging my wetness up to circle it.

I watch his face until he surprises me again by lowering his head to kiss my private parts.

I suck in a breath as his lips touch me down there, a breath that turns into a gasp when he drags his tongue through my folds and flicks it over my clit. My bottom would have shot off the desk if he hadn't been holding me down.

"Be a good girl and let me make you feel good, blossom."

My head rolls to the side. I fist my hands, one above my head, the other at my side.

He strokes my tender skin with his thumbs, driving me bananas. "That's a good girl. Don't move."

I hold my breath as he lowers his mouth again. He seems to lick every inch of me before suddenly sucking my sex into his mouth.

BECCA JAMESON

I cry out. It feels so good. I had no idea.

He's relentless too, pushing me higher and higher with his sucking and whatever he's doing with his tongue against my clit. In seconds, I'm close to orgasm, and I know it's going to be one of the strongest I've ever experienced.

Without warning, his mouth is gone, and he releases me.

My knees draw partly together as I whimper. "Sir..." I beg. I'll die if he doesn't let me come. I tip my head to see him unbuttoning his pants and lowering the zipper.

When his penis pops free, engorged and bobbing in front of him, I lick my lips. I want to taste him again, but I'm not sure I could even get my mouth to work properly considering the way he's left me wanting.

He grabs my waist again, leaning over me. "Wrap your hands around my neck, blossom."

I do as he asks, loving the way his erection rubs against my heated skin.

As he backs up in a return to the sofa, I wrap my legs around him again, pressing my swollen folds against his hard length.

Master Roman lowers himself to sitting on the sofa. "Plant your feet next to my thighs, blossom, and ride my cock. I can't think this morning until I've been inside you. Naked. Raw." He cups my face as he speaks, forcing me to meet his gaze.

Ride him? I have no experience with this, and I feel awkward.

He smiles. "You can control the speed and depth in this position. I don't want to rush to thrust into you this morning. Your cunt is going to be sore."

My desperation to have him inside me emboldens me to lift my bottom.

He lines his penis up with my opening, and I lower onto him. My dress flares out around me, blocking the view, hiding our love making.

272

My eyes roll back at the stretch. Nothing hurts. Pure, intense, all-consuming pleasure. I moan loudly when I'm fully seated, instinctively grinding my clit against the base of his erection.

"God, Lucy. You have no idea how good that feels…" His voice is tight, and it trails off.

I search his face, but his eyes are closed, his mouth open. Once again, I realize what power I have over him when he takes out his penis. Will it always be this way?

I lift almost off him and slam back down. I'm going to come. Soon. I was so close from his mouth already.

He cups my bottom, his fingers digging into my flesh. "Fuck me…" It's not a demand. It's more of an exclamation of shock. But I speed up as if he's instructed me to. He gasps, his lips parting.

I squeeze my eyes shut, the need building. I'm going to come around his penis, any second. He starts to lift his hips into me, helping me, increasing the friction.

I scream out as my body convulses around him, my channel throbbing. I dig the tip of my fingers into his shoulders, my breasts bouncing under my dress, the smocking rubbing them to stiff points.

Seconds later, a rumble leaves his chest, and I know he's coming inside me. He grips my waist and holds me down, keeping himself deep as his erection pulses inside my channel.

When he's spent, we are both panting, and then his hands are on my face and he kisses me all over my cheeks and neck until his lips find mine and deepen the kiss into something far more intimate and sweet.

I'm still gasping when he releases my lips. "I think I'll like this addition to our relationship," he states.

My face is heated, but I smile. "Me too, Sir."

I wince as he lifts me off his erection and sets me on my

feet. "Don't move." He stands, zips himself back into his pants, and then pads across the room.

When he returns, he has my panties in his hand. His orgasm is running down my thighs. He crouches in front of me. "Step in, blossom."

I balance myself with my hands on his shoulders as I lift first one foot and then the other. I'm mortified as he drags my panties up my thighs, his come catching in the elastic until he has them tugged over my hips, fully in place. He presses his palm against the crotch of my panties, soaking them with his come.

I'm shaking. My panties are dripping wet as he stands.

He cups my face and kisses my nose. "You aren't permitted to wash my come off you this morning, blossom. I want you to feel me up inside you and drying on your legs. I want you to remember who you belong to all morning. I'll clean you up before your nap after lunch. Understood?"

"Yes, Sir." My voice quivers. I'm so turned on. The thought of going to breakfast with my panties soaked with his come makes my face heat. I'll leave a wet spot on the chair. What if Evelyn sees it?

Master Roman pats my bottom. "Go eat your breakfast, blossom. If you're a good girl, I'll take you out to the backyard this morning. You can play outside for a while."

"Yes, Sir." My face feels warmer than ever as I step away from him. His come is dripping down my legs, oozing from the sides of my panties. It's so naughty. And so arousing.

CHAPTER 45

Master Roman

It's been two weeks since I first entered Lucy's sweet cunt. Two weeks since she agreed to start studying so she can take the SAT. Two weeks since I contacted the PI...

I'm reading another email from him now. He easily tracked down the man in question. He indeed lives in rural Missouri. Daven Neill is his real name. Hersh is certain Daven's father is the same man who fathered Lucy. Their birth certificates match. Charles Neill fathered Daven out of wedlock and left Daven's mother before Daven was even born.

Daven never met his father. It appears Charles never paid a dime of child support and Daven's mother, Katherine, never pursued Charles. "Probably because the man was an asshole, and Katherine was glad to be rid of him," I mutter under my breath.

Daven is ten years older than Lucy. He lives in rural Missouri. His farm is deep in debt. He's close to foreclosure.

Katherine indeed died a few months ago, so it's believable that Daven found information about his father and half sister after her death.

I lean back in my chair and inhale deeply. I should tell Lucy. I really must. Keeping this from her is unconscionable. But I can't shake the feeling that this man's timing is impeccable. Until a month ago, Lucy had nothing to offer him. I'm suspicious. Even though I can easily see the death certificate for his mother, I'm mistrustful. There is no proof that Daven hasn't always known about Lucy and kept tabs on her. He could have found out about me and decided to profit from her newfound wealth.

If he does know about me, he's not wrong. Lucy does have newfound wealth. I'd give her anything in the world. If it made her happy, I'd save her brother's farm.

What I don't know is Daven's character, and his intentions where Lucy is concerned. She's fragile. Lucy would be devastated if she found out she had a brother and he turned out to be as disappointing as every other blood relative. I can't take the risk. Not right now. Not while she's focused on studying and getting into college.

I'll wait. At least until after she takes the SAT.

I glance toward the door to her office. I can't see her. She's been in there studying for hours. It's time for her to take a break.

CHAPTER 46

Lucy

"Lucy."

That one word, spoken as a harsh reprimand, makes me freeze. I recognize the tone. I've heard it often enough in the last month. I slowly lift my gaze to the door to my playroom and find Master Roman strolling toward me, hands on his hips.

"Is there something wrong with your dress, Lucy?"

"No, Sir." I put my hands in my lap.

"Then how come every time I enter this room, I find you fidgeting with the material instead of studying?" He sets his hand on my little desk, the one he bought me almost two weeks ago after we first had sex. It's small, the size used in middle school. It's just my size since I didn't get much taller after seventh grade.

I'm wearing a pale blue frilly dress that has white lace around the poofy sleeves, the neckline, and around the hem. It doesn't have a waistline. It does have several layers of tulle under it. It's not remotely age appropriate. In fact, it's more suitable for a toddler. It doesn't come even close to covering my bottom, and I'm wearing matching frilly, poofy bottoms over my panties. My socks are also ruffled, and my white patent leather shoes have buckles across the top of my feet.

I've gotten used to the fact that I never know what Master Roman might choose for me to wear each day. Most days he dresses me as a twelve-year-old, but he likes to surprise me now and then and dress me as someone much younger. He still treats me as a middle no matter what I wear, but he watches me closely on the days he experiments. I think he's making sure he keeps things interesting and also probably double checking my headspace.

I'm pretty solid as a middle. It suits me. I have no interest in behaving like a baby, a toddler, or even an older child. I like that I have knowledge and the ability to do most anything even in the role. It's liberating to be too young to make my own decisions, but old enough to hold a conversation without breaking the constant scene.

The truth is that the tulle under my dress is touching my nipples—which he knows—and driving me bonkers. He hasn't let me come yet today, and my panties have been soaked since I put the dress on. It may be too young for me, but I'm aroused anyway.

I'm supposed to be studying this morning. We have an agreement. If I study for three hours every morning, I get to play for an hour before lunch, and then I work for him as his assistant after my nap. He has not relented about me having a nap, and I've gotten used to the time alone.

"You're supposed to finish that section of math so I can check your work. How many problems have you done?"

I glance down. I've done twelve out of fifty problems. I haven't been able to concentrate. He knows this. It's why he's hovering over me. He planned this.

He doesn't wait for me to answer. "You have two weeks until the SAT test. If you don't study, you'll end up having to take it again. And that's fine. But if you don't score well enough on it, you also can't start classes next semester."

I nod. "I'm sorry, Sir. I'll try to focus."

"I know you will, because I'm going to give you an incentive."

For a moment, I think he's going to offer me ice cream or cookies after lunch if I get all my math done. But I'm so very wrong.

Instead, he comes around my desk. "Stand up."

I slowly come to my feet, facing him.

"Arms in the air."

Yeah, I'm in trouble. He rarely makes me strip in the playroom. I lift my arms. He hauls my dress over my head. After setting it on my beanbag chair, he turns around and faces me, pulling something out of his pants pocket.

I'm extremely nervous, more than I have been in several days. I glance at the floor-to-ceiling windows, even though he's told me over and over that no one can see in. Not even if they plaster their face to the glass. It's still weird being naked in my playroom.

In addition, I constantly worry that someone will walk in. They won't, of course. Master Roman is meticulous about who comes in and how far they advance toward his desk. I might hear voices, but no one ventures close enough to see me around the corner.

"Don't slouch, Lucy."

I'm hunching a bit because I'm so exposed. I'm still wearing the ruffled bloomers that make me look like I should have a diaper underneath. In truth, they are a diaper cover. I know this. Between those and my baby shoes, I now look like I must have spilled something on my dress. Except my breasts are not flat.

Master Roman lifts up something that looks like hoop earrings. I don't have pierced ears. I never have. I've even asked Master Roman if I can get them, but he's told me I'm too young. Maybe when I'm older.

For half a second, I think he's going to let me get my ears pierced. That's the surprise.

He shakes his head. "These are not earrings, Lucy. They go on your little titties."

I freeze. I should have known. I've seen them in books and read about them. I'm not remotely interested in wearing them. I take a step back.

He shakes his head. "How many times a day do I have to tell you to stop fussing with your titties, Lucy?"

I swallow. "I'm sorry, Sir. They rub against my clothes." If he would give me a bra…

"And you need to learn to control your impulse to squirm. That's going to start now." He reaches for one of my nipples and tugs it, pinching and twisting it until my panties are soaked and I think my knees will give out. When he has the tip hard and engorged, he quickly clamps one of the hoops on my raw flesh. It grips my nipple on both sides. Obscenely.

I bite my lip, trying not to cry. While I'm fighting the urge, he grabs the other nipple and treats it the same, pinching hard and then pulling it toward him until he's pleased with how swollen it is. That's when he clamps it to match its twin.

I'm used to how rough he is with my breasts. He's gotten rougher every day because my reaction pleases him. It hurts, but it also makes me extremely aroused. He says I have a nipple fetish. I think he's right.

"You can sit down now." He points at my chair. "The clamps stay until you have ten more problems done. Don't move and you'll get used to the sting. If you squirm, you won't be able to focus. The longer they stay on, the worse it's going

to hurt when I remove them. If you think I'm kidding, try me."
His brows are furrowed.

"Yes, Sir." I sit very still. My nipples are throbbing. I don't
know how I will concentrate on math. It's not like I've never
done these problems. It's just been a while. I was an excellent
student, but I need a refresher before I can take the SATs and I
can't apply for the local university until I have those scores.

I'm motivated because I've grown increasingly excited
about going to school since the day Master Roman mentioned
it. But he makes it very hard to study. On purpose. He's
training me to do better and learn to focus with distractions.
Distractions being tormenting my titties, as he crudely refers
to them.

I force myself to focus on my math problems, distracted
not just by the pain that is slowly ebbing, but the fact that I
can't look down without seeing my poor swollen offended
nipples.

I work fast, finishing in fifteen minutes. I'm not allowed to
raise my voice to yell or call out to Master Roman, so I have to
rise from my chair and gingerly cross the room. I stop in the
doorway, relieved to have arrived. The jiggling was almost
more than I could bear. I hold up my paper. "Sir? I finished." I
don't enter the room. It's my only form of protection. That
doorway and my playroom. My haven.

"Good girl. Come here."

I pray he's shut the door and am relieved to see he has
when I step into his office.

"Let me look it over. You rushed through your work. If
you were sloppy, I'll send you back." He takes the paper from
my hand, and I wait next to his desk, arms clasped behind my
back as I've been taught.

It takes him forever to examine my math. Finally, he smiles
at me. "Good job, blossom. See what you can do when you
concentrate?"

"Yes, Sir." I'm trying not to move. Even speaking draws my attention to my aching nipples. Breathing is a chore.

He faces me. "I'm going to remove them both at the same time. The pain will be sharp." He pops them both off at once, and I cry out. Seconds later, his fingers are rubbing my offended flesh. He even leans in to suckle one and then the other.

Finally, he pulls me closer. "I know that was hard, blossom. I'm proud of you. I'm sure your panties are soaked, but I'm not going to reward you by letting you come. Go put your dress back on and see what Evelyn's made you for lunch. If you don't want to wear those clamps on your titties again today, you'll think twice about fidgeting after your nap."

"Yes, Sir."

He swats my bottom. "Go on."

CHAPTER 47

Lucy

Two days before my SATs, I'm sitting at my adult desk, hurrying to get eight hours of work done in four. It's what I do every day. I won't let up or relent because I don't want Master Roman to hire someone to replace me. I like being near him every day. I like that he takes breaks in the mornings while I'm studying to play with me and tickle me and sometimes even let me orgasm under my dress.

Usually he rubs me over my panties because he is truly stunned that I'm sensitive enough to come day after day through the cotton barrier.

I love that he does this to me. When I'm fully clothed in whatever scandalous outfit he's chosen that day, my sex drive goes through the roof. I get off faster while I'm in my little girl outfits than when I'm naked.

He knows this. He knows everything.

He also lets me come at night most of the time. If I've been a good girl, when he tucks me in, he pulls my comforter down, pushes my babygirl nightie over my chest and rubs my pussy until I scream.

We have sex too. Not every day, but most days. Sometimes we have sex at his desk. Sometimes in my playroom. Up against the wall. On my desk. On my beanbag chair. We've had a few movie nights too that always end with his penis deliciously filling me.

What we don't do is have sex in my bedroom. And to this day, I have not even seen Master Roman's bedroom. I've never been permitted to go anywhere else on the second floor.

I've asked him about this on three occasions. Every time he has flatly denied my request. He says I need my sleep and my alone time in my own little girl room. My special place where I get to be alone for a few hours before he tucks me in. He says he wouldn't be able to keep from mauling me all night if I were in his bed. He's adamant about this point. I haven't asked for over a week.

I love being his cherry blossom, and my life is almost perfect, but I hope I can wear him down on this issue eventually. I want to sleep in his arms at night. At least sometimes. Why does he turn me down? It feels like a rejection, and it hurts deep in my heart every time he reiterates that policy.

I have another concern I haven't voiced, and that's about school. He wants me to go to college. He's the one who brought it up. Made me think. Offered to pay for it. Has arranged for me to have everything I need to study for my SATs.

I'm grateful, but I worry I have another battle on my hands. Master Roman wants me to take online classes, at least at first. The problem is that I picture myself on campus with people my age, learning and laughing and living.

Meanwhile, I realize Master Roman pictures me working

alone in my office, studying on my computer, taking online classes.

This doesn't appeal to me, and I have no idea how to broach the subject. All I know is that it isn't worth going to bat over until I know if I even have the scores to get in.

"Lucy."

I jerk my gaze up and to the left to find Master Roman standing in the doorway. I've been daydreaming and fretting for I don't know how long. I need to get my work done.

If he knows this, he doesn't let on. "I have a meeting with a client across town. I'll be gone for a few hours. Will you be okay?"

I nod. "Yes. Of course, Sir."

"There's a pile of things on my desk that need to be filed or mailed. Can you grab them?"

"Yep."

He lifts a brow. Every once in a while, I slip up and respond to him in disrespectful slang. "I mean, yes. Sorry, Sir."

"Come here." He doesn't move. He likes to make me come to him. It's a way he exercises his dominance. I never hesitate or complain. I like going to him also.

I stand, instantly aware of my traitorous nipples that have never stopped driving me to distraction in the many weeks since I've last worn a bra. I don't think I'll ever get used to the sensation. And Master Roman obviously intends to ensure I do not by insisting I wear blouses, shirts, and dresses that bring attention to my always sensitive titties.

The word he uses for my breasts has practically imbedded itself in my mind now. Every time I hear or think the word, I slide into a deeper level of submission. It's instantaneous. My panties get wet, and my nipples stiffen.

I come to his side quickly. Today I'm wearing a white cotton tank top dress. White is the worst of all the colors Master Roman chooses for me. I've never said a word, but I suspect he knows. He can read me better than I can and usually knows what I'm thinking or feeling even before I do.

White is pure and youthful. It is also more revealing. The material used to make my clothes is usually thin, which means everyone can see not only the outline of my breasts against the tight T-shirt material, but the color and pucker of my nipples also.

Making things worse, Master Roman almost always chooses colored panties for me so that they are obvious through the skirt, and he likes to spend those particular days tormenting my breasts in the morning so that I have to go to lunch with swollen, erect nipples.

When I reach him, he dips down to wrap his arm around my thighs and lift me into the air. His hand rests on my bottom under my dress.

I giggle. I love it when he cuddles me. I love every type of attention he gives me.

"Kiss me like you mean it, blossom."

I bring my lips to his and kiss him with all the lust I feel, making sure he knows it. He's worked with me, teaching me to kiss him just the way he likes. With tongue and lips and passion. I enjoy it as much as he does.

As he slowly lowers me to the floor, my dress rises up my body, exposing my panties and my midriff. I shiver.

"I'll be back soon. Let's have a quiet dinner together." He lets go of my waist and reaches to tweak one of my obvious nipples. I giggle again. "If you're a good girl and you have all your studying and work done, I'll let you ride my cock after dinner."

I smile. "I'll be good, Sir. I promise." My panties are wet now, of course. It's going to take me a while to get my heart rate down before I can resume working.

"Good girl." He swats my bottom and turns to leave.

I step into his office and watch him exit the room with

sure steps, his height and size and broad shoulders making me drool. I'll never get enough of him. I haven't said the words yet, but I love him so much.

There's something else I haven't said to him yet. I'm holding back. I don't know what I'm waiting for, but I think it has to do with him letting me the rest of the way in. Into his bed and his room and his private space. I need that.

I know I need to ask for what I want, but I don't want to rock the boat right now when things are going so well. I'll wait until after I take the SATs. After we've hashed out my desire to go to school on campus. After he finds out I crave those hours each day in public with adult clothes on.

I know it will hurt him. I know he wants to keep me locked up in his mansion for the rest of my life, his special little girl. And I love being his. I love how he cherishes me. I love how he dotes on me and how connected we are and how in tune we are with each other and how our needs mesh and how I can be myself with him and how he thrives on my age play. I love all of that. But I want more.

The question is, can Master negotiate something we can both live with? I'm afraid he will see my independence as me pulling away from him. He'll worry I might leave him. He'll fret all the time that I might meet someone else.

But that doesn't change the fact that I have to confront him and voice my desires.

Later, I remind myself. After the SATs. After all, if my scores aren't good enough to get into the university, our probable disagreement would have been for naught.

CHAPTER 48

Lucy

After grabbing the pile of folders off Master Roman's desk, I settle at my own desk and take several deep breaths to chase my arousal and my middle role to the back of my mind. I've gotten good at compartmentalizing. I'm a pro. Most of the time.

I realize the top few files in the pile I've picked up actually belong in Master Roman's desk. He's never had me deal with his personal files, but I recognize them because the tabs are blue instead of red.

I rise from my desk and head back to his office. He wouldn't have included the additional folders if he hadn't intended for me to file them. When I open the deep drawer on his desk, I realize I'm going to need to familiarize myself with the system he's using here. I scan the files to figure out if they are alphabetical or organized in another way.

Suddenly, the tab on one of the files catches my attention.

Lucy Neill. Private.

I stare at it for a moment, wondering why he has a file on me. After a second, I chase away my concerns. It's probably medical records from my visit to the doctor. My school transcripts he's requested so I can apply for college. Stuff like that.

Curiosity eats at me though, urging me to see what information he's got on me.

Against my better judgment, I pull the folder from the drawer and open it. It's thicker than I thought. The page on top is a handwritten note. It says,

Roman,

I hope you know what you're doing. You're messing with a woman's life.

Nevertheless, this is what the PI has been able to find on Lucy Neill. Her past is clean as a whistle. No prior arrests or even a traffic ticket. She doesn't even have a driver's license. No living relatives. Her last residence was with a maternal grandmother in Chicago. She died a year ago.

Be careful. You're playing with fire on this one. That girl is sweet and innocent. I hope you know what you're doing before you mold her to fit your expectations. If you hurt her, you'll regret it for the rest of your life.

Julius

I can't breathe. My legs are shaking so badly that I have to back up and sit down before I fall. I set the folder on the desk and move the note to the side so I can see what else is in this folder. I no longer feel any remorse or hesitation. I shuffle quickly through the pages.

My life. Everything. Every detail.

My childhood home and address and school.

My grandmother's information. My grandmother is dead? I didn't even know that. Apparently Master Roman did. Fuck him.

My medical records going back for years. Medications. Copies of receipts. Every personal detail about me.

When I get to the piles of pictures of the inside of my apartment, my throat drops. I'm going to be sick. He was in my apartment. He went through my belongings. He stole information from me.

There are details about Martin and Sons. My vision swims when I realize he paid them to fire me. There are detailed notes about his conversations with them. He's even included a receipt showing how much he bought me out for. Why would he do that?

Duh, to make it so I was in need of a job and would apply to work for him.

My God. He had me fired. I try to process that detail.

He manipulated me into accepting a job with him and took over my life and moved me into his home and dressed me up the way he wanted me and touched me. He fucked me. He put his cock inside me.

I flip to the next page. A handwritten letter on notebook paper. Odd. I blink several times as I read it. It's a letter to me from someone claiming to be my half brother. I'm shaking as I read it again. Where did this come from? When? What the fuck is happening here?

I grab the folder and throw it across the room. The papers fly all over the place. I've never been so angry. So violated.

I run from the room, down the hall, and up the back stairs. Before I enter my bedroom, I pause to listen. No one is up here. I can't hear a sound. I think Nancy and Evelyn were going shopping. Weston might have taken them.

I spin around, hell-bent on seeing the rest of this floor in Master Roman's house. I run down the forbidden hallway and around a corner. There are two more wings. So many doors. I race down one, opening every door. Most are guest rooms. Bathrooms. Empty rooms even.

Finally, I come to a set of double doors and know this room is Master Roman's. I yank on the handle, stunned to find it unlocked.

When I enter, I let my gaze roam all around the space first.

It's an ordinary bedroom. Was I expecting a dungeon or something?

The bed is king-sized and four-posted. The comforter is a deep navy blue. The bed is made. Everything is in its place as if no one has ever set foot in the room. In fact, the carpet has been recently vacuumed.

I scuff at it furiously with my toes, hating Roman—if that's even his name—and everything about him. Fuck his perfect room. I turn toward his dresser and open it. Underwear in the top one. T-shirts next. Socks. White and then dark colors. I abandon the dresser to open his closet. It's an enormous walk-in.

No, it's bigger than my bedroom. The left side is lined with suits and dress slacks separated by colors and shades. The right side stops me dead in my tracks. I can't breathe.

It's my side.

It's filled with my clothes. The ones he dresses me in every day. All my pretty little-girl outfits. I can't bring myself to touch them, but I wander down the row, realizing they are in order of age. The first ones are for newborns and they progress all the way up to my current age, twelve. Nothing beyond that.

Some of them I've seen several times. Others I've never been presented with. The first few make me cringe. Onesies and footed pajamas. Baby mittens. Booties. All in my size.

I turn from this shrine and rush toward his bathroom. It's also pristine, like no one's ever been in it. The bathtub makes me drool. It's large enough to hold two people comfortably. They wouldn't even have to touch. It has jets too.

The shower is a walk-in. No doors. I'm jealous. No, I'm pissed. Why has he kept me on another wing all alone in a small little-girl room with a tub that doesn't even have a shower?

So many questions.

I rummage through the drawers under the vanity. Two sinks. Empty drawers. Just one has his razor and toothbrush and a comb.

Why?

Why, why, why?

I run out of this room. I need to get out of his house as fast as I can. Before anyone gets home. I run back to my designated wing, the only space I'm permitted to see. I enter the room I have loved for all these weeks and head straight for the closet. It's locked. I yank on it. It won't budge. Are my personal belongings in there?

"Lucy?"

I jump and spin around at the sound of Weston's voice from a bit of a distance.

"Lucy? Are you in your room?" He's getting closer.

I spin around. There is nothing in this room I can use to cover myself. I haven't liked exposing myself to Weston ever. I'm way too pissed right now to confront him.

I finally yank back the comforter and tug the sheet off the bed. I'm grateful that it's white this week. I hug it to my chest and lunge for the bathroom, shutting myself inside and locking the door just as he knocks on my bedroom door.

I'm gasping for breath. My heart is pounding. My ears are ringing. I've never been so angry in my life.

On top of everything else, I'm kind of trapped here. I have nothing. I can't just leave. I have no clothes. I would get picked up and put in a mental ward if anyone caught me wandering the streets in this outfit meant for a child.

What was I thinking letting someone take over my life, move me into their home, cut me off from the world? I'm so stupid.

"Lucy? Honey, what's going on?" Weston sounds panicked. Has he already called Roman?

I yank the pink fluffy towel off the rack and throw it down the chute. I don't want to look at it. I don't want to look at anything.

I need to think. I need a plan. And fast.

I wonder if Roman will keep me here against my will? Are all of his employees accomplices? Surely four people can't hold a woman hostage and get away with it.

Then again, I have no one. I have no family. No friends. No one. Not a single soul knows I even exist. Or maybe that isn't even true. Maybe I have a half brother. I can't even process that thought. I could die in this house and no one would ever look for my body. Is that why he picked me?

I wrap the sheet around my shaking body and climb into the tub, curling up on one end, trying to think. My brain is rushing around. It's a hurricane in there. I can't think. I can't catch my breath. I'm going to faint or vomit or have a stroke or a heart attack.

I tuck my head between my knees and try to draw in oxygen.

"Lucy, are you sick?"

I ignore Weston. He's the least of my concerns. He's feeble enough that I could get by him without issue and escape. But that presumes no one else is home. He must have seen me on the monitors, running around upstairs like a crazy woman. Which I am.

I close my eyes, trying to come up with a plan. Any plan.

I have no money. No clothes.

Everything I've believed to be true for weeks has been a lie. I can't stop the tears that begin to fall.

Was this all a game? A plot to find some petite young woman who looked like a girl and train her to be a little? Is Roman that devious? If he's sick in the head, why do so many people go along with it?

I stiffen at my next thought. How many women has he kept in this mansion? In this bedroom? Kept as his little girl?

Tears run down my face. I trusted him. I turned my life over to him. I let him manipulate me into his pet project.

I'm sobbing now. And I know that isn't entirely true. I wanted this. I craved it. Did he see me in his club and figure out I was a good target? He could have. I spent a lot of time watching other people play. If he saw me watching littles with their Doms, he would have easily suspected I was fair prey.

I squeeze my eyes shut. A wealthy businessman who owns a club surely doesn't kidnap women and hold them against their will. It paralyzes me to think that way.

I slide down into the tub in a fetal position, the sheet tight around my trembling body. I can't come up with any viable options. Now that I've figured out what a con man Roman is, what will he do to me when he gets home?

I don't move. I can't. I concentrate on breathing. It's all I can do.

CHAPTER 49

Lucy

I'm not sure how much time passes, but I flinch when I hear Roman's voice through the door. "Lucy? Blossom. Can you open the door?" His voice is high-pitched. Frantic. Good. Let him suffer. He's destroyed me. He can go fuck himself.

I hear other voices. I think one of them is Julius. The others are Nancy and Evelyn. They're mumbling.

"Lucy, at least answer me so I'll know you're okay."

"Fuck you," I state loud enough for him to hear.

There is no response.

"Dude, I told you this would bite you in the ass. You wouldn't listen." Yep. That's Julius. The accomplice. Does he always help his friends kidnap women?

"Shut up, Julius. I need your help, not your criticism. Call Claudia."

"Sure. That'll help." I hear the sarcasm in Julius's voice. Good. Fuck them both.

"Lucy," Roman says again. "Can we at least talk? Please. I fucked up. I'm sorry. Please give me a chance to explain."

At least he obviously knows what I've found.

"Fuck you, Roman. What I need is some motherfucking adult clothes. Let me leave. That's all I want." My ID and credit card are in the drawer in the bathroom still.

I hear his breath hitch even through the door. "Lucy, please. I don't want you to leave. I want you to let me explain."

"Explain what? Explain how you got me fired and took over my life and moved me into your home and cut me off from the world and turned me into your pet project? How you picked a petite woman who was small enough to be a girl and naïve and stupid and innocent? Someone no one would ever miss? How long were you planning to keep me here? A decade? Two? The rest of my life? Until you got tired of fucking me?"

I'm on a roll here. My voice rises. I'm fucking furious. "How many other women have fallen for this? How many have stayed in this room? How many have submitted to you and let you parent them and take over their lives? How long did they last? Were they small like me? Did they have families?"

I'm shaking and screaming, and I doubt anyone can even understand me, but I can't stop. I can't. I have to get it all out. "Did you let anyone else sleep in your bed? Use your fucking bathtub? Did other women wear the same clothes as me? Do you keep those for all your littles? Do you only kidnap girls my same size and stature? What the fuck do you want from me?"

I don't think I've ever used the word fuck in my life. It's getting easier. It's flowing off my lips. It's appropriate.

"Who is Daven? When did you get that letter? Why would you keep something like that from me? Fuck you."

I'm sobbing hard. Tears are running down my face. I don't

have the energy to continue. I just want one outfit so I can leave this fucking mansion and never look back. Hell, I don't even fucking need clothes. I just want to walk away.

I can't catch my breath. I'm crying so hard. I'm scared and shaking and even cold in this bathtub with this sheet. I kick off my shoes and throw them at the door one at a time. I peel off my socks next. I'm out of energy though, and I don't want to be naked when someone inevitably breaks down this door.

I close my eyes and tuck my head against my knees again. And then I wait. Eventually Roman will have to come in. What he does with me next is out of my control. I'm not strong enough to fight him.

I'm so freaked out that it's hard to remind myself that obviously he's not going to hurt me. It's not logical.

I hear a noise. The doorknob. It clicks a few times, and then it opens. Of course. Duh. A key.

I don't lift my head to look.

When the door shuts seconds later, I'm too exhausted to care.

"Lucy, hon. It's Claudia."

I'm kind of shocked, but I don't move a muscle.

"I'm just going to climb in there with you so we can talk, okay?"

Climb into the tub with me? What? Why?

I hear two soft thuds. Her shoes. And then I sense her stepping into the tub. She's on the other end. I'm in such a tight ball that there is plenty of room. She doesn't touch me.

For several minutes we sit there in silence.

Finally, I speak in a low voice. I don't want Roman to hear me. I'm sure he's right outside the door. "I want some clothes. That's all. Will he let me leave?" My voice is strained.

"Honey, you're not a prisoner here. You can definitely leave anytime you want, but I think you should hear what Roman has to say first. I know you're hurt right now. I totally understand. And it's possible the damage is insurmountable. But maybe we could talk for a bit and I can help you better understand where Roman's coming from. Yeah?"

I don't see how that's possible. I also don't see how I have a choice. I say nothing.

"You're hurting. You have every right. What Roman did was wrong. I know that. You know it. But his intentions were pure. I promise you."

I sniffle.

She pauses and then continues. "I've known Roman for twenty years. We met in college. He and Julius were at a club together. I was there. We started talking. They both hit on me. And then I told them I was a Domme. That was the last time they tried to dominate me." She chuckles lightly.

I cringe. This is not funny.

"Sorry." She sighs. "Anyway, Roman has spent his entire adult life looking for you. He's known he wanted someone exactly like you since before you were probably born. I used to think he would never find the right woman to be his little girl. Now I know why he was so lonely for so long. He had to wait for you to grow up."

I squeeze my knees closer, not lifting my head. I have yet to look at her.

"Julius and I have both been pleasantly surprised by how relaxed he's been since you came into his life. I've never seen him smile this much. He has never given any other woman even a full evening of his time."

I flinch.

"I'm serious. I know you have about a thousand questions. I heard some of the list before I came in, but what you need to know is that he loves you so much that he will let you walk out the door right now without a word if you insist. He set some clothes in a pile outside the door. If you want me to grab them and let you dress, I will. If you want me to take you somewhere, I'll do that too. You don't even have to see him first. We can go right out the back door if you want."

I lift my gaze. New tears are falling. I'm so uncertain about so many things. I know she speaks the truth, but is it enough? Can I ever forgive him for getting me fired and luring me into his life and keeping things from me, including the fact that I apparently have a brother?

Claudia stands and climbs out of the tub. She picks up her heels, and I notice for the first time that she's in a pencil skirt and gorgeous deep purple blouse. She looks perfect, just like the last time I saw her.

She smiles down at me. "Do you think you could give him a chance to explain himself? Maybe he could come in? I'll wait right outside the door. If you decide you want to leave at any time, you could yell my name."

I inhale slowly and nod. It's obvious I'm going to have to let him speak his piece. Might as well get it over with.

CHAPTER 50

Lucy

A few moments after Claudia slips from the room, Roman
fills the doorway. I've lowered my face. My chin is on my
knees again. I don't acknowledge him.

He eases into the small space and sits on the toilet. For
several moments, he says nothing and then he takes a deep
breath and speaks, his voice low and soft. "The first night you
stepped into Surrender, I nearly swallowed my tongue. I
knew. Even though my friends tried to tell me I was crazy and
that no one could possibly be that certain, they were wrong. I
knew. I knew you were it for me."

I want to point out that he has a funny way of showing it,
but I purse my lips instead, keeping my face down.

"I followed you around the club that first night, shaking. I
wanted to approach you, but I held back. I was scared out of
my mind that you might not return. Even though I don't
frequent the club as much as I used to, I did that month. Every
second the club was open, I was there. Waiting. Praying you

would come back. And then you did. Every Friday. And I knew the clock was ticking. I knew I had to do something. Anything to capture your attention before your six visits were up."

Everything he is saying rings true. In fact, my heart rate slows as I picture him frantically trying to figure out how to approach me. I can totally see it in my head. When he wants something, he gets a little crazed about it. It's exactly why I haven't told him I want to go to school. I worry about the nervous, jealous, fearful, possessive, insecure side of him he tries to hide. The man who took so long to have sex with me because he was afraid I would destroy him if I left. That is the man sitting on the toilet baring his soul.

He continues. "I made some poor choices. Julius and Claudia told me I was crazy. I wouldn't listen. I insisted you were it for me. So I dug into your life. I know it was nefarious, but my intention was to know enough about you to figure out how to get you to see me."

"You got me fired," I finally interject without lifting my gaze. That part is unforgivable.

"Yeah. I did. That wasn't my finest hour. I couldn't figure out how to make sure you would give me a chance. I justified it in my mind by making sure my offer was much better and providing you with more benefits. Every dime of your fulltime salary, overtime, and the severance pay we discussed is in your account. It's yours. I can't take it back.

"Before you moved in here, I got you a new apartment. I've been paying the rent on it all this time. It's next to the university. All your things are there. Every single item from your other place. In addition, I added new furniture. A better bed. A sofa. Table and chairs. Television. It's been a side project of mine, making sure you would be taken care of and have everything you need when and if you change your mind."

I'm stunned. I had no idea.

He shifts on the toilet seat, his voice lowering further. "I have never had another woman in this house, Lucy. Not even for a night. I've never had a little or a middle. No one has slept in this room. No one has slept in my bedroom either." His voice trails off.

I remember he kept something else from me. "Where did you get that letter?" I whisper.

"It came to your apartment. Weston brought me your mail when he finalized things with your landlord." Roman audibly swallows. "It was stupid of me to keep it from you. I just..." He pauses. "You were settling in. Happy. Studying. I didn't want to upset you. I didn't trust this man who says he's your half brother. I had him investigated. It would seem he's legit, but I still don't trust him. I have to question his timing. After twenty-two years, he pops out of nowhere the moment you are no longer destitute? I should have told you. I still think we need to tread carefully where this Daven is concerned. I seem to get a little crazed when it comes to protecting you."

A little crazed? I almost laugh. Understatement of the year. I can't believe I might possibly have a half brother. I also can't focus on that right now. I have so many questions, and I'm sure Roman knows most of the answers, but I'll leave that subject for another time.

Roman clears his throat. "I'm sorry about your grandmother. It must have been jolting to realize she died."

I nod.

"I looked into her estate. It was worth nothing. If I had discovered she had anything of value, I would have secured it for you."

I hadn't considered that either. I wouldn't expect my grandmother to have had any money. That's not shocking. But a hint of warmth seeps into me amidst the anger, that at least Roman was looking out for my best interests, even if he did go about doing so in the wrong way.

Roman blows out a breath. "Lucy, I can't tell you how sorry I am. Idiotic. I've made horrible choices. I manipulated your life to get you to see me. It was inexcusable. All I can do is beg you to forgive me and promise to never do anything like that again."

I try to think. Yes, it was stupid of him to interfere in my job and speak to my bosses and make it so I was desperate, and he could hire me. Would he have been able to talk me into submitting to him if he'd simply been honest and walked up to me at the club?

It doesn't really matter now. Obviously, he didn't think he could win me over that way. It was devious, but it also speaks to his vulnerability and how scared he must have been. So desperate to get us together that he did some stupid things. Really stupid things.

If I dig deep, I have to admit, he was not wrong about me. He was spot on. He didn't force me to submit to him. Not even that first time when I kneeled before him to let go of some stress. He gently guided me to see myself for who I am. A middle.

In my heart, I already knew I wanted to belong to someone. Otherwise I wouldn't have gone to Surrender in the first place. I went there to *surrender*. I didn't have the strength to put myself out there, but I did learn a lot. I would have eventually realized I wanted someone to care for me. Protect me. Guide me. Even discipline me.

And the reason I like to age play as a young girl is so that I can let someone else make all the decisions for me, allowing me to relax for the first time in my life.

I can't know how long I will want to play this role. No one can ever be sure of something like that. But for now, it fills a need, a void created by not ever having a father figure in my life who cared. Not even a mother, really. No one ever paid attention to me. I didn't have toys or clothes or bedtimes or rules or any attention at all.

I'm smart. I know I like this arrangement because Master Roman fills all those holes. He does so perfectly. Seamlessly. He lets me live as the young girl I didn't get to be when I was her. He makes it perfect by recreating every detail I needed at twelve and never had. Rules. Discipline. But also love and commitment and a roof and food and clothes and toys and books.

He's given me the world. I never dreamed of finding someone like Master Roman. Someone who wanted to give exactly what I needed to receive.

I could leave. But I know in my heart I will never find love like this again. Not in a million years. It's rare.

We have so many things to work out. I need to know why he doesn't let me sleep in his bed. I need him to let me go to college even if he thinks it's a risk and he spends all four years worrying. I need to know that he will love me no matter what and that he will always be willing to negotiate with me.

I need him to be the father figure I never had and all the things that go with it. I want that to be our lives for as many hours of the day I can manage. I thrive in that role. It frees me and soothes me and relaxes me.

I also want the sexual side. No one will ever be able to make my body sing the way he does. It's unconventional, but it's who we are as a couple.

I'd kind of like to see the apartment he arranged for me. Its existence is just one more thing he kept from me, but the fact that he went to so much trouble to make sure I would be taken care of if I left speaks volumes. I could go stay there for a few days. Think. But I would only be doing so to make Master Roman suffer a bit longer. In the end, there is no way I'm going to leave him. I'm going to yell at him some more later, but I'm not going to leave.

Right now I'm too exhausted to continue this discussion. I hope he can accept that. At least for tonight.

He rises from the toilet and lowers to his knees beside the bathtub. "I'm so sorry, Lucy. I'm an idiot." He leans his forehead toward me until he rests it on mine.

We stare at each other.

I lick my lips. "I'm too tired to talk about this anymore tonight, but if you have any other skeletons or secrets, you should probably gather them all up and introduce me to them in the morning."

He nods, his expression solemn.

"Dig deep. You only get one pass," I warn him.

"I will." He sets his hand on my shoulder and pushes himself to standing. He stares at me for a long time, his expression sorrowful and grim. His tail is between his legs.

Finally, he leans over the tub to lift me easily into his arms. I let him, though I can't relax against him as he carries me to my bed and gently sets me on the mattress. He hesitates and then walks to the door. He reaches around to the outside and turns out the light. For a moment, I stare at his silhouette in the dark, thinking he will leave me to my thoughts until morning.

Instead, he seems to change his mind. He turns around, pads back to my side, and tucks his hands under my small body again and lifts me in his arms. Without a word, he cradles me against his chest and carries me from the room.

I know exactly where he's taking me, and it makes my heart soar.

Down the hall, around the corner, another hall, and finally he enters his bedroom. It's dark in his room, but the light coming from the hallway lets me see the drawers are closed now, as is the closet. I wonder who cleaned up my snooping mess.

He holds me with one hand and uses the other to tug back

the comforter. And then he settles me on the bed, sheet and all. After kicking off his shoes, he climbs over me and hauls my back against his chest.

He's fully clothed in slacks and a white shirt. His tie is gone, and the top button of his shirt is undone, but that's it. I'm still in my white dress and panties with the sheet from my bed cocooning me.

Master Roman strokes my hip and up my arm and then my cheek. He tugs the hairband from the end of my braids and starts to unravel them. It takes him a long time, but finally, he runs his fingers through the length, over and over. Nothing has ever felt so good. Not even my mother ever took the time to care for me like this.

Roman doesn't speak for the longest time. I begin to think he won't. And then he says, "I love you so much, cherry blossom."

I turn my head to meet his gaze and give him the only thing I have left. "I love you too, Daddy."

CHAPTER 51

Master Roman

I haven't slept. Not a single moment. I couldn't. Every time I closed my eyes even for a minute, I saw Lucy in that bathtub, curled in a ball. Hurt. Broken. Defeated. Mistrusting.

She was right to feel those things. It was wrong of me to take over her life and not discuss it with her. Julius warned me. I didn't listen. I had a one-track mind. Making Lucy mine. It wasn't fair to her.

I died a thousand deaths while I paced outside her room, Julius holding me back, insisting that I let Claudia have a moment with her first.

I owe Claudia. I owe her my life. I know she talked my girl down off the ledge. And I'm grateful.

The sun is just coming up when Lucy stirs in my arms.

I stroke a finger over her brow. I've been dying to touch her for hours. But I let her sleep instead.

She whimpers as her eyes slowly blink open, and then she

BECCA JAMESON

rolls onto her back, looking up at me. Her brows are drawn together. "I'm in your bed."

"Yes." I smile. "And I like you here."

"Why have you kept me down the hall?"

I lick my lips. I owe her an explanation. I owe her a lot of explanations.

"Marbles," she murmurs.

I nod, remembering our assigned word for "Let's talk frankly." I lean my chin on my palm, keeping my face inches from hers, holding her gaze. "This house was much crazier and more chaotic when I was growing up in it. For several years my grandfather lived here with me and my parents. He was a Dominant in his own right, and even in his eighties he was still practicing."

"That must have been strange."

I shrug. "I didn't know any different. My father, on the other hand, wasn't just a Dom. He was a philanderer. There were always women around here, often dressed scantily. Even when I was young."

"Where was your mom?" Her eyes pin mine.

I sigh. "She was here too. She played the role of the dutiful submissive wife, but I'm not sure it suited her. In addition, my father expected her to accept that he had other women on the side. He even flaunted it in her face. I learned at a young age that she didn't approve. But she never said anything."

"Kinda like my mom," Lucy points out.

"Yeah. Though my dad never yelled at us or did anything I recognized as abuse at the time, it shaped me. In many ways. I hated how my father used women and discarded them with no regard for their feelings. I believe my mom also felt used.

"By the time I was an adult, I knew I never wanted what my father had. I was a one-woman man. I also knew I didn't want to bring a woman into my home unless and until I was ready to commit to her." I close my eyes for a moment, not sure what her expression might be.

"You decided you were willing to commit to me before you even hired me," she stated. It wasn't a question.

"Yeah."

"That's a bit over the top, you know."

I give her a slight grin. "Yes. I just knew. I had a feeling. I still do. I know."

"What does this have to do with your bedroom?"

I take a slow breath. "I left that one last wall up as a barrier to protect myself in case you left me. I knew I would be shredded if I brought you to my room and then you left. I couldn't face it. I was too chicken."

"And now?" Her voice is soft.

"I realize I was wrong to keep you at arm's length. I need to trust that you won't walk away from what we have without a fight. It was wrong of me to take over your life. Selfish. You're a grown woman with a mind of your own. I should have asked you out like a decent human being and then let our relationship progress naturally."

Her lips part, but she hesitates before speaking. "I'm not sure that would have worked. I would have been too intimidated and turned you down." She narrows her gaze, "But your way still sucked."

I nod. "You're right."

"I'll forgive you on two conditions."

"Name them."

"Never ever ever do something that hairbrained again."

"Done."

"And let me sleep in your bed." She turns to face me more fully, her sheet falling away. "I'm in love with you. I want to sleep with you. I want to have sex in the middle of the night and wake up in your arms."

"How about a compromise."

She rolls her eyes.

"I decide where you sleep each night. Most nights it will be here in my room. Some nights you'll sleep in your little girl room. You'll never know what I'm going to choose, but you can rest assured if you've been disobedient on any given day, you will likely end up in your twin bed." I lift a brow, waiting for confirmation. Before she has a chance to respond, I add, "Oh, and I'm putting a camera in your room."

She squirms, her entire demeanor sliding into one of submission just before her soft voice changes to the pitch she uses when she submits to me. "Yes, Sir."

I give a mental fist pump. I know things are going to be rocky between us for a while, but I love her, and I'll do anything in my power to ensure she knows it every day, especially ensuring that I'm the best Daddy I can be. I know what she needs from me. I've known it from the moment I first laid eyes on her.

She needs someone to cherish her and take care of her. She needs to know she can count on her world always being a soft place to fall. She needs guidance and direction and discipline and structure and rules.

I can do all that for her and so much more. We're just getting started.

CHAPTER 52

Lucy

Four months later...

It's freezing outside. And Raining. I hate the weather in Seattle in the winter. I'm so glad to be home from school though. As I bust through the back door, I shake my hair out, letting the drips of water fall everywhere in the entry to the kitchen.

Evelyn rushes over to meet me. "Good grief, child. You'll catch a cold if you don't start wearing a hat and mittens. That coat is too thin for this weather too. I'll talk to Master Roman about getting you a thicker one this afternoon."

I smile at her. "Thank you, ma'am." There's no sense arguing with her. When she wants to fuss over me, she does. Our relationship may be odd, but it's not awkward. She fully understands the nuances of my arrangement with Master Roman. She mothers me in a way. Far more than my own mother did.

I want for nothing in this house. Evelyn sees that I'm well

fed. Nancy makes sure I have everything else I need. Weston drives me around. Sometimes they fight over me and what they anticipate I might want or need.

I know several other interesting bits of information. Weston is Evelyn's husband. Not only that but I'm fairly certain she is his service sub. They have a suite of rooms on the main floor, and I'd bet my last dollar that when they close themselves off from the world, she submits to him.

Nancy is not married, but she once was. Her husband died about ten years ago from a heart attack. I hate thinking that she is lonely, but I've come to realize that since I moved into the house, she has changed. I see it in everyone's faces. She has a new purpose in life. Taking care of me.

They all do. It's a group effort. Like an extended family of grandparents I never had. They all love me dearly, and I feel the same about them.

"Lucy?" Master Roman's voice booms from his office. He does that. He worries about me every day until I return from school. I don't think he breathes until I'm back in the house. His shoulders visibly relax when I round the corner to his office, and I scurry to do so now.

"Don't run, child," Nancy reprimands when she sees me coming down the hallway at a skip.

"Sorry, ma'am." I slow my pace.

She smiles at me and shakes her head. "Master Roman is going to have a fit when he sees your hair."

Don't I know it.

I round the corner to step through the open office door, my smile broadening when I see Julius lounging on the couch. Sometimes when I see him, Levi and Beck are with him, but I've learned the two of them own a business together, Vanguard Media Specialists. Julius is their third, but silent, partner. Levi and Beck are often at photo shoots.

Roman is perched on the armchair, but he rises when I

enter and comes to me. That's new for us. Sometimes he comes to me now. It's like he can't wait for me to close the distance, so he does it himself.

He cups my face and kisses my lips gently as he does every day, his eyes searching mine as if he might be able to detect if I have something I need to tell him. I don't. Unless he wants to hear about my psychology exam. And he will. Every detail. Later. After.

"Your hair is soaked," he admonishes.

"I know. It started raining."

"Didn't you bring an umbrella?" His expression makes me smile. I'm used to it. He's overbearing. I go with the flow.

"I forgot."

He narrows his gaze, his mouth opening to say more.

I cut him off and round him to speak to Julius. "How are you, Master Julius?"

"Can't complain." He winks at me. "Did you cut your hair?"

Master Roman groans, and I want to toss a glare at Julius, but I don't. I might find myself in the corner if I'm disrespectful to Master Roman's best friend. "She insisted. They took off too much though."

"I looked too young with it down to my butt at school, and you know it. I'm already weird enough. I don't need to stand out."

Julius glances down at my legs. "Roman lets you wear those jeans out of the house?" He's fighting a grin. He's baiting me. Now I really want to shoot him daggers with my eyes.

Master Roman grumbles as he resumes his seat. "Why anyone would ever want to wear something torn like that is beyond me."

"Come on," I whine. "You knew I was buying them. You even sent Evelyn with me to approve my clothes." I turn toward Julius, rolling my eyes. "He gives me an allowance, but then he insists on seeing every single thing I want to buy and giving it his approval first."

"And I can put a stop to that any time I want if you don't watch that sassy mouth, little girl." He snaps his fingers. "Almost forgot. A package came for you. It's on my desk."

I glance that way. I have no idea what it is.

He nods that direction. "I ordered it the other day. Go look."

I skip across the room and grab the package, tearing into it as I return. My face heats up when I hold up the package of panties. He tricked me into opening them in front of Julius. Not that Julius isn't completely familiar with my wardrobe. I'm positive he's seen every pair of panties I own at some point or another.

"Cute," Julius says. "Are those butterflies?" he teases.

The package contains six new pairs of extremely babyish full-cut panties in pastel colors with butterflies all over them. "What they are is Master Roman's form of a chastity belt."

Master Roman chuckles loudly. "Is that what you say behind my back?"

"What else would you call them?"

"Insurance?" he suggests.

I roll my eyes. I'm going to pay for my attitude later, but for now I'm having too much fun. I spin back to face Julius. "Master Roman thinks if I wear these under my grownup clothes, I'll be too embarrassed to let anyone see them and thus he won't have to worry about me letting any boys into my pants."

Julius laughs so hard he tips his head back. "That's brilliant." He reaches out to his friend and gives him a high five.

I continue. "And that's only half of it. After agreeing to let me wear a bra at school, he had them specially made to be exactly like the training bras preteen girls wear before they have boobs, in that stage when they want to feel older."

"Hey," Master Roman interjects, "you're the one who insisted on having them. It's your decision to wear them or not. You asked for bras. We negotiated. I got your bras. You either wear them, or you don't. Your choice."

"They cover more skin than most of the dresses you choose," I point out.

"Yep, and you wouldn't dream of letting any college boys see them either. Would you?"

Julius starts laughing again. "Chastity panties and chastity training bras. You're a genius."

Master Roman smirks. He's beyond proud of himself. He has also calmed down significantly since we negotiated this trade. I get to wear jeans and sweaters and fashionable clothes that don't raise eyebrows on campus, and in exchange, I agreed to let him select every undergarment I own. The panties I expected. The training bras I did not.

Every one of them is cut the same and made out of thin cotton material in pastel colors with every sort of rainbow, unicorn, or butterfly pattern he could find. They don't have wires. They are more like short, cotton undershirts with an elastic band that lands just below my breasts. The straps are wide and thick. They don't have a clasp. I have to put them on over my head. My nipples poke through the cotton.

Honestly, they probably make me look more ridiculous than if I just didn't wear a bra, but I put them on every day on principle. And every article of clothing I've purchased with my allowance covers so much skin that no one will ever see. Even my jeans are cut high on my waist. I would be mortified if my panties stuck out over the top. So I'm super modest, and that was undoubtedly Master Roman's master plan.

The truth is that for all my groaning and complaining, I secretly love that every morning when I wake up Master

Roman has chosen my panties and training bras. He says girls my age don't need a bra, but he'll let me pretend if I want to.

When I'm at school I'm always wearing Master Roman's choices under the layers. It's a constant reminder of who I am inside.

Daddy's little girl.

I usually call him Daddy now. It was weird at first, and it took me a long time to rationalize it in my head. The term was on the tip of my tongue for weeks before we fought that night, and it slid out easily when we silently made up. It's not that I think of him as my father. He's not. He's my lover in every sense. It's more a term of respect. When I call him Daddy, it tells him that I acknowledge his role in our life and defer to him on all things.

"You've dawdled long enough, Lucy," he chastises. "Go change into your play clothes. Julius is staying for dinner. Claudia is coming too. You can join us if you get your homework done on time."

With those words, I know my few minutes of joking around as if I'm an adult are over. He's reestablished control.

"Yes, Sir."

"I want that hair off your face too, Lucy. Ponytails or braids. You choose. Come back here after you change. Your sassy attitude earned you a sore bottom for the afternoon."

"Yes, Sir," I murmur as I slide more fully into my role. He can do that with the tone of his voice alone. It only takes seconds.

"And since you thought it would be cute to whine to my guest as if you are so mistreated, I think it only fitting that he watch as I take you over my knee."

I flush, heat rising on my face. It was fun making jokes about my undergarments with Julius, but now I'm wondering if the price was too high.

Master Roman pushes me in different directions all the

time, helping me reach deeper into my inner self and expand my hard limits. Apparently today he intends to expose my bottom to Julius.

I'm mortified, but as I shuffle from the room, I realize I'm also aroused, as usual. I'm growing into the role more with each passing week. Several months ago, if Master Roman had suggested spanking me in front of anyone, I would have died. Today I'm the exact perfect balance of horrified and titillated.

CHAPTER 53

Master Roman

I watch Lucy's back as she leaves my office, smiling. She is my life. My cup runneth over. I can't believe my good fortune. We click.

Sure, I throw new things at her all the time to keep things spicy, but she takes every new challenge in stride.

"You gonna stare at the door until she comes back or what?" Julius is chuckling. I can't blame him. "You're whipped."

"I am. Wait until you meet the *one*. I'm going to laugh every day until my side hurts. She's my family. My soul. My heart. You'll see." I settle back in my chair. Lucy knows I'm going to punish her. I'm sure she's going to dawdle.

Julius rolls his eyes. "Speaking of family, have you contacted her brother yet?"

I shake my head. "I tried. I couldn't find him. It seems he sold the small farm he lived on and changed his cell number. I'm sure if I dig deeper, I could locate him, but Lucy doesn't want me to right now. Not yet anyway. She says she's not ready. I shared everything I know about him. She's curious, but she's also skeptical. As am I. I suspect one of the things holding her back is that she can't imagine sharing our unconventional relationship with anyone. We live so deeply in our roles that it's hard to imagine stepping out of our comfort zone and pretending like we're a vanilla couple. Eventually, we'll need to do so, but she insists she's not ready."

Julius nods. "Makes sense. But he's her only living relative. Don't let her put it off forever."

"I won't." Julius is right.

He looks toward my desk, grinning now. "I've never seen your desk so messy. Is Lucy still giving you a hard time about hiring an assistant?"

I groan and roll my eyes. "Don't remind me. I finally have someone starting on Monday. We've argued about it so many times, it's gotten to the point where I want to slam my head into a wall."

"Hey, you can't blame her for not wanting another woman in your home. And you know she doesn't feel comfortable with age play in front of strangers, especially men. So, how did you work this out?"

I grin. "She finally agreed to someone after dozens of applicants."

Julius lifts a brow. "Is this someone I know?"

"Yes. Easton Rogers."

"Easton? The kid who just joined Surrender?"

"That's the one."

Julius's smile widens. "Why didn't I think of that? Perfect."

"Yep. He's gay, submissive, and in the lifestyle. Finally, someone Lucy could agree on." I couldn't believe my luck when he applied. I nearly tripped over myself bringing the application to Lucy's desk where she was studying in her playroom. "She was never going to consent to me hiring a woman, and I was never going to agree to hire a straight man. We might have a growing period while she adapts to submitting to me in front of someone, but I think she's ready to branch out a bit. She's growing more comfortable in her role. I'm hopeful that Easton can mind his own business while I make my woman squirm in front of him."

"I'm sure Easton is up to the task. He's a natural submissive. If you tell him to look the other way, he won't hesitate to obey." Julius leans back in his seat and glances at the doorway, lowering his voice as he speaks again. "You think Lucy will be able to expose herself to Easton?"

I nod. "I think she's ready. Hopefully I'll be one step closer to getting her to go to the club with me."

"Good luck with that."

I sigh. I'm going to need luck. We've been together for six months. I love her with all my heart. She's an amazing submissive and middle. Our dynamic is beyond anything I could have hoped for.

Nevertheless, she has not set foot in Surrender or any other club since the day she applied to be my assistant. At first, I was greedy and unwilling to share her, so I didn't even blink twice. But as the months have gone by, I find I want to branch out. I want to take her with me, as my middle. She has never left the house dressed as my little girl.

I would never let her scene with another person in my club or any other location, but I long for the day that she will scene with me in a more public setting.

I'm hoping the addition of Easton to our lives will help her loosen up on this topic. Sure, she plays the role of a twelve-year-old girl in front of my staff and my closest friends, but I do not expose her pussy or her tits to any of them. It's been a hard line for her.

She's about to get her bottom spanked in front of Julius though. Any moment now. It will be a first. We've discussed this several times. It's one step toward easing her into exposure. It's just Julius. He's seen naked bottoms before. It's just a spanking. I'm not going to fuck her or even fondle her in front of him. He won't see more than her sexy cheeks with her panties bunched in a wad under them.

I'm hopeful. She's growing. Eventually, I'd like to be able to take her to the club when I work. Right now, when I go to Surrender, she stays home with a "sitter." Nancy or Evelyn.

She doesn't mind. Both women dote on her. I'm pretty sure they let her eat too many sweets and stay up past her bedtime. I'm suspicious because every time I tell her I have to work and she'll be home with a sitter, she perks up.

I smile inside even now. I love that my staff adores her and treats her like she's their own. It's as if she has three grandparents in the house.

It's rare that Lucy is out of my sight or that of my staff. I know I'm overbearing and insist on far more supervision than a girl her age requires, but the truth is I'm calmer when she's in my direct line of sight. It's mostly selfish, but I believe she is more relaxed when she can see me too.

She grumbles on occasion when I don't give her permission to go outside alone or free rein of the house, but I know she secretly thrives on my authoritarian ways. It makes her feel cherished and safe.

In fact, after months of closely monitoring her reactions to everything I do, I've added to the list of things she isn't permitted to do without supervision. She isn't allowed to use the stove or oven unless Evelyn is helping her. Likewise, the sharpest knife she may use is a butter knife. The basement is also off limits. I don't want her playing around my weights in case she drops one on her foot or something.

Of course, there are preteen girls all over the country who stay home alone, use the oven, and have permission to wander free in the house. But none of those girls are mine. I'm overprotective. Lucy knows it.

But most importantly, Lucy gets aroused when I put my foot down. It's comforting to her. Boundaries give her peace.

"Earth to Roman."

I jerk my gaze to find Julius smirking. "Sorry, I was in my head."

"I noticed. Are we waiting for Lucy to get back before we continue discussing work?" He lifts his brows.

"No. We should get back to it. I'm sure she'll drag her feet. She's less than excited for me to spank her in front of you."

Julius laughs again. "You're very patient. She'll get there."

I know she will. She's come so far.

So have I.

She's mine.

But I'm also hers.

AUTHOR'S NOTE

I hope you've enjoyed *Raising Lucy* from my Surrender series. Please enjoy the following excerpt from *Teaching Abby*, the second book in the series.

TEACHING ABBY

SURRENDER, BOOK TWO

It was my idea.

I thought we should hire an intern for the summer. Julius and Beck both think I'm crazy. And maybe they're right. But I still think it's the right thing to do.

Our business has been stagnant for the last few years, and I attribute part of that to lack of change. We need a female perspective. We do fine without one, but occasionally we lose a potential client because they prefer a female to do their photo shoot.

It's just a trial run. We aren't keeping this woman. She's not even available past August. I've selected her intentionally so that Julius and Beck won't worry about her possibly overstaying her welcome.

If this works out, I'll have proven my point. That we need to add a woman to our staff.

I get that it's complicated. Our arrangement is complicated. It will be difficult to keep our private lives private. But surely we can manage to do so for one damn summer. It's not like we haven't gone three months without a woman in our beds before.

I shift in my chair as I flip through the pictures of her on my computer screen for the tenth time today.

Abigail Wise.

I received a dozen applications from females for this internship, and I immediately looked every one of them up on social media. It's the natural thing to do.

Abigail stood out to me from the moment I saw her smile. Yes, she's incredibly gorgeous, but that's not the only thing that caught my attention. She's obviously carefree and fun. Her social media is clean as a whistle. The only pictures she has are off her with her grandfather and her with a woman I assume is her best friend.

She doesn't have pictures of drunken nights in bars or boyfriends or even dates. She looks younger than I know her to be also.

There's something about her. I knew she was the one the moment I set eye on her pictures. My partners are right. I'm crazy. I should not be choosing an intern based on her looks or even her smile. And I definitely shouldn't pick someone who makes my cock hard and my mouth dry.

It's a horrible idea.

It's also done.

Reviving Bianca

Reviving Olivia

Project DEEP Box Set One

Project DEEP Box Set Two

SEALs in Paradise:

Hot SEAL, Red Wine

Hot SEAL, Australian Nights

Dark Falls:

Dark Nightmares

Club Zodiac:

Training Sasha

Obeying Rowen

Collaring Brooke

Mastering Rayne

Trusting Aaron

Claiming London

Sharing Charlotte

Taming Rex

The Art of Kink:

Pose

Paint

Sculpt

Arcadian Bears:

Grizzly Mountain

Grizzly Beginning

Grizzly Secret

Grizzly Promise

Grizzly Survival

Grizzly Perfection

Arcadian Bears Box Set

Sleeper SEALs:

Saving Zola

Spring Training:

Catching Zia

Catching Lily

Catching Ava

Spring Training Box Set

The Underground series:

Force

Clinch

Guard

Submit

Thrust

Torque

The Underground Box Set

Saving Sofia (Kindle World)

Wolf Masters series:

Kara's Wolves

Lindsey's Wolves

Jessica's Wolves

Alyssa's Wolves

Tessa's Wolf

Rebecca's Wolves

Melinda's Wolves

Laurie's Wolves

Amanda's Wolves

Sharon's Wolves

Wolf Gatherings Box Set One

Wolf Gatherings Box Set Two

Claiming Her series:

The Rules

The Game

The Prize

Emergence series:

Bound to be Taken

Bound to be Tamed

Bound to be Tested

Bound to be Tempted

Emergence Box Set

The Fight Club series:

Come

Perv

Need

Hers

Want

Lust

The Fight Club Box Set

Wolf Gatherings series:

Tarnished

Dominated

Completed

Redeemed

Abandoned

Betrayed

Wolf Gatherings Box Set

Durham Wolves series:

Rescue in the Smokies

Fire in the Smokies

Freedom in the Smokies

Stand Alone Books:

Blind with Love

Guarding the Truth

Out of the Smoke

Abducting His Mate

Three's a Cruise

Wolf Trinity

Frostbitten

A Princess for Cale/A Princess for Cain

ABOUT THE AUTHOR

Becca Jameson is a USA Today best-selling author of over 90 books. She is most well-known for her Wolf Masters series and her Fight Club series. She currently lives in Houston, Texas, with her husband and her Goldendoodle. Two grown kids pop in every once in a while too! She is loving this journey and has dabbled in a variety of genres, including paranormal, sports romance, military, and BDSM.

A total night owl, Becca writes late at night, sequestering herself in her office with a glass of red wine and a bar of dark chocolate, her fingers flying across the keyboard as her characters weave their own stories.

During the day--which never starts before ten in the morning!--she can be found jogging, running errands, or reading in her favorite hammock chair!

...where Alphas dominate...

Becca's Newsletter Sign-up:
http://beccajameson.com/newsletter-sign-up

Join my Facebook fan group, Becca's Bibliomaniacs, for the most up-to-date information, random excerpts while I work, giveaways, and fun release parties!

Facebook Fan Group:
https://www.facebook.com/groups/BeccasBibliomaniacs/

Contact Becca:
www.beccajameson.com
beccajameson4@aol.com

facebook.com/becca.jameson.18

twitter.com/beccajameson

instagram.com/becca.jameson

bookbub.com/authors/becca-jameson

goodreads.com/beccajameson

amazon.com/author/beccajameson